FROZEN IN TIME

Also by Ali Sparkes:

Out of This World

Dark Summer

Wishful Thinking

The Unleashed series:

A Life and Death Job

Mind over Matter

Trick or Truth

Speak Evil

The Burning Beach

The Shapeshifter series:

Finding the Fox

Running the Risk

Going to Ground

Dowsing the Dead

Stirring the Storm

FROZEN
IN
TIME

Ali Sparkes

OXFORD
UNIVERSITY PRESS

OXFORD
UNIVERSITY PRESS

Great Clarendon Street, Oxford OX2 6DP

Oxford University Press is a department of the University of Oxford.
It furthers the University's objective of excellence in research, scholarship,
and education by publishing worldwide in

Oxford New York

Auckland Cape Town Dar es Salaam Hong Kong Karachi
Kuala Lumpur Madrid Melbourne Mexico City Nairobi
New Delhi Shanghai Taipei Toronto

With offices in

Argentina Austria Brazil Chile Czech Republic France Greece
Guatemala Hungary Italy Japan Poland Portugal Singapore
South Korea Switzerland Thailand Turkey Ukraine Vietnam

Oxford is a registered trade mark of Oxford University Press
in the UK and in certain other countries

British Library Cataloguing in Publication Data

Data available

ISBN: 978-0-19-273400-6
1 3 5 7 9 10 8 6 4 2

Printed in Great Britain
Paper used in the production of this book is a natural,
recyclable product made from wood grown in sustainable forests.
The manufacturing process conforms to the environmental
regulations of the country of origin.

This edition is warmly dedicated
to the memory of Kate Williams
and her brilliant editorial
eye for detail.

ACKNOWLEDGEMENTS:

Many thanks to the listeners of BBC Radio Solent and readers of the *Southern Daily Echo* for sending me their memories of growing up in the 1950s (and to Julian Clegg and Dave King for helping that to happen). Also to Freddy and Pauline Sparkes and Vera and Bert Warner for their memories and photos and guidance. Thank you, also, Ralph Montagu, for digging out a very special edition of the *Radio Times*, June 1956 ...

Oh—and thank you very, very much, Enid.

LONDON, TWO YEARS BEFORE

The man in the dark grey trench coat walked briskly along the Embankment, cursing the cold and his lack of gloves. It had been years since he'd been called out to a secret rendezvous—he was past this kind of thing. But the name rang a bell. Made him curious. Astonished, in fact.

The old boy was waiting under Westminster Bridge, as promised, his thick coat cut like a Russian's. He didn't try to shake hands, but nodded slowly, several times, when he saw his old, old colleague.

'By God, it *is* you, Dick. I can't believe you have the nerve—even after fifty years!'

Dick smiled. A miserable smile. 'I came to give you information. About Henry. I have to clear my conscience. It wasn't him . . . it was me. I was your man—not Henry. He had no choice. That's all.'

The man in the dark grey trench coat shook his head. 'What do you want?'

'To be here again, in England, for the rest of my life . . . It won't be long.'

'And Henry? And his children? What about *them*?'

'His *children*?' The old man looked shocked.

'You didn't take them?'

' . . . Didn't you?'

1

Chapter 1

The satellite falling to earth changed life for ever for Ben and Rachel Corder. It was catastrophic.

One day their world was full of colour and light and sound—and the next, in just a few terrible seconds, it was grey and swarms of insects engulfed it.

'No! No! No! No!' wailed Rachel, panic rising through her, while Ben aimed the remote at the TV and pressed the buttons again and again, as if this could make a difference.

'We should never have let Uncle J put it up,' said Ben. 'Satellite dishes should be put up by the men from Sky, not by random uncles! Now we've only got the old aerial. Press the TV button . . . see if there's anything coming through at all.'

Rachel crawled across the room and prodded the TV button below the screen, which switched the system to the old free terrestrial channels . . . if there were any left these days. It was a desperate measure. Only minutes ago they could have watched hundreds of different channels, from music to documentaries to cartoons . . . Pop divas wiggling their hips at the camera, ravening dinosaurs plunging through realistic CGI swamps, real people arguing spitefully with other real people in live reality shows, unreal Disney teenagers with perfect teeth, singing and dancing . . . and now . . . what?

The tall ancient oaks which surrounded the house made it barely possible to get even BBC1 through on the old aerial. BBC2 was slightly better and Channel 4 would come and go. Forget the rest.

By 11 a.m. Ben and Rachel were slumped back in their usual position—the position they'd been in for almost all that wet, wet, wet summer, sprawled across the old parquet flooring in the sitting room, propped up on their elbows, watching a repeat of a 1970s detective series.

'We'll have to ask Uncle J to phone up Sky,' sighed Ben. 'It'll take him for ever to get around to it though.'

He absent-mindedly scored the damp dark stain on the floor with one fingernail, while Rachel toggled a loose woodblock up and down, and they both squinted at the 1970s detective who was solving crimes through a relentless attack of bees. The bees were not part of the plot—it was just *really* bad reception. There was a hot, dusty smell coming from the overworked set, but they were both too dull and damped down that morning to do anything about it.

They would have liked to go outside, but the endless rain made playing in the huge and wild garden almost impossible. A deep valley of overgrown shrubs and trees, it had become a vast mud bath, especially on the lower lawn by the stream, where they usually liked to play. You'd go in up to your ankles there.

Sadly, playing inside, when Uncle Jerome was working, wasn't easy either. Ben and Rachel would tend to get noisy, and then he'd tend to get angry, because he couldn't concentrate. Uncle Jerome wasn't bad really. He was just very brainy and intense and when he was caught up in his work upstairs he had no patience for anything else. It was easier when Mum and Dad were around, but this summer, like most summers, they were away again, on tour. They were a magic act. Truly. Ben and Rachel's dad could eat fire and sawed their mum in half on a regular basis. They were very good and much in demand—and their high season was always May to September, and Christmas, of course. Right now they were on a cruise ship somewhere.

This meant that Uncle Jerome, who lived with them all in the large old house on the outskirts of town, became their guardian whenever high season came around. He was quite a good guardian, in the way that he didn't really care *what* his thirteen-year-old nephew and twelve-year-old niece did—as long as it didn't end in death or, worse, a lot of noise.

'Do you think he'd notice if we were dead?' Ben mumbled, resting his chin in his hands and staring at the Seventies TV detective, speeding along in his open-topped car, through the swarm.

'Who—Uncle J?' said Rachel, rolling onto her back and staring at the high, ornate ceiling with a lacklustre yawn. 'Not for a few days, probably. Unless we managed to be dead *and* very noisy at the same time.'

Ben grinned. 'Maybe if I fell on the remote control with my last breath and pinned down the volume button. If *Scooby Doo* was on and the weight of my corpse made it go louder and louder and louder.'

Rachel giggled. She was too floppy and bored to stop herself. 'Or if I got caught up on the ceiling fan in the dining room,' she improvised. 'If it was strong enough to hold a dead body, that is. And if it was switched on—I could just go round and round, over the table, with my dead feet kicking the biscuit tin every time.' She laughed, limply. 'You'd have to switch the fan on for me before you fell dead by the telly.' They both started giggling helplessly.

Then the telly blew up. There was a blue flash and a loud bang, and the sharp smell of singed dust hit them both on a sudden draught of air. They both sat up and stared at the dead screen for a moment, before Ben jumped up and ran to the socket and pulled the plug out.

'Ow!' he said. 'It's hot!'

Fearfully they looked around the back of the TV. The hot and dusty smell was strongest under its rear outcrop of dark grey plastic moulding and wires. Luckily, nothing seemed to be on fire.

They sat back down again and looked at each other. True, they had probably experienced more excitement around the TV in the last twenty seconds than they had for the past five weeks—but now even Seventies TV detectives were denied to them. The final week of school holiday stretched ahead bleakly. More rain. No telly.

'Oh no,' murmured Ben, weakly. 'I think we'll start playing Monopoly soon.'

'It hasn't come to that yet,' said Rachel. 'Maybe it'll stop raining.'

They both looked forlornly out at the deep, dark green, slithery, slippery garden. Under the beaded curtain of endless drops of water, it fell away down steep slopes towards the lower lawn and the stream.

Their parents were hopeless gardeners, but that didn't matter. In a normal summer the garden was perfect for playing in. It had many tall trees: old oak, rowan, ash and elder; several good apple trees, and hazels, which were a larder for a dozen or more squirrels.

Through its overgrown grass and thickly spreading bushes, foxes would flit. Jays would clack noisily in the trees. It was a wildlife garden. That's what their mum called it. It was the way she justified never mowing the lawn. Once or twice a year they would get in 'contractors' to hack it back a bit—so they could actually get out of the house.

But for most of the time it was left to do its own thing—as was the tangled wood beyond the stream, also part of the grounds which went with the house. The garden was great, thought Rachel, resting her forehead against the old, wobbly glass of the sash window and steaming it up with her sigh, but when it was this wet—*this* wet—you just couldn't *do* the garden. You couldn't even get down the bank, unless you were happy about going head first.

'Bum,' said Ben. He sat heavily on the old leather pouffe next to Rachel and also rested his forehead against the window.

Then it stopped raining. Just like that. Then the sun came out.

'What's that weird light?' said Ben and Rachel wasn't sure that he was joking. For the first time in more than three weeks, the summer sun finally smiled.

They whooped. They cheered. They jumped up and down and then ran for the hallway.

Uncle Jerome emerged at the top of the stairs, blinking. 'What's all the racket about?' he demanded fiercely.

'The sun! The sun!' Rachel was bouncing up and down, while Ben was flinging their wellingtons out from under the stairs. 'Look!'

Uncle Jerome squinted down at the large front door, with its stained-glass windows. The green, red, and yellow in the leaded panes were actually reflecting in the unpolished tiles on the hallway floor. Even Uncle Jerome smiled.

'Good news!' he said. 'Now you can get outside for a bit and we can stop driving each other batty.'

Ben was hit in the face by a soggy honeysuckle bloom as soon as the door was open. He didn't care. He and his sister scrambled past the porch and stood on the narrow gravel path above the bank, raising their pale faces to the sky and feeling the warm sun pat across their noses and cheeks with her soft, fond, long-lost fingers.

'Oh! Oh! At last!' beamed Rachel, feeling as if she might possibly cry with delight. Even the sight of the fallen satellite dish, dangling next to the porch on its flex, didn't bother her now.

They pelted past the ornamental well and across to the giant acer which grew at the top of the bank in a wriggling tangle of pale trunk and branches. It was the perfect hand-hold for lowering yourself carefully down the first few metres of slippery greenery. Then there was a leap down to the rhododendrons, which would hopefully break your fall before you scrambled through some knee-high shrubs and lilies and out onto the lower lawn.

The lower lawn looked like a huge chocolate blancmange. Its grass was drowned in ten or eleven centimetres of muddy water. The stream had over-flowed. On the opposite bank the land began to rise again, held firm by the gnarly roots of trees which had been there for hundreds of years.

Ben and Rachel waded across the lawn in their wellingtons and splashed more deeply across the stony bed of the stream. Grabbing the roots, they hauled themselves up on the far bank.

'Den?' said Ben.

'If it hasn't been washed away!' said Rachel and they made their way to a collection of planks and old doors which they had made into a den last summer, leaning them up against the almost horizontal bough of a beech tree, like a sort of tent. Inside, their plastic crates were soaked and a wooden tea chest they'd used as a table was growing mould.

'We should have covered it with plastic sheeting,' sighed Rachel.

But Ben wasn't listening. He was peering hard through the triangular entrance at something through the trees. His brow was furrowing and he was narrowing his eyes.

'What is it?' asked Rachel, trying to follow his gaze.

'Dunno,' said Ben. 'Something—something shiny. Down there. There's something shiny stuck in the ground.'

Rachel pushed her shoulder next to Ben's and stared in the direction he was pointing. He was right. There *was* something, smooth and glinting in the pale sunshine, deep between the roots and the ivy and the rich brown earth.

'Probably an old hub cap off a car or something,' she said. 'Probably someone's been dumping stuff again. Hey! Wait for me!'

Ben was already running and slithering across the knotty woodland floor to examine the thing. Rachel scrambled after him. It was probably rubbish, but she didn't want to be left out. By the time she caught him up, Ben was hunkered down, wiping away the dead leaves and peat from the thing. It looked a bit like a car steering wheel. An old style, large metal one, like you might see in classic cars, lying at a slight angle in the earth. The remains of a very decomposed old log lay over part of it. It looked as if the log had slid down the bank slightly in all the rain.

'What is it?'

'I don't know,' said Ben, grunting with effort as he tried to prise the wheel thing out of the soil. He had managed to hook his fingers around the curve of metal tubing on each side of its circumference, but although he was tugging hard, it wouldn't give. Rachel crouched down beside him and dug her fingers into the cold earth around it too. They both, instinctively, took a breath and then pulled hard, together.

Grunts of effort rang through the small copse and startled the wood pigeons, which flapped clumsily among the higher branches, bumbling and cooing in an offended tone.

The wheel wouldn't give.

'I reckon it's attached to something in the ground,' said Ben, poking his fingers deeper into the dark earth around it. 'Help me dig.'

Rachel didn't know why he was getting so excited. It was a just a wheel. Still, she shrugged and knelt down, oblivious to the water squeezing out of the wet sponge of earth into the denim knees of her jeans, and made her fingers into spade shape, like her brother.

Utterly soaked by nearly a month of unstoppable rain, the soil gave up its hold quite readily, and soon they had cleared a sort of crater around the wheel, down to a thick metal post at its centre.

'What metal is it?' asked Rachel, flicking a squirming, annoyed worm off her fingers.

'Steel, I think,' said Ben, although he didn't know. 'Really hard and solid, whatever it is. Keep digging.'

They were getting filthy, but did not worry. Uncle Jerome wouldn't notice, and as they did their own washing, there was nobody to give a sharp exhalation and fold their arms in annoyance when they traipsed back to the house later.

Soon the crater was a few centimetres deep and the soil was damp rather than saturated. Ben was getting fed up. He grasped the wheel and tried to shake it but it absolutely wouldn't budge. He sat back on his muddy heels and wiped his dark blond fringe out of his eyes, leaving a wide trail of woodland ink across his brow. 'It should be budging by now!' he said, crossly.

'We should be able to get it out! We can make a go-kart or something with it.'

Rachel sat back too and sighed heavily from the spent effort. 'Maybe it's not a steering wheel,' she pondered. Ben creased his muddied forehead and thought. He stood up and looked at the trees around them. Then he made vague measuring shapes with his soil-caked hands, turning them vertically and examining the sky through the chinks in the gently dripping leaves, before peering back at the wheel.

'It's dead horizontal!' he said, thoughtfully.

'Is it?'

'Yes. You can't tell at first, because the ground's at an angle here—it's a bank.' He sank down again, kneeling on the edge of the crater and resting his elbows and forearms on the obstinate wheel. He chewed on his lower lip, as he always did when an idea was coming to him. 'I think it's joined to something big and heavy under the soil. It must have been here for years—but that log was on top of it. Come on!' With renewed enthusiasm he ducked down into the crater and dug harder.

Rachel joined him, raking her fingers deep down into the soil, tearing through its network of fine roots, dragging up clumps of matter and hurling them off away from the excavation. They were both feeling excited. It beat watching telly. After another five minutes Ben gave a shout. His fingers had met with more metal—the thick column under the wheel was joined to a flat surface under the soil. They both tried to make it tilt in its dark brown bed, but it was as immovable as the wheel.

Intrigued, they knelt back and stared at it. Then Ben gave an exclamation and rubbed quickly at the metal surface five centimetres from the column. Under his fingers Rachel could see the earth catching. The metal was raised here, in relief. A curve around the base of the column tapered to a triangular point.

'It's an arrow!' gasped Ben. 'An arrow!'

'What does that mean?'

Ben was looking at her with gleaming eyes and an excited grin. 'It's an arrow! Like you get on taps or bottle lids. It's telling us which way to turn the wheel!'

Rachel stared at the wheel and the arrow.

'Don't you get it?' demanded Ben, in a voice which was squeakier than usual. 'It *opens*! There's something down there—and it *opens*!'

Chapter 2

In the large shed that had been built on to the side of
the old Victorian house they found spades and forks
and trowels. They each took what they could carry in
one arm and slid awkwardly down the soaked bank.

Back at their excavation site they dug around
the wheel and its metal base, dragging the earth, roots,
stones, and affronted creepy crawlies off its surface.
The flat base was, in fact, very slightly curved, like a
dome.

'What do you think it *is*?' gasped Rachel, her
cheeks crimson with effort under the streaks of mud.

'I dunno,' Ben gasped back, equally florid and
muddy. 'Maybe some kind of fuel tank. We'd better
be careful not to light a match near it when we open
it.'

'We haven't got any matches!' pointed out his
sister.

'Well—just don't make a spark then.'

Rachel gave him a look. 'I'll try not to. It'll be hard though.'

They laughed while they dug on.

'Hey!' Rachel knelt up and yanked Ben's arm. 'Look!'

The edge of the dome could now clearly be seen. They could see that the whole thing must be about a metre across and perfectly round. It took half an hour to reveal the complete, raised circle of metal and the beginning of another level, about ten centimetres beneath it. At length, they stood back, resting on their shovels and measuring the circle with their eyes. For several seconds, both were silent, before slowly turning to look at each other.

'You know what I think . . . ?' murmured Ben in wonder. 'I think it's a manhole.'

Rachel felt suddenly frightened. 'It might be,' she said, with a gulp. 'But we don't know that it's actually for *men*.'

'What *are* you on about?'

She looked slightly embarrassed, but also stubborn. 'It might *not* be for men!' she repeated. 'Haven't you ever heard about this sort of thing? It might be,' she dropped her voice low, 'an alien spacecraft!'

Ben stared at her and then burst out laughing.

16

'What? With these markings from a distant galaxy?' he snorted, pointing to the furthest edge of metal he'd been clearing. On it were the letters 'H J E' followed by a '1' and a '9'. The rest, if there was any more, was still covered in soil.

Rachel laughed shakily. 'Well, I read a book once,' she began, but Ben wasn't listening. He was again trying to turn the wheel. Now that its shaft and the circular cover were revealed, it was obvious that it was *meant* to turn, and he meant to turn it. He leant his chest across it and grasped it hard with both hands, pushing and pulling in the direction the arrow suggested. Nothing happened and he grunted with frustration. 'Come on! Help me!' he shouted at Rachel, and she grabbed the wheel too, pulling and pulling in the same direction, anchoring the heels of her mud-caked wellingtons at the foot of the column and leaning her whole body weight round.

Still it did not move. They both flopped down on the metal base angrily and as they did so, they felt, rather than really heard it. The metal sang a low, subterranean note, which spoke of empty space below. They stared at each other and then dropped their eyes to the cover, almost fearfully. Ben stood up. 'Oil!' he said. 'That column is caked with dirt. We need poky things—kitchen knives or something—to dig it out.

17

Maybe some hot soapy water and brushes. Then we need oil to rub into the moving parts.'

They raced back across the wood, splashed across the stream and waded over the lower lawn, where tips of grass were gradually emerging as the flood began to ebb away. Back at the house they stopped only to pull their extremely muddy wellingtons off at the door before running down the hallway in socks and straight into the kitchen.

Here Ben collided head on with Uncle Jerome and both ended up on the terracotta tiled floor in a heap of mud and leaf litter, apple pie and orange juice. Uncle Jerome had been on one of his occasional forays to the fridge when his nephew had struck like a mud and flesh tornado. The man looked dazed for a moment, and then opened his mouth to bellow his annoyance.

'Benedict!' he roared, and Ben quailed and Rachel winced. Their uncle really could have been a huge hit in the opera. The volume, percussion, and resonance he could create from just one word was quite remark-able. It clanged against the kitchen walls and the pans that hung above the sink vibrated.

'Sorry, Uncle J!' gasped Ben, rubbing his elbow which had struck the floor hard. Uncle Jerome looked ready to unleash another terribly loud complaint, but a piece of sugary apple slid over his grey hair and fell into his eye, behind his spectacles, and this distracted him.

Getting to his feet, he began wiping his snack off his head, neck, and shoulders. Rachel quickly ran to the sink and wetted a tea towel and then began to sponge off the fruit, pastry, and sticky orange juice, while Uncle Jerome grunted in annoyance.

After a minute he noticed the state of his niece and nephew. 'Have you been *mining*?' he asked, aghast. They realized they must look pretty bad, because Uncle Jerome almost *never* noticed what they looked like, so distracted was he by his science projects, which he worked on ceaselessly in his attic laboratory.

Ben decided to be straight. 'Yes,' he said. 'We've found something in the wood. We were trying to dig it up.'

'Oh, I see,' nodded Uncle Jerome. 'Good. Better than watching television all day. Children should dig more. All children should dig.'

Ben and Rachel smiled and nodded. Uncle Jerome took off his spectacles, wiped them on the tea towel and put them back on his nose.

'I'm sorry, you two,' he said. They stared at him in surprise. 'It's not much fun, is it? Stuck out here all summer, with only an old scientist for company. I know it's dull for you.'

'Well,' began Rachel, 'it's not that bad now the rain's stopped.' She was itching to get what they'd come for and get back to the wood. Uncle Jerome had picked the worst moment to come over all reflective and understanding.

'It's just that I've got to get this project finished— or at least to the next stage—by September, or I'll lose my funding,' said Uncle Jerome. They nodded sympathetically. Uncle Jerome was working on something for some government body. They had tried to understand what it was once, when he'd been in the mood to explain it to them. They hadn't understood a word he'd said.

'Perhaps you could have some friends to stay?' he suggested. 'Get some school chums over for a week.'

Ben and Rachel sighed. It's not that they didn't have school 'chums'—it's just that none of them much wanted to stay beyond a day in a leaky old house with no decent computer games. Mum and Dad had promised them a games console at the end of their summer tour, but until then, now that the telly was dead, the most hi-tech distraction they had was the toaster. They both had some little hand-held computer games, but those had run out of batteries days ago. There *were* computers—about three of them—in Uncle Jerome's laboratory, but he had always made it quite clear that prodding even one button on one keyboard could lead to a cataclysmic disaster in the world of science beyond all measure. Likely to end in a death. Probably of the button prodder.

The house was on the outskirts of the town and quite remote. People didn't just drop by, apart from the postman and Percy, an old man who occasionally toiled up the stony lane and leant on the gate, staring at the woods beyond Darkwood House. He always moved off before Ben or Rachel could talk to him, although they had heard him speak to Uncle Jerome once in a while.

'Give it some thought! Let me know!' said Uncle Jerome, retrieving more apple pie and orange juice from the fridge. Then he was gone, back upstairs, humming softly to himself as he went.

Ben and Rachel ran to the cupboard beneath the sink. Getting the hot soapy water in a bucket down the steep slopes and over the stream was very difficult, but they had at least half of it left by the time they reached their excavation site. Never had anyone been more excited about scrubbing brushes and floor cloths. They worked around the earth-choked ins and outs of the metal wheel on its shaft and soon streams of brown water were running across the gentle dome of the metal under their knees. When they had poked out all the mud from every channel with barbecue skewers and washed the whole wheel and column clean with a final upending of the bucket, they dried it all with the floor cloths and then Ben poked the 3-in-1 oil nozzle into the channel that ran around the column beneath the wheel.

'Turning it should undo some kind of catch inside, and then I reckon it'll tip up,' said Ben, gnawing on his lower lip. They threw all the cleaning and oiling stuff in the bucket and put it to one side as they stared at the gleaming results of their work. The metal shone pale grey—there was no rust on it. The lettering at the base of the dome had been fully revealed now. HJE—1955.

'It's been here more than fifty years,' whispered Rachel, and a shiver ran through her, making the hairs stand up on her arms. 'What could it be?'

Ben shrugged. 'I dunno. Probably just some water workings or something. Anyway . . . let's find out.'

They both took hold of the wheel and pulled in the direction of the arrow for half a minute, straining and gasping and screwing up their dirty faces with the effort. They stopped and stared at each other, frustrated. 'It's no good,' panted Rachel. 'It's stuck.'

'No,' grunted Ben and narrowed his dark grey eyes. He was not going to give up on this—not if he was still here, tugging at this wheel, at midnight. 'Come on—again!'

They bent to the wheel once more and hauled at it with aching hands, and maybe their previous efforts had helped, because, to their utter amazement, this time there was a gritty, grating sound, and the wheel actually began to turn. Ben shouted and Rachel squeaked with excitement. It *was* turning—faster and faster. It turned a full 180 degrees, with the brother and sister hanging off it and grinning at each other in delight, before it stopped. They stopped too and stood up and just as they were about to reach over and try to yank the hatch up in some way, there was a clunk and then a low metallic ring, deep in the earth beneath them. Then a sound like a metal chain being dragged across something. Three clicks and then a hiss. They stood, gasping, as the hatch dropped *down* and then slid sideways, smoothly, revealing a crescent of black emptiness which grew and grew until it was a full circle. With a final clunk, the movement stopped and the black circle gaped up at them—a replica of their own shocked mouths.

Rachel grabbed Ben's arm and found that he was shaking as much as she was. They looked at each other, identical eyes wide with amazement and fear. A musty old smell rose from the black circle

23

and Ben could feel the cold of it curling around his ankles.

'I don't know if I want to do this,' said Rachel, sounding very young. Ben had been thinking the very same thing.

'We'll need torches,' he gulped, his voice shaking. But just as he said this there was a click and a humming noise started up and then a pale orange light glowed up from the hole, revealing a metal ladder set into the side of a deep shaft. 'Wow!' breathed Ben and they leaned over, staring down.

'How far does it go?' Rachel leaned on his shoulder.

'Not that far—about four metres maybe . . . ?' said Ben. And they could see where the ladder ended at a dull grey concrete floor. 'There must be a corridor leading off it,' breathed Ben, excitement fighting with fear inside him. What if Rachel was right? What if there *were* aliens or something?

'Come on then!' said Rachel, much to his surprise, and she was stepping down onto the first rung already.

'No! Let me go first!'

'Why? Because you're a *boy*?' she snapped. 'Don't be sexist.'

'No—because I'm the eldest! And it might be dangerous. And Mum and Dad always say I have to

look after you, so get off there and let me go first . . .
we don't even know if it's OK to breathe down there,
do we?'

Rachel looked mutinous so he added: 'And I bet
the spiders are *huge*.' That did it. With a shudder she
stepped back up again and let him go first. He did
expect, in fact, to have to flap his way through a lot
of cobwebs as he went down, and was surprised to
find that there were actually hardly any. Maybe there
was no point in a spider being down here. Not much
in the way of flies would have been through for a very
long time.

The ladder, as he tested it with a few sharp kicks,
seemed perfectly sound. It was bolted securely into the
shaft wall, which was circular, like the hatch, and
made of smooth concrete. He realized that the lid of
the shaft, which had slid away into the side, must be
thirty centimetres thick. Whatever mechanism had made
it move must be very strong. As he descended he saw
a pull-lever switch, like the kind of thing you see on
generators, which must work the hatch lid from the
inside. Next to it was a bright yellow notice. Black
lettering on it read: **Check all sensors. Do not attempt
exit before blue light. STOP. CHECK. Are you wearing
your suit and breathing equipment.**

He also saw that there were lights, domed and

covered in metal grilles, at intervals, alongside the ladder. The one next to the yellow sign looked blue, although it was not lit.

Ben felt scared. Very scared. He looked up at Rachel who was making urgent 'get a move on' gestures, ready to follow him down.

'Look . . . let's just go to the b-bottom and see what's there. I don't think we should go any further . . . not until we know a b-bit more about this . . . ' he said. It was no good. His stammer was starting up, so she would know he was scared.

'OK, OK!' she said. 'But hurry up! I want to see.'

He descended then, steadily, determined not to look frightened, and Rachel swung her muddy wellingtons over the edge, dropping a small clod of earth on his head, and followed fast. The deeper they went the thicker the fug of mustiness. It swam into his nose and throat like gas and made him gulp rapidly. Rachel felt it too, but having given way over the spiders thing, she was equally determined not to look scared in front of her brother.

At last they stood at the bottom. They turned in one direction. The only direction they could turn. A concrete corridor led away, its grey walls lit with more orange lights, to a closed metal door about five metres away. The door had curved corners, like something from a submarine, and another one of those wheels to turn to get it open. They looked at each other as they reached it.

'C-can we do this?' asked Ben, no longer trying to look un-scared.

Rachel stared up at him, eyes huge with fright and excitement. 'Yes,' she said. 'We can.'

They grabbed the wheel together and this time, without fifty years of mud and roots embedded in it, it turned quite easily. Finally it stopped turning and there was another hiss and clunk, like the first time, and the door seals abruptly snapped. It moved inwards slightly, propelled by the breaking of the seals, and a blackness stole around the edge, as it had done at the hatch. Ben reached out a shaking hand and poked at the door and it swung open into the next room a little more.

As it did so there was a sudden click and a zooming noise, like something powering up—orange light flickered and then glowed steadily through the gap they had made and then, to their utter amazement, they heard a voice.

Chapter 3

Rachel shrieked. So did Ben. Then they hitched in their shocked gasps, holding their hands to their mouths, and listened with eyes wide and glassy.

'YOU ARE ENTERING A SECURE ZONE,' warned a stern male voice. 'IF YOU ARE CONTAMINATED TURN BACK NOW.'

They gasped and clutched at each other. Who could be down here? Who was this man?

'YOU ARE ENTERING A SECURE ZONE,' repeated the man. 'IF YOU ARE CONTAMINATED, TURN BACK NOW.'

When he said it for the third time, Ben's hammering heart at last began to slow down. 'It's OK,' he whispered to Rachel. 'It's just a recording.' And he reached out and pushed open the door, embarrassed that he'd been so scared. 'It must have been triggered by the door unlocking. Come on!' Now he pushed open the door and light flooded out. Inside was a chamber, about the size of their living room, stacked with floor to ceiling shelving, which was filled with all kinds of boxes and tins and bottles and packets. As the stern man continued to warn them off, Rachel stared around in a daze. She saw OMO and VIM and Brown & Polson, and other names which didn't mean much to her, in old-fashioned writing. The floor was covered in a green swirly carpet and there was an old-fashioned leather sofa and two armchairs, grouped around a table—and between the sofa and armchair was the source of the voice. An old-fashioned reel to reel tape recorder was turning, a small pale cloud of dust rising from it.

Ben wandered across to the machine and pressed a clunky STOP button on its surface. At last the voice stopped, plunging them into an eerie silence, under which ran the soft hum of some kind of power generator, Ben guessed. He noticed that the air seemed a little fresher too—perhaps it was some kind of air conditioner.

'Ben—look—it goes on,' whispered Rachel, standing transfixed in the middle of the room, pointing to another door in the opposite wall. This one was an ordinary door, painted white, with an ordinary handle. Rachel was already opening it and Ben hurried across to stop her going through.

'Wait!' he breathed. 'Me first—remember? I'm the eldest!' She let him go willingly enough and he realized she was as scared as he was.

The door opened normally, and beyond it lay another room, also lit by the orange lamps set on the walls. There was more shelving ahead, filled with more curious stuff, on one wall, and two sets of metal bunk beds, complete with mattresses and dark grey folded up blankets, lined the walls on either side of the door. Another door led off to their left. They walked to it as if mesmerized and pushed it open. Now another room—a kitchen, with small units painted cream and blue, slanted glass doors on the cabinets above them, filled with floral-patterned china. A low white sink with metal taps shaped like carrots was set into a pale blue work surface, decorated with little grey specs. 'Formica,' Ben mouthed. He opened one of the base cabinets and saw pots and pans.

Rachel pulled open a cupboard set into a wall and found more packets and tins and bottles. 'Look!' she said. 'Heinz! It can't be *that* long ago . . . ' She pulled out a tin and the familiar Heinz label glimmered in the orange light—although Ben could see that it was an old-fashioned design on dull paper. He walked over and looked into the cupboard and saw stack upon stack of square tins with SPAM on them.

The label carried the promise 'REAL MEAT FOR YOUR MONEY' in old style letters.

'Come on—we should keep going,' he said, quietly, as if he might wake ghosts hiding among the stacks of tins.

'Wait! Look—sweets!' Rachel scooped a waxed paper tube out of the cupboard. It was orange with yellow stripes and apparently cost 3d. 'Spangles,' murmured Rachel, turning the square tube in her palm. 'Deliciously fruity—excitingly new . . . ' she turned to a new side of the tube. 'The sweet way to go gay.' She giggled and Ben snorted.

'Oh-kay,' he said. 'Let's leave the fruity excitement alone . . . there's another door.'

The next room was a bathroom, with black and white tiles on the floor and green paint on the walls. There was a bath and a toilet with its cistern high up, and a wall-mounted sink on iron brackets, with a lozenge-shaped mirror over it—and a corner shelving unit filled with stack upon stack of toilet paper in boxes. 'IZAL,' read Ben. 'Must be about three hundred boxes of it! Blimey! Either they were planning to stay a long time or they used to eat some really mean curry.'

Rachel looked disgusted. 'It's the stuff that Gran used to have—do you remember? It smells funny and feels like sandpaper!'

There was soap on the sink, in a dimple of ceramic between the metal taps. It was dark red and looked almost fossilized under its light layer of dust.

'What was all this *for*?' wondered Rachel. 'Why would anybody want to live underground?'

'Another door,' said Ben, nodding off into the corner of the bathroom where a square of mottled glass was lit from behind. It made the hairs prickle on his neck again—because this light was different. It wasn't the regulation orange that they'd grown used to over the past few minutes—but a soft, blue-white glow. 'Come on.'

The temperature dipped noticeably as they stepped into the next room. The last room, Rachel realized, as soon as the door had swung shut behind them. It was painted white and no more doors led on from it. One wall was filled with machinery—a kind of huge metal console with knobs and levers and buttons and three small screens, dead and showing nothing. From the top of the console three channels of tubes and wires and ducting pipes led up, across the ceiling and down into the centre of the room. Each group of pipes and wires descended to a large torpedo-shaped thing, which was bolted to the floor. The three torpedo things were lightly covered in dust and stood like small monoliths, silent and odd.

'What *is* it?' whispered Rachel, shivering with more than just the cold.

Ben looked all around and up and down and still found it really hard to take even one step forward. He felt terrified and didn't want to speak, because Rachel would hear it in his voice. His stammer was sitting in his clenched throat like an impatient cricket, waiting to mess up his words and drive a blush up his cheeks. He noticed that there was a kind of desk area protruding to one side of the console, and heaped upon it were books and notepads and even a couple of pencils, under a thin layer of dust. In fact, he thought, the dust wasn't nearly as heavy as you'd expect, if this place had been here as long as the furniture and the tins of food suggested. Probably because it was underground and there wasn't much down here to *make* dust. At last he found his feet and stepped towards the console. He cleared the dust off the open pages and saw spidery handwriting compressed into the narrow lines of the paper. There were figures and diagrams and words that he could barely read. It looked scientific, which was not surprising. This was a laboratory of some kind, surely.

Rachel had gone over to one of the torpedo things. 'You don't think . . . ' she breathed, 'that it could be a bomb . . . ? Do you?'

Ben shrugged. 'C-could be, I suppose.' She gulped. 'But I don't see why it would be bolted to the floor, if it was.'

She reached out and gently wiped away the thin skin of dust. The torpedo thing gave up some dimly gleaming grey metal, reflecting the white orb-shaped light that hung above it. She took a spare floor cloth out of her pocket and gave it a more thorough wipe and then let out a shout of surprise. 'It's—look—it's glass!' Ben spun around and stepped over to see. 'Or plastic or something,' she went on. 'Look!' Set into the smooth curve of the torpedo was a glass window. It wasn't a bomb—it was a chamber of some kind.

'It's like a—you know—a diving bell thingy,' said Rachel, who had been to a sea life centre recently and seen a display of old diving equipment.

Beneath the glass lay nothing except what looked like a cushioned leather base to the torpedo. It certainly did look a bit like a diving bell . . . sort of. 'Does it open?' he asked, and they began to wipe more dust away and run their hands over the chamber, trying to find buttons or levers or any clue at all to how they might get into it. But they found nothing other than a fine seam around the base of the torpedo, too narrow to even get a fingernail into.

'Weird,' said Ben, leaning back against the

neighbouring torpedo, his arm wiping a track through the dust on its curved glass window. 'Really weird.' He felt suddenly exhausted by the excitement and fear. 'Maybe we should get Uncle J down to have a look.'

'He'd *love* all this!' agreed Rachel. 'It's so weird! Amazing.' She too, leaned on the second torpedo thing, resting her cheek on her palm, her elbow on the bit that Ben had just dusted. Then she opened her eyes wide. And then her mouth.

And began to scream.

Chapter 4

Ben had heard his sister scream quite a lot. She was a girl, after all. But he had never, in twelve years, heard her scream like *this*. He jumped violently and grabbed at her and saw that her eyes were bulging with shock and horror. She was pointing and screaming: 'A body! Oh, Ben! It's a dead body!'

Ben stared into the glass and saw a face. Eyes closed, pale pink lips very slightly open, revealing milk-white teeth. Dark hair curled across an alabaster forehead. It was a girl—about the same age as Rachel. It made him think of Snow White in her glass coffin. A shudder of fear went through him, making his heart thud and his legs feel weak. Rachel had stopped screaming now, and was holding her hands across her mouth, her eyes shut, shaking and crying. They should get out of here—now! And yet, something inside him couldn't let him walk away, just as it had barely allowed him to walk *in* a few minutes earlier. This girl . . . this cool, still, sleeping girl . . .

'She doesn't look dead,' he said, finally, still holding on to Rachel's shoulder. 'Maybe they had a way of p-preserving them. You know—embalming—like they did with Lenin and Eva P-Peron . . . '

Rachel stared at him. 'What are you *talking* about?' she gasped.

'I just mean—that she looks . . . pretty good for a dead person.'

'Oh—my—God . . . ' said Rachel. 'You fancy a corpse!'

'Don't be stupid,' he said, with an exasperated click of the tongue, and suddenly he realized he wasn't really *that* scared any more. He was more fascinated—as if he'd stumbled into Tutankhamun's cave. 'Come on—we can't go back now. We have to know . . . '

Rachel gave a little shriek as he vigorously wiped the top of the last torpedo chamber. Ben caught his breath in shock, even though he'd been half expecting it this time. Another face lay beneath the curved glass window. Also dark haired. His eyes, too, were closed, and his features were similar to the girl's. Perhaps they were related. He seemed, thought Ben, to be smiling. As if he was having a bit of a joke. At any moment his eyes might spring open and he might shout 'SURPRISE!!!'

'He looks like her,' breathed Rachel, who had overcome her fear to move around to lean on Ben's shoulder. 'A bit older. He's probably her brother. Maybe this is some weird kind of mausoleum . . . you know . . . like when they buried Egyptian kings and put all the stuff they'd need in with them, to take them into the afterlife.' Ben nodded—he'd been thinking similar thoughts.

'But if someone took this much care over burying their kids,' he pondered, 'you'd think they'd've put up a headstone or something . . . wouldn't you?'

'It's creepy,' shivered Rachel. 'I can't believe I'm still standing here.'

'Well, they're hardly going to spring up and bite you, are they?' said Ben. 'They must have been dead for decades. I wonder what killed them . . . and who they were . . . Maybe . . . ' He walked back to the console, ducking past the pipes and wires that went into the top of the torpedo chambers. 'Maybe there's something about who they were in these notebooks.'

Rachel hurried after him. She did *not* want to be standing on her own between two dead bodies, no matter how healthy they looked. Ben was flipping through the notebook, coughing now and then as the dust from it caught in his throat. She glanced at the other books, but they looked like textbooks—the kind of stuff she hoped never to have to get down off the shelf in maths class. She studied the console with all its old buttons and levers. Everything looked as dead as the boy and girl in the torpedoes. As if it had lain there for centuries. She could probably press all the buttons and flick all the levers without anything happening but a bit of a dust storm. Although the square plastic or glass one down on the left looked as though it might do something. There was a very faint red glow about it—but that was probably just a reflection of the red top she was wearing. She flicked it idly and, of course, nothing happened.

'Anything?' she asked Ben, who was squinting at the book.

He shook his head . . . 'Nah . . . it's all just equations and numbers and stuff. Science stuff. Weird things to leave in a burial chamber. Maybe they were both . . . you know . . . geniuses or something, like Uncle J. What's that noise?'

Rachel listened, her fair head cocked to one side. Something was hissing. Not like a snake, but steadily, like escaping gas. She stared up, scared again, at Ben. 'Shhhh!' he said, in an imitation of the noise. But now she realized something else was threading through her ears . . . beneath the hissing . . . a low hum, almost below the range of hearing, it was more as if they could *feel* it, vibrating through their bones.

Now the hiss and the hum were joined by a regular beeping noise, like a slowed down alarm clock.

'Oh no—what did you do, Rachel? What did you do?'

'Me? What did *I* do? I didn't do anything!' she squawked.

'You must have! What did you touch?'

'Only that red square button—but it didn't work. It's not even lit up—it's—oh!' Now that she looked at it again, she could see that the button *was* lit up. Quite definitely. And next to it a row of other buttons, in various colours, were also beginning to light up, some glowing steadily and others flashing.

'Oh no!' moaned Ben. 'We've set something off! We've got to get out of here.'

They both ran towards the door but as they reached it there was a click and a metallic thud and they saw that on *this* side of the door was not just an ordinary knob, but a turning wheel type thing like on the outside of the shaft . . . and it was turning. Rachel screamed again and Ben grabbed the wheel, trying to turn it back—but was completely unable to make it stop turning. He could hear the cogs and levers of a strong locking mechanism moving relentlessly inside it. Why had he shut the door behind them? Why?

Rachel was now banging against it, crying, 'No! No! No! I'm not staying in here! Get me out! Get me out! I don't want to die down here.'

Ben felt fingers of dread creep coldly over his shoulders and make for his throat. He and his little sister were being entombed. Buried alive with the dead. He shouted too then—he didn't know what; he just bellowed with fear. The hissing went on, the hum grew louder and even the light seemed to get brighter as the beeping got faster. Rachel crumpled against the door and slid down its unyielding surface, crying uncontrollably, her nose running and her eyes screwed up. He felt himself beginning to pitch into hysteria with her . . . what was the point of trying to stop himself? They were done for. They would never get out and it would take several days for Uncle J to even notice they were missing. There was no food or water stored in this room. They were dead. As dead as the girl and boy in their metal coffins.

'I do wish you'd both stop that racket. It's like a blasted kindergarten in here.'

Rachel turned around and stared at the owner of the voice. Then her eyes rolled up into her head and she keeled over, unconscious, onto the floor.

'For goodness' sake!' said the boy, after Ben had gaped at him for thirty seconds or more, making faint gurgling sounds of shock and horror. 'You might stop looking at me as if I'm a ruddy ghost! And what the blazes are you doing in my father's vault? He'll go off like an atom bomb when he sees you here.'

The boy wiped back a dark fringe which hung across his brow from a neat side parting and rubbed his hands together, sitting on the edge of the torpedo under the glass which was now suspended above him at an angle, like the bonnet of a sleek racing car. 'Shocking cold,' he muttered and then leaned over and hammered unceremoniously on the torpedo next to him. 'Hey! Polly! Get up, you lazy coot!' At this there was a higher note of hissing and the girl's glass cover suddenly popped up too, like the boy's. A draught of cool, slightly sweet air flowed from it and Ben heard a sleepy murmuring from inside. He smacked himself on the face with both fists. It hurt. Yep. He was still awake. The boy was giving him an odd look.

'I say, Poll—wake up fast will you? There's a lunatic boy and a half dead girl here.'

Rich, thought Ben. *Considering*.

Polly sat up, yawning and scrubbing at her eyes.

'Who? What? Oh, dash it! I'm frozen. He's done it again, hasn't he? Left us in too long. It's really too bad. I bet I've missed Hilary's party!'

Ben simply could not get his jaw to close. He kept gasping and blinking and shaking his head and trying to wake himself up and then he realized that Rachel was coming round at his feet and he simply did not know what to do.

'Who's he?' asked Polly, sitting up fully and also rubbing her hands. She peered at Ben as if he were another species.

'Can't say,' said the boy, who was getting out of the torpedo now, somewhat unsteadily. He was wearing a short-sleeved shirt and grey flannel shorts. 'Oh heck— I think you're right. He's left us too long again. I've never been *this* wobbly before. He probably got going on some new experiment and hasn't eaten for two days—much less think about *us*. I'm jolly well not doing this again, I tell you. Look, *will* you two stop all that gibbering! It's perfectly all right. The door will open again in a few minutes. It's just a time delay, you ninnies.'

'T-time delay?' gulped Ben. Rachel had just sat up and begun all the gaping, gasping, blinking, and pinching stuff he had been doing himself only seconds ago. She looked like a mad fish.

'Yes. The air pressure has to be equalized before the lids can be sprung,' explained the boy. 'It's probably a bit too complicated for you to understand. Don't worry. I'd like to know how you got in here, though.'

'We—we d-dug . . . ' said Ben, and Rachel, who was now past the mad fish stage and getting unsteadily to her feet, nodded feverishly.

'Yes . . . we dug.'

'We . . . dug . . . ' repeated the boy, slowly, a patient smile on his face. 'Well—we . . . *Freddy* and *Polly*! Are both of you called Doug then?' He raised one eyebrow and gave a slightly wonky grin.

'No! We *dug*—we dug down. With spades! That's how we got in!' said Ben, his more normal voice finally bursting through. He felt that this was not the time for sarky humour.

'Right-oh!' said Freddy. 'If you say so. But you'd better scarper or you'll be in a lot of darn trouble when my father catches you. And if you tell anyone you've seen this place, you'll be in even more trouble. There are forces, you know, more powerful than . . . '

'Oh pish! Don't be such an idiot, Freddy,' said Polly—who was clambering out of her own torpedo now. 'They must be Father's students. And they must be trustworthy, or he wouldn't have let them in.' She

44

wore similar shorts to her brother and a pale pink blouse with a neat round collar. Her clothes looked as if they'd been washed, pressed, and put on that morning. She dropped off the edge of the torpedo and her legs immediately gave and she crumpled to the floor with a surprised squeak.

'I should go easy,' said Ben. 'I don't think you've used those for a while.'

'Thank you,' she said, primly. 'But I don't think I've forgotten how to *walk* in one week!'

'One week?' echoed Rachel and she and Ben exchanged appalled glances.

'Yes—it's beastly, isn't it?' said Polly. 'That's what you get when your father's a genius. You might think we'd get two motorcars, a twelve inch television set, and a trip in an aeroplane, but oh no—we get to be suspended for days on end, just to help out. I'm jolly sick and tired of it. I'm not ever doing this again. Not even for a ten shilling note!'

'Your dad—he was a genius?' asked Ben and inside him the fear and amazement were beginning to mix with the most awful sense of pity. Something really terrible had happened to these two children and they had absolutely no idea.

'Oh yes—he is,' said Polly, rubbing her ankles through her short grey socks, to warm them up. Her buckle-up sandals were navy and polished. 'He built all this stuff. It's all terribly hush-hush, of course, but now that you've seen it there's not much point in fibbing, is there? He's a genius and he knows how to make your heart freeze . . . and then just start up again! Whenever you like. Isn't that fantastic?'

'Oh yes—jolly fab-oh,' muttered Freddy, who was also fully out of the torpedo by now and gingerly walking around to his sister, on very shaky legs. 'I think he should go back to using rats. I'm sick of waking up feeling all queer and then finding out I've missed *Journey Into Space*.'

'So—so you've had your heart stopped . . . and then just started again?' said Ben. 'You've just been frozen in time? I mean—that's cryonic suspension, isn't it?' He liked sci-fi stuff and stored up these kinds of phrases. The brother and sister looked at him in surprise. And then at each other.

'Gosh—Father must have told you quite a lot,' said Polly, a new respect creeping into her high, elegant voice.

'Um . . . no. Not really,' said Ben. 'Look—there's something you two should know—but . . . look, have you got any sweet drinks or anything?' He looked wretchedly at Rachel and she returned his expression. How on earth would a bit of sugar help a shock *this* big?

'Heaps!' said Polly, proudly. 'Tizer! We'll get some from the refrigerator as soon as the door opens.'

'*What* should we know?' asked Freddy, and he was looking hard at Ben. *Man to man*, thought Ben. 'What's going on?'

Ben shuffled his feet. His fear was quite gone now, but he found his stammer was back, all the same. 'When d-did your d-dad put you under?' he asked.

'Wednesday,' said Freddy. 'Why?'

'What *date*?'

'The sixth. Of June. What are you driving at?'

Ben closed his eyes and it was Rachel who said, gently, her voice full of sadness for them. 'What . . . *year*?'

Freddy gulped and Polly paled. '1956, of course,' said the boy. His eyes glittered and he stood up straight and then shouted '1956! 1956!' And he watched their faces and his eyes skittered around the room while he chewed on his lower lip, and he finally said, 'When . . . what . . . is the date now?'

The door hissed and clunked and the mechanism reversed. Rachel pulled it open. 'You stay here—with them—I'll find the Tizer. Don't let them out . . . not yet.'

'What the heck do you mean?' shouted Freddy, and he tried to stride angrily across to the door but his legs gave way under him. He sank down next to his sister and she grasped his hand tightly and bit her lip.

'Oh, Freddy,' she said. 'What has he done?'

Rachel ran through the bathroom and into the kitchen. The fridge was still working although its light didn't switch on. It was still full of tins and boxes. There were bottles of Tizer in its door—and they looked OK. She hoped the lids wouldn't have gone rusty or something on the inside. She ran to the drawer, looking for a bottle opener—these weren't the kind that unscrewed—and found one, quickly. Awkwardly she fumbled with it until at last the cap shot off and danced across the Formica worktop. She did a second bottle and ran quickly back through the bathroom with both. Before she reached it, the door at the other end opened, and Freddy and Polly staggered through, Ben behind them, shrugging at her and shaking his head. 'I couldn't stop them,' he said.

She and Ben had both realized that the sight of the dust all over the things in the living areas would provide the clue that they had been left, hearts stopped, for a bit longer than a week. As Freddy and Polly moved through the bathroom and into the kitchen, they were already beginning to slow down and sweep horrified glances from one side of the room to the other. In the chamber with the torpedoes the dust had not been so obvious, somehow. Everything in there was pale and grey-looking anyway. But here, on the blue and cream kitchen furniture, across the draining board of the sink, over the curved metal toaster and the pale lemon biscuit tins, the layer of dust was mournfully obvious.

Rachel pulled out two low stools from beside the sink. 'Please,' she said. 'Sit down and drink this. You really, really need it.' Dazed, they both sat and accepted a bottle. They drank a little, and then pulled faces. 'Flat,' said Freddy.

'Drink it anyway,' said Ben. 'You need the sugar.'

Freddy took a long drink and then sat up, looking levelly at Ben. 'All right. Don't try to fudge us. You'd better tell it to us straight. How many months have we been down here? And what's happened to our father?'

Ben winced. *Months*. They still thought it was only months. But then—why not? Dust like this *could* build up in months . . . maybe. And it wasn't as if he and Rachel had arrived in shiny silver cat-suits, waving ray guns, like anyone after the year 2000 was supposed to have looked like to people living back in the old days. They wore jeans and sweatshirts, and many kids in 1956 probably wore something similar. 'Look—I don't know what happened to your father,' said Ben, as kindly as he could. 'But you ought to know this. It's going to be a bit of a shock. This isn't 1956 any more.'

They stared at him from round blue eyes—desperately unprepared for what he was about to say.

'Freddy . . . Polly . . . This is 2009.'

Chapter 5

There was an incredibly long pause. Then Freddy let out a shuddering breath and his shoulders started to hitch and his head dropped and he rubbed his eyes. When he looked up his face was pink and he was shaking his head. He was in fits of laughter. Polly was staring at him, a shaky smile beginning to dawn on her face.

'You—you—you must have thought we were born yesterday!' hooted Freddy, slapping his thigh like someone in a pantomime. 'Honestly—I—I really, nearly . . . you nearly had me! That was good—that was . . . I have to say . . . really the tops! The tops!'

Ben and Rachel looked at each other, aghast. Now what?

'We're not joking,' said Ben, but now Polly was laughing too. 'We're not!' he shouted. 'Look—look—have you seen anything like *this* in 1956?' He pulled up his sleeve and showed them the watch he'd got for Christmas. It was a gleaming dial of digital numbers, the liquid crystal display twinkling with blue-green light, offering up the time of day, the date, a stopwatch function and even a calendar and calculator if you wanted it. It kept exact time, as it was connected to a global satellite, and it was sleek and fantastic and totally twenty-first century.

Freddy grabbed hold of his wrist and stared at it. 'Wizard!' he said, respectfully. 'I've heard you can get those in America.'

'Oh come *on*! In 1956? Not on your life!' Ben began to flick through the different modes of the watch, like a desperate timepiece salesman, urging Freddy to believe the unbelievable. 'See—it can do *that* and *that* and . . . '

'Stop it,' said Rachel. 'They'll know soon enough. We need to take them back up the ladder. Back to the house. That'll settle it.'

'You bet your life it will! Father will soon sort *you* out,' said Freddy, slamming the Tizer bottle down and getting to his feet.

'D-did you live in Darkwood House too then?' asked Ben.

'We *do* live in Darkwood House!' snapped Freddy. 'And you don't! So pack it in! Stop being such an ass!'

He pulled Polly up with him and they walked smartly, although still rather unsteadily, through to the bunk bedroom and on into the sitting room with its silenced reel-to-reel machine. Ben and Rachel watched them take in more dust on all the surfaces but they didn't slow down. They strode across to the door which lay open to the corridor—a shaft of pale daylight showing at the end by the wall ladder.

'Careful—you're still really weak,' said Ben, as they both flung themselves righteously up it. He was right too, they had to pause halfway up, but eventually they were on the surface and when Ben and Rachel had caught up and clambered out onto the soggy mud around the hatch, they found the brother and sister standing staring around them in silence.

'Well,' said Rachel, at length. 'I guess you can see it's not June any more. It's August. Nearly September.'

They continued to stare. Stricken and still. 'Where's the garden?' said Polly, in a choked whisper.

'Oh—um . . . well it *is* a bit overgrown,' said Rachel, apologetically. 'Mum and Dad aren't great gardeners . . . and Uncle Jerome wouldn't know a lawnmower if it bit him.'

'It's . . . it's a jungle . . . '

Freddy was slowly turning around, taking in the

trees and bushes. Ben could guess that he was sizing them up and remembering them as they had been . . . just a day ago in his world. He gulped several times and his hands went into fists. His skin went pale. Then he stepped across to Polly and rested a hand on her shoulder. 'You're not to panic, Poll. All right? Don't have hysterics. We'll work this out. It's probably not . . . I mean, it needn't be as long as they say.'

But Polly had turned and was taking in the evidence of all the digging Ben and Rachel had done around the hatch. 'Look,' she whispered. 'Look how far under it was. They really *did* dig us out! Why would he have done that? Why would Father have buried us?'

Tears welled up in her round blue eyes and began to spill silently down her cheeks. Rachel felt her throat constrict. She tried to imagine how she would feel if *she* had woken up that morning only to find more than fifty years had passed. She moved over to Polly and took her hand, amazed to find how normal and warm it felt. 'Look—don't worry. It's OK.'

'How?' said Freddy, and his voice sounded hard— tightly controlled. 'Exactly how is it oh-kay? If you're telling the truth . . . '

'Freddy—look,' sniffed Polly, pointing to the crumbly remains of the log. 'The drop log. That . . . that's all that's left of it.'

54

Ben felt out of his depth. He wanted to do something, to help in some way, but he couldn't think how—except to get them back to the house and give them a cup of tea, with lots of sugar. That's what Mum always did when someone was upset.

'Come on,' he said, sounding much more decisive than he felt. 'Come back to the house with us. You can have a cup of tea and we'll talk about this.'

To his immense surprise, Freddy and Polly just nodded and as he moved away towards the stream, they simply followed. They were in shock, of course. They hopped over the stream, Freddy taking Polly's hand, and climbed up the slope, hanging on to branches as Ben and Rachel did, looking around bleakly.

At least, thought Rachel, they won't find too much to startle them at the house. It couldn't have changed much in a hundred years, let alone fifty. But, of course, she was wrong. As soon as they were through the front door, Polly cried out, 'No!' and put her hands to her mouth. Freddy stood still and slowly took in the hallway. It certainly had many of its original features, like the floor tiles, the stained-glass door, and the picture rail and old coving on the ceiling. Obviously, though, it had changed a lot.

'Where's the clock?' whispered Polly. 'And the occasional table? And . . . the wallpaper? The pictures?'

She spun slowly around, staring at the hallway as if she'd just landed on another planet. Rachel took her hand again and led her along to the kitchen. It didn't help. Although the old ceramic sink and a built-in wall cupboard were original, the units were only a few years old—pale oak and very twenty-first century.

'Come on—sit down. I'll put the kettle on,' said Rachel, and began to fill the jug kettle at the tap. Freddy stared at it.

'You can't put that on!' he said. 'It'll melt!'

'Oh—oh no.' Rachel looked down at the kettle, seeing it with new eyes. It was made of plastic, of course, and connected to a round base which was plugged into the socket. In 1956 the kettle would probably have still been put on the hob. 'It doesn't work like that any more . . . and it's a really tough kind of plastic. Look.' She plonked the kettle jug down onto its base and switched on the socket. Immediately the water level gauge on the side of the jug lit up blue. Freddy and Polly blinked and then stared at each other and then back at the kettle. Their eyes were now wandering all over the very average twenty-first century kitchen they had stepped into.

As Ben got milk from the fridge Polly whispered, 'Is that a sort of television set?'

'Ah—no. No, that's a microwave,' explained Rachel

and Polly looked scared. Freddy stood up with a clatter of his chair on the tiled floor.

'Are you sure that's safe?' he asked.

Rachel shrugged and opened the door. The light went on, revealing the revolving glass plate inside and two baked beans which had been welded to it for some days now. 'It cooks food. Really quickly. That's all.'

'We know what it *does*,' said Freddy, much to her surprise. 'Father says they're not safe. He doesn't trust the inventor—that American chap, Spencer. Father says these things could cook your insides if you stand too close to them.'

'You mean, you had microwaves in 1956?' Ben was amazed.

'Well, *we* haven't, of course!' said Freddy. 'Some swanky American restaurants have got them—and I wouldn't go near one. You can cook your brains!'

'Look—it's OK,' said Rachel. 'They've done lots of tests on them and they're not at all dangerous now. We use them all the time—you know, for ready meals and stuff—when Mum and Dad are away. Uncle J can't cook for toffee and we just live on cook-chill chicken tikka massala and moussaka and stuff.'

'Chikka tikka *what*?' said Polly, looking appalled.

The kettle was bubbling urgently now, so Rachel shut the microwave door and took the jug off its stand. Ben had got four mugs and now dropped round tea bags into each of them.

'No—no teapot then,' said Polly.

'Well, yeah, we do have a teapot,' said Ben. 'We get it out for visitors sometimes. You know, old people. They like teapots and all that cup and saucer stuff. We just dunk teabags in the mug, though. Less washing up.' Rachel poured the boiling water in and Ben squished the teabags around with a spoon. Freddy and Polly watched, wordlessly, as the squashed tea bags were scooped out and fired into the bin in the corner.

'Milk—sugar?' said Ben, unscrewing the lid of a plastic milk container.

'Yes, please,' said their guests, looking extremely uneasy.

At last their tea was in front of them. Polly took her mug with a shaking hand. As she sipped her tea, her face relaxed. It obviously tasted all right.

'Is it OK? Sweet enough?' asked Rachel, anxiously. She had put two heaped teaspoons of sugar into each of their mugs.

'It's very nice, thank you,' said Polly with a polite smile. Then her eyes widened in shock as she watched her brother drink *his*. Freddy drank from one of Ben's mugs. It had a picture of Bart Simpson on it, showing off his yellow cartoon bum. Beneath the cheeky image were the words 'Eat my shorts!' Polly spluttered through a mouthful of tea and looked away, blushing furiously.

Rachel shot her brother a disapproving look. '*Ben!*' He shrugged, looking bewildered.

'Sorry,' said Rachel. 'Um . . . it's kind of a joke— you know? From a TV show.'

'Oh yes. Yes, of course,' said Polly, but she was still staring into her own mug. Freddy had turned his around and was gazing at it in amazement.

'Eat my shorts? What does *that* mean?'

'Um . . . it's kind of . . . a . . . a challenge,' muttered Ben.

'Are you feeling any better?' asked Rachel, drawing up a chair and sitting down with the brother and sister. 'This really must be a terrible shock for you.'

'What—what year did you say this was again?' asked Freddy, and Ben and Rachel looked at each other, wondering whether to start him off once more. Then Ben had an idea.

'Wait,' he said. 'I'll show you.'

Under the stairs was a box where they kept news-papers for recycling. Uncle Jerome picked up the *Guardian* in town from time to time, and the local free paper found its way, somewhat infrequently, to the house. Ben hauled out two *Guardians* and

The Advertiser, and took them back into the kitchen. He spread them out on the table. 'Look, Freddy,' he said. 'Look at the date—and—and—just try to stay calm.'

Freddy pulled the newspapers towards him. The front cover of one showed a picture of soldiers in the Middle East somewhere. The other one had a photo of the Prime Minister attending a ceremonial event in Westminster. *The Advertiser* showed a local carnival queen in a very skimpy shorts and a crop top and a sash.

'Gosh!' gasped Polly, pulling the local paper towards her. 'You can see her underwear!'

'Poll—look,' said her brother gravely, pointing to the date at the top of the page. For a long while neither of them spoke. Then Polly began to cry again.

'It's true,' she said. 'It's true. He's really gone and done it! He left us! How could he? How *could* he?' She buried her face in her hands and sobbed loudly, without restraint; and why should she restrain herself? thought Rachel. If she were in Polly's place, she'd be beyond hysterical.

'What *is* this row?' barked an impatient voice and everyone jumped and looked round. Uncle Jerome had come down from his attic and stood in the doorway. He was clearly rather alarmed. It took a lot for Rachel to cry like that. Now he saw that it was *not* Rachel, Uncle Jerome looked even more alarmed.

He took a step inside the kitchen and looked at Polly and then at Freddy. He clutched at the side of the fridge and pushed his spectacles up his nose, blinking repeatedly. Then he took his spectacles off, rubbed his eyes, put them back on again, and just *stared*. Then, like Freddy and Polly twenty minutes earlier, his knees gave way and he sank to the floor. 'Ghosts . . . ' he breathed. 'I always knew this place was haunted . . . '

'No—they're not ghosts,' said Rachel, standing up. 'They're—'

'I know who they are. Who else would they be?' gasped Uncle Jerome, resting his head against the fridge and stretching his eyes as if he just could not fit what he saw into them. 'It's Frederick and Pauline.'

Chapter 6

Ben got his uncle to put his head down between his knees until the faintness passed, while Rachel made another mug of sweet tea.

'Are they still there?' Uncle Jerome's voice was weak and muffled by his corduroy trousers. 'Have they faded from view yet?'

'They're still here—and they're not fading at all,' said Ben. 'They're not ghosts. How do you know their names?'

'Have they made contact?' asked Uncle Jerome. 'Ask them to knock three times if they can see us.'

'They're *not* ghosts!' insisted Ben. 'Honestly, Uncle J—I'm surprised at you! You're a scientist!'

'How does he know your names?' asked Rachel but Freddy and Polly just shrugged, distracted from their own grief and shock by the arrival of the man who was insisting they weren't real.

'Uncle, please!' said Rachel, sounding as much as she could like her mother (Uncle Jerome's younger sister, who never did take any nonsense from him). 'This is Freddy and Polly—we found them in an underground vault in the woods.'

'They're not ghosts,' repeated Ben. 'That would be ridiculous. They've just been held in cryonic suspension for fifty-three years.'

Uncle Jerome shot his head back up from between his knees. 'What did you say?' he gasped.

'I said, they've been in a sort of cryonic suspension . . . down in the vault in the garden . . . since 1956. We just dug them out.'

Uncle Jerome looked across at the brother and sister, who were regarding him nervously across their half-drunk tea, and suddenly he gave a wild chuckle and a tear rolled down one cheek. 'I knew it . . . I knew he couldn't have done it. I knew it!'

'What? What do you mean?' Ben shook his uncle's shoulder.

'Everyone said he did—but I *never* believed them! Never! And I was right!'

'What are you talking about?' said Ben.

'Ben—be a good boy and bring the wooden chest in from the sitting room,' said Uncle Jerome,

63

who was now getting to his feet, still chuckling, his moist eyes fixed upon Freddy and Polly. 'Hurry up!'

When Ben returned with the small chest, Uncle Jerome was sitting at the table, shaking his head in amazement, looking from Freddy to Polly and then back again. Rachel was trying to get him to drink his sweet tea. 'You look exactly—*exactly*—as I remember you,' he was murmuring.

'I'm sorry, sir,' said Polly. 'But I don't remember *you*. Ought I to?'

'Not like this, certainly,' laughed Uncle Jerome. 'You need to knock fifty-three years off. I was only six when it all happened.'

'When *what* happened?' asked Freddy. 'I want to know what happened. What happened to Father? Where is he?'

Ben dropped the chest at his uncle's feet and Uncle Jerome quickly undid it to reveal books and old faded papers. He pulled out a grey foolscap folder and put it on the table. Inside were yellowed newspaper pages. 'Prepare yourself,' he said, quite gently for Uncle Jerome, and opened up what turned out to be the front page of the local daily paper. Across it, in thick black headlines, they read:

SCIENTIST BELIEVED TO HAVE MURDERED
CHILDREN AND FLED

Polly cried out and put her hand to her throat while Freddy inhaled sharply and pulled the elderly paper closer to him, staring down at it in horror. Ben and Rachel peered over his shoulder and read the story. Of course, they had *heard* about it, long ago . . . everyone had.

Renowned scientist Henry Emerson is being hunted by police after the sudden and suspicious disappearance of his son Frederick, 13, and daughter Pauline, 12, from their Hampshire home. Professor Emerson, who was commended by the Government for his invaluable research during the war, has not been seen for two weeks. His children were reported missing after failing to arrive back at their boarding schools for the second half of term.

Headmaster Jonathan Harlow, of Plumstead Boarding School for Boys in Wiltshire, first attempted to contact Prof. Emerson by telegram, letter, and telephone but was eventually obliged to call in the Hampshire Constabulary. Detectives have reported signs of a scuffle and bloodstains on the floor of the Emerson family residence at Amhill.

Mrs M. Minstead, the family housekeeper, told police she was asked to take holiday over Whitsun and leave the family to look after itself. She reported that Prof. Emerson sometimes performed some of his experiments upon his children, despite the concerns she expressed. A thorough search of the family house and gardens has revealed no trace of the children, but many of the scientist's books and notes appear to have been taken from his attic laboratory, along with his passport. The children's belongings were left behind, according to Mrs Minstead.

'We can't be sure,' said Detective Inspector Percival Shaw, 'but it does look very suspicious. Professor Emerson kept very much to himself and was known to be short-tempered with his children. We do fear the worst.'

Ben and Rachel stared at each other, amazed, across the table. Why didn't they think of this sooner? The mystery of the missing Emersons had been talked about for years around Amhill, but to be honest, everyone had got used to the story by the time Ben and Rachel had moved into Darkwood House. It only tended to come up at Hallowe'en.

Freddy raised his eyes to Uncle Jerome. 'Does—did—everyone believe that? That my father killed us?'

Uncle Jerome shook his head and shrugged sadly. 'It was a big shock, of course. Nobody wanted to believe it—but the evidence, such as it was in those days, stacked up against your father. I was too young to be told much, but I remember everyone in the town talking about it.'

'How do you come to have this?' asked Freddy. 'How do you come to be living here—in our house?'

'Well, you see, Frederick—you're my uncle. And Pauline is my aunt,' explained Uncle Jerome, with a smile. 'My mother Ivy was married to your big brother, William—who died of TB when you were little and I was only a baby. Do you remember? So that made her your sister-in-law—your father's daughter-in-law. When *your* mother died after having Pauline, my mother would sometimes come and help out at Darkwood House, and bring me along too—remember? My sister, Annabel, was born about ten years later after mother remarried—you never met her. Annabel is Ben and Rachel's mum. Do you see?'

Freddy was screwing up his face. 'You mean . . . *you're* JJ? That snotty little infant who tried to eat my chemistry set?'

Uncle Jerome laughed. 'Yes! Yes—it's me. I always loved your chemistry set. I loved your father's lab too, although he only rarely let me see it. He was amazing. I couldn't believe he was a murderer. I really couldn't. He—he inspired me! I inherited his house and his laboratory . . . even some of his notes. I'm a scientist, too, but, oh my word, nothing like as great as he! He actually did it! He actually *did*! He perfected cryonic suspension. And here you are! The living proof! Tell me—what can you remember? What can you remember about—'

'Yesterday?' said Polly and Uncle Jerome shut up, stricken, as they were all reminded that for this girl it really *was* yesterday that she last saw her father.

'Yesterday was sunny,' said Polly, in a small, high voice. 'We were going to have Battenberg cake at teatime, as a treat. Because Father said he'd really done it. It was perfect. He said when they dropped the atom bomb we'd all be safe. We could all just sleep for years until the radioactivity was gone—and wake up good as new. He wanted to do a one hour check and then we were going to have Battenberg . . . '

'So it's a *bomb* shelter?' gasped Ben. 'Of course! Why didn't I think of that?'

'Father said there could be a strike at any time,' said Freddy. 'He said we had to be prepared. He had the shelter built last year . . . I mean . . . in fifty-five. But we weren't to tell anyone about it. He said neighbours would all come running when the sirens went off, and we didn't have enough space or supplies for them all—especially if the sleeping chambers didn't work. But they did. They did . . . ' He looked down at his feet and then suddenly up at them all again. 'Did they drop the bomb? Did it happen?'

'Well . . . no,' said Rachel. 'We wouldn't all be here if it had, would we?'

Polly stood up and began to walk around the

kitchen in agitation. 'Who cares about the bomb? What happened to Father? Where is he? Is he . . . is he still alive? Did they put him in prison? What?'

Uncle Jerome sighed. 'I'm so very sorry, Pauline. We just don't know. He was never found. Some people thought he had fled abroad after killing you both—perhaps in an experiment which went wrong—others said he was a spy for the Soviets and had defected—'

'Never!' shouted Freddy, also standing up again. 'My father did everything for his country! Everything! He was a hero! And he never did experiments on us, whatever Mrs Minstead said—that's just tosh!'

'Well . . . er . . . he *did* put you in suspension a few times . . . didn't he?' ventured Rachel.

'Well, we helped him sometimes, that's all. And that's not the same as—I don't know—sticking needles in us or making us eat radioactive pudding or something,' said Freddy. 'And that's exactly what it sounds like in that shabby newspaper. What else do they say about him?'

Uncle Jerome pulled out some more cuttings, all following the story of the missing children and their father with headlines like: '**MISSING SCIENTIST & CHILDREN—MYSTERY DEEPENS**' and '**COULD HE HAVE KILLED HIS OWN?** *VANISHED SCIENTIST*

69

EVIDENCE POINTS TO MURDER'. The bloodstains, they read, had been identified as the children's blood group.

'But our father was the *same* blood group as us. He did tests on all our blood!' said Freddy. 'What if it was *his* blood? It must have been *his*.'

'Yes—I think that was said at the time,' said Uncle Jerome. 'None of the family wanted to believe he was a killer—but the press really got their teeth into it. The investigation went on for months and months before they just had to give up. They didn't find any bodies and no trace of any of you . . . which puzzles me now. How is it that they didn't find the entrance to the shelter? I know Rachel and Ben dug you out today, but that was after fifty-odd years—you'd expect it to get covered over, in the middle of a wild wood, over the years—but surely it wasn't at the time? And they must have searched the wood.'

'Well, Father set up a system in case he needed to cover it up in a hurry,' said Freddy, looking proud. 'We even practised it with him, like a drill, a couple of times, in case of emergency. We had a pulley system in the trees. There were ropes which held some leaves and earth in a bag—and a log suspended upright near the hatch. When you wound the handle, this great load of mud and sticks and leaves would fall into the hole that the hatch was set into—then the log would drop down across it. Then it looked just like the rest of the wood floor, with a jolly heavy log on top. You could do it in a minute if you needed to and all the ropes and pulley stuff was hidden in the trees. Father made it work from the outside *or* from the inside, so we could cover our tracks if we all had to go in. I expect the police *did* search the woods, but if you didn't know what you were looking for, well . . . you'd never have found it. Not until the log mouldered away, at any rate. And it worked, didn't it? It took fifty-three years.'

'Astonishing!' marvelled Uncle Jerome. 'So we can see *how* it was done . . . but *why*?'

Everyone thought about this but nobody could come up with any answer. Why *had* Freddy and Polly been buried and abandoned?

'Didn't your housekeeper, or anyone else, know about the shelter and what your father was doing?' asked Ben.

'Oh no—definitely not!' said Freddy. 'She was a decent sort, I suppose, but a frightful gossip. Father wouldn't have trusted her with our secrets. Like I said, we didn't want a great crowd of neighbours rampaging up to us when the sirens went off . . . and . . . they never did . . . ' He shook his head in amazement.

'Everyone was so scared, with the Soviets working with the Arabs . . .'

'Why?' asked Rachel.

Ben snorted. Rachel was never that great at history. 'Don't you remember? 1956! The Suez crisis! Everyone thought they were going to get nuked over that one.'

'Suez crisis?' echoed Freddy.

'Yeah—you know . . . when the Egyptians grabbed the Suez canal and the Russians sided with them and everyone thought . . . ' Ben tailed off and glanced at Uncle Jerome.

'That was in the *November*,' he said. 'Freddy and Pauline disappeared in the spring of that year . . . May or June, I think it was.'

'I don't care about some rotten old canal!' burst out Polly. 'What about Father? What about *him*? If it was his blood on the floor—what—what happened to him? Someone must have attacked him! What—what if—?' She put her hands over her eyes and shook her head. 'No! No—this can't be real. It can't be!' Suddenly she ran out of the kitchen and back down the hallway, shouting: 'Father! Father! Daddy—oh, Daddy! Make it stop! Make them all stop and come back! Come *back*!' She flung open the front door, fought her way past the wisteria and out into the garden and ran.

Freddy raced out after her and the rest of them followed. Rachel felt her heart contract with sorrow for Polly as she heard the girl stumbling and slipping back down through the wet garden shouting 'Daddy! Daddy! Come back!' over and over again. Eventually they found her, crouched, hugging her knees, in the damp little cave space which had been beaten into the rhododendron bushes on the bank by years of den making. Tears streamed down her face.

Freddy gave her a hug. 'Come on, old girl,' he said. 'It'll be all right. It'll be all right . . . I mean, at least we've still got family, eh? Even if one of them *is* the oldest nephew in living history . . . '

Uncle Jerome followed Ben and Rachel into the tight, leafy cave, hanging awkwardly from a slippery green branch. 'Yes, quite right too, Freddy. You and Polly will be fine with us. You'll stay here with us and we'll look after you. And I promise you, I'll do everything I can to find out what happened to your father. And imagine! You're fifty-three years in the future— all kinds of things for you to see and experience! Ben and Rachel will be your guides and keep you safe. What an amazing thing! What a challenge!'

'Yes—that's right. It's a challenge,' said Freddy, briskly, as Polly wiped her eyes, sniffed and nodded. He nodded too and added, robustly: 'Eat my shorts!'

Chapter 7

'I hope you don't mind sharing,' said Rachel as she showed Polly into her bedroom, which was at the front of Darkwood House, overlooking the driveway and the five-bar gate that led out onto the lane. 'There are other rooms but they're a bit dusty and old. There's a spare bed that comes out from under mine—it's really nice,' she explained, pulling out the red mattress on a low frame on little wheels. 'I've used it for sleepovers and it's comfy.'

Polly gazed all around her. She said nothing. Rachel's heart suddenly thudded with realization. 'Oh . . . was this *your* room, before?'

'Yes,' whispered Polly.

'I'm sorry. It must be really weird seeing all my stuff in it.' Rachel glanced around at her books and stuffed toys and clothes and teen dolls, all mixed up with magazines and CDs for her mini sound system, her digital camera, the fibre optic lamp in the corner and the yellow bead blinds that hung over the high sash window, matching the lemon paint on her walls and the duvet cover on her high pine cabin bed. She saw it with different eyes now. 'What was it like in nineteen—I mean—yesterday?'

'It was green,' said Polly, softly, her eyes travelling the walls. 'Wavy green leaves on the wallpaper and cream paint on the ceiling.' She glanced up to the white ceiling which had yellow and orange stars randomly painted on it, at the yellow glass bead lampshade over the light, and then across to the window. 'With a dressing table there—by the sash—a glass topped one. I had a silver-backed brush and comb set on it and a mirror on a stand. And a pot of Yardley's face cream. There was an oak tallboy near the door. My bed was where yours is—but a proper iron-framed bed with a lace counterpane on the eiderdown. I had my dolls on a shelf. Miss Rosebud used to sit on my bed. She's my favourite doll. Of course, I'm a bit old for dolls now, really, and Freddy laughs at me—but I do love her.'

'Oh—I love dolls too!' said Rachel, cheerfully, although it wasn't strictly true. She quite *liked* dolls, but certainly didn't love them—she'd pretty much grown out of them a year or more ago. She seized one now, though, to show to Polly. It was Ritzy—a Chatz Doll—one of a collection of funky teenage figures with oversized eyes, glossy pouting lips, and dreadlocked hair. This one wore hotpants and a crop top and leather-look boots. The designers had given her a navel with its own piercing and she came with a choice of belly-button rings and studs.

Polly took the doll in her hands, eyes wide. 'She doesn't look like a little girl at all. She's got a . . . a bosom! Oh! And someone's stuck a pin in her tummy! How horrid!'

'No—that's . . . ' Rachel tailed off. Polly didn't even have pierced ears, she could see. This was going to take a while to explain. She changed the subject. 'I'm sure we've got lots in common!' she chirruped. 'What's your school like . . . er . . . *was* it like? I bet you had a horrible maths teacher. Every school has a horrible maths teacher!'

'We went to boarding school,' said Polly. 'So Father could concentrate on his work. We didn't mind. Grange Court was all right. The girls were mostly quite decent although you had to fag for the older ones and that was jolly hard work when I first went.'

'Fag?' Rachel queried.

'You know—do all their chores for them! Because I was in the first year, of course. It's to teach you your place! And how to shine shoes and sew and all that. Just because we're at boarding, it doesn't mean we all have butlers, you know. We don't have anyone at home except Mrs M and she only comes in three times a week. But you're right—mathematics is ghastly! I detest it. Mr Bullford is *awful* whenever I get my times tables wrong and I'm wrong a *lot*. Freddy's good at maths, of course—and sport and all that boy stuff—but I'm a total clot when it comes to that kind of thing. I'm good at English though, and Domestic Science. I can make hotpot and neck of lamb and all sorts.'

Rachel noticed how Polly kept saying 'is' instead of 'was' and 'have' instead of 'had'. Maybe she still thought it was all a bad dream and she'd wake up tomorrow, back in 1956, in time to go to Hilary's party after all.

'Ooh! I've read this! I just *love* this!' Polly pulled a dusty red book off Rachel's shelf, beaming. It was *Five Go To Smuggler's Top*. 'I'm in the Famous Five fan club! Are you? I've got the badge—it costs a shilling to join and you get special letter and your badge. Enid Blyton is just super! I mean—gosh—to think! You've got *this* book after all this time! It's just like the one I had—it's—' She paused, opening the cover, and then gasped. 'It *is* mine!' She showed Rachel the neat, rounded writing, in blue ink, on the first page. '*This book belongs to Pauline Emerson.*'

'Wow,' said Rachel. 'I never thought I'd get to meet the girl who first got that book!'

'Do you have any more?' asked Polly, looking eager and bright for the first time.

'Yes—I think so—downstairs mostly. I've kind of moved on from Enid Blyton now,' confessed Rachel. 'More into mags really.'

'Mags? Who's Mags? She can't be better than Enid!'

'No,' laughed Rachel, 'magazines . . . like this.' She handed *SWEET* over to Polly—a flimsy cluster of luridly coloured pages, all about the latest music in the charts, pop groups, girl bands, boy bands, film stars, and celebrity stuff. The front cover featured a sulky looking pop starlet, her tanned arms around the neck of a boy band star who was wearing only jeans. Polly stared at it, her mouth dropping open in shock, and went crimson. Next to the photo were the words: *JAMIE RICE—HOW SNOGGABLE IS HE?!* Polly read the words, mouthing them silently, and then stared up at Rachel.

'Does your father *let* you read this?' She looked absolutely appalled and Rachel began to shuffle, embarrassed, on her wood-effect flooring. Listed down the front page she could see further shocks in store for poor Polly. **STEP IN TO SEXY SUMMER SWIM-SUITS** had Polly's hand flying to her mouth and **DOES MY BUM LOOK BIG IN THIS?** had her eyes ready to pop out of their sockets.

'Um—didn't you have magazines like this?' she asked, feeling peculiarly self-conscious.

'Well—I get *Girl*, of course,' said Polly, still staring at *SWEET* as if it was the work of the devil. 'But that's *nothing* like this!'

'What *is* it like?' asked Rachel, taking *SWEET* out of Polly's hands and tucking it hurriedly under her bed with *MISSS* and *JJEM* and other shocking publications.

'It's super! Full of adventures stories, like "Wendy & Jinx" and "Belle of the Ballet". They have the most amazing things happen to them—and they certainly don't worry about the size of their backsides! I love them. I always wanted to have adventures and amazing things happening to me . . . ' She tailed off, gulping, and her round blue eyes fixed upon Rachel with a wet glitter. 'And now I've got my wish.'

'This used to be Father's room,' said Freddy, as soon as he stepped into Ben's bedroom. It was a wide room

79

with a double sash window which overlooked the wild garden and the woods beyond. Ben slept in the top of a metal bunk bed. The floor was covered in blue carpet and drifts of Star Wars Lego, and luminous 'glow-in-the-dark' planets were stuck all over the ceiling. Ben kept meaning to take them down—he was thirteen now, after all, and they'd gone up when he was six—but he still liked the way they glowed gently in the night.

'This must be really weird for you,' said Ben. 'What did it look like?'

Freddy shrugged. 'Cream and beige. Oak stuff. Ghastly old curtains which must have been there since 1900, I reckon! It's better now, I can tell you. That bed is whizzer! Can I have the top bunk?'

'Well,' Ben shuffled, awkwardly. 'It's kind of m-my bed. It's got all my books and stuff on the shelf.'

Freddy grinned. 'It's all right, you clod. I'm just joshing you. I'll be perfectly happy in the bottom bunk. I say—this is going to be fantastically odd. Maybe I'll wake up tomorrow in 3009! Maybe *you* will too!'

Ben sat down on the spinning metal seat which went with his white desk unit (also covered in Star Wars Lego) and stared at his great-uncle. 'You really are something!' He shook his head. 'You're just super-cool about this, aren't you?'

'Certainly have been,' said Freddy, opening the built-in wardrobe and eyeing Ben's clothes and shoes. 'Super cooling is part of the process. That's how Father put us to sleep.'

'Did you ever think that was—a bit—dodgy? Him putting you to sleep like that?'

Freddy shrugged. 'It was the obvious thing to do. He needed to do research and it's no good always doing it with rats or dogs. He only did it after he was absolutely certain it was safe. We didn't mind. He never put us in any danger.'

Ben found it hard to agree. What if those cryonic torpedo things had gone wrong? Freddy and Polly would surely have suffocated. 'He'd never get away with it today,' he said. 'Social Services would be round before you could blink. Mind you—I bet there's not a parent alive that wouldn't hope it could work. I mean—my mum and dad often talk about how great it would be to put *us* to sleep. In long car journeys mostly. They say they'd like a glass screen to slide up between the front seats and the back seat, and some kind of gas to pump in, so as soon as we went "Are we nearly—" they could freeze us. Five hours later when the car got to Cornwall they'd just hit the defrost button and we'd go "there yet?".'

Freddy chuckled. 'That would be the tops!

Imagine—I could freeze Polly and never have to hear her drooling over Miss Rosebud all the way to the seaside! When we find Father, I'm going to get him to invent that! It'd sell like hot cakes! Good grief! Is this *yours?*' He pulled a hanger out, from which dangled a colourful floral Hawaiian-style shirt, which Ben had worn to a beach barbecue last summer. Freddy was looking at it incredulously. 'It's your mother's, right? In the wrong wardrobe.'

Ben bit his lip. 'Didn't you ever see Elvis in that kind of gear?'

Freddy squinted at him. 'Elvis?'

'Yeah! Elvis! Don't tell me you've never heard of Elvis Presley!'

Freddy stuffed the shirt back in the wardrobe. 'Elvis Presley . . . Oh—*that* Elvis. Yes—I've heard of him. He's an American, isn't he? I think he's doing quite well in the popular music charts with his song—top ten, I think. My chum Frankie's got the record. He thinks it's whizzer. He does this lunatic dance to it, all hips wiggling and stuff. What's it called? Something about a hotel, I think.'

'"Heartbreak Hotel",' said Ben, at once. He wasn't really into Elvis, but his mum had a 'Best of Elvis' CD which she sometimes played at parties.

'Yes—that's it. Gosh. He must have made it to

number one then. Father thought he was dreadful. I thought he was a bit of a peacock, really. He sounds as if he's being hit in the chest with a road drill. Did he do well then?'

Ben laughed. 'You have *no idea*!'

'Well, I can see I'm going to have to go back down the hatch,' said Freddy, closing the wardrobe door decisively. 'There's no way I'm wearing *your* stuff! Honestly! Your clothes are all shiny, like girls' clothes. I prefer to look like a boy!'

'With a haircut like *that*?' retorted Ben. 'You look like the Prince of Wales. And trust me—that is not a look you *want* nowadays!' His own hair was a fairly credible mess. In spite of all the drama of the past couple of hours, Freddy's straight dark brown hair was still neatly parted to one side. 'Anyway, that's just party gear. I normally wear T-shirts and jeans. Don't you have any jeans?'

Freddy shrugged. 'Not me. Some of the town boys do, but Father says they're working men's trousers. I think they're all right, actually. Wouldn't mind some. The Americans wear them all the time, according to Poll. She wants some.'

'Do you think she'll be OK?' said Ben. Polly seemed very young compared to Rachel, even though he now knew they were about the same age.

'What, Poll? Certainly. She's tough as old boots, that girl. She'll stop the blubbing soon and start having fun. She's just worried about Father.'

'Aren't you?' asked Ben. He knew he would have been blubbing worse than Polly if *his* father had vanished without trace and was wanted for murder. Freddy stood up straight and shoved his hands deep into the pockets of his grey flannel shorts.

'As I see it, this is a mystery,' he said. 'Nobody knows anything for sure, so what's the point of blubbing about it? I want to find out what's happened to him, of course.'

'B-but, even if he's still alive he'd be . . . what . . . ninety—a hundred?'

'Ninety-one,' said Freddy. 'And he is still alive. I'm certain of it. I'll get a good night's sleep and some decent food in me—that's if you still *have* decent food these days—and then I'm going to search for him. First thing in the morning. Until I find him. Emersons don't give up. That's what Father always said and that's why he did such amazing things. You wait, Ben—you'll see. I'll find him. Emersons don't give up.'

Ben nodded, impressed. 'You're not really like a teenager, are you?' he said, folding his arms and peering at Freddy.

'What's a teenager supposed to be like?' asked Freddy.

Ben opened his mouth to answer, but then he was silenced by the door being bashed open violently, and Polly hurtling in, followed by a confused looking Rachel.

'FREDDY!!!' yelled Polly, in panic. 'FREDDY! We've got to go back down! Now! Oh, Freddy! WE FORGOT BESS!'

Chapter 8

Freddy looked stricken.

'Oh no! Poor Bess! We left her down there.'

'Who's Bess?' asked Ben and Rachel, at the same moment.

'Oh, how dreadful we've been!' whimpered Polly. 'So selfish and caught up about ourselves that we left her down there, all frozen, on her own!'

'Well, come on then!' Freddy propelled her back through the door and soon all four of them were racing down the stairs, slithering through the garden and splashing across the stream to get back to the hatch. It was hugely different from their first trip. Now, instead of fearful, Ben and Rachel were utterly intrigued by it and thrilled beyond measure that someone *else* was about to be defrosted, before their very eyes.

Uncle Jerome had been down there for the past

fifteen minutes, while they'd been showing Freddy and Polly their rooms. They found him in a state of absolute rapture.

'It's perfect! Just perfect!' he gasped as soon as they ran into the sitting room. He'd been rifling through some of the supplies boxes. 'It's a 1950s time capsule! Imagine! Untouched for fifty-three years, until today!'

'Yes, yes . . . amazing!' said Freddy as they all flew past him and straight through the next door. By the time they reached the torpedoes chamber Uncle Jerome was right behind them, demanding to know what was going on.

'Come right in,' ordered Freddy. 'We have to seal the room again first.' He ignored Uncle Jerome's urgent questions in a way which hugely impressed Ben and Rachel, while he went to the console and punched the red button which Rachel had first hit that morning. Once again there was the hissing noise, followed by the mechanical workings noise, and the door locked itself.

'That's what happened the first time,' Rachel whispered to Uncle Jerome. 'We thought we were sealed in like Egyptian mummies, for ever.'

'It has to seal, to equalize the air pressure before the chamber can be opened,' said Freddy.

'You mean to tell me there's someone *else* in

here?' gasped Uncle Jerome. 'But I looked in them all. The end one is shut, of course, and I couldn't open it, but I could see through the glass—there's nobody else in it!'

Freddy went to the first chamber and peered into the glass. He gave a grin and said: 'You didn't look hard enough.' As the hissing noise eased off there was a click and the glass window smoothly rose up, as it must have done for Freddy and Polly earlier, only Ben and Rachel had been too hysterical to notice. Polly ran to Freddy's side and gasped 'Bess! Oh, Bessie! Are you all right?' Then Freddy leaned over, reached right down into the chamber, to where his feet would have lain had he been in it, and pulled something out. Something sneezed. Something snuffled. Polly took the something from him and cuddled it with a sigh. 'She's all right! She's waking up!' And she turned to face them, delight all over her face, and a puppy in her arms.

'Good lord!' said Uncle Jerome, while Ben and Rachel just groaned with delight. The puppy was a brown Labrador with liquid eyes and shining fur, floppy ears, and big paws which dangled sleepily from Polly's arms as she hugged it to her. 'A fifty-three-year-old puppy!' added Uncle Jerome. 'Astonishing! Truly astonishing!'

'We only got her a week before we got frozen,' said Polly. 'We came home from school and found that Father had already frozen her six times. She's actually six months old, but she's spent half that time frozen, so she's only three months really . . . if you know what I mean.'

'He froze a *puppy*! How *could* he?' said Rachel—even more shocked about puppy-freezing than child-freezing.

'Well, it doesn't hurt her,' said Freddy. 'Any more than it hurts us! Don't make him out to be some kind of monster. He's not. He's a genius!'

'I know, I know,' said Rachel, playing with Bess's silky brown ears as the dog nuzzled into Ben's palm. 'And, actually, I'm really glad he did. We've never had a puppy!'

'Well, she'll be very useful,' said Uncle Jerome. 'We can test her—see how she's holding up biologically and physiologically after such a long time in stasis. We'll have to test you two, as well. Just make sure the extended suspension hasn't caused any damage. Don't want you going over too fast, like frozen strawberries. They never last an afternoon after they've been defrosted!'

'*Uncle!*' Rachel shoved his arm and glared at him and whispered, '*Don't! You'll scare them!*'

Uncle Jerome nodded and tapped his nose. 'Yes, good point,' he muttered and went to run his hands over the cryonic machinery, his face a picture of reverence. Ben thought it was a bit like watching a pilgrim arrive at a holy shrine. 'So,' breathed Uncle Jerome, 'the liquid nitrogen—I *assume*—must pass through these pipes and circulate around the interior of the chamber . . . cold enough to chill you into suspension, but not making actual bodily contact, thereby not burning your skin off or leading to a nasty multiple-fracture situation when you go to move again . . . Oh! This is magnificent! How does it feel? When you're suspended?'

'Um—I don't know really,' said Freddy. 'We just go to sleep.'

'Ah yes, of course, yes. Are there any special preparations beforehand? Do you have to eat or drink anything specific or . . . ?'

'Not really. We just get in. Although Polly always makes a point of going to the lavatory first. Don't know why. I've told her enough times, her bladder's just as suspended as the rest of her. You know what girls are, though. Bess just snuggles down in the bottom bit where your feet go. She likes it there—that's why you couldn't see her.'

'And when you wake up again? Do you feel odd?'

'Pretty queer sometimes,' said Freddy, now stepping over and joining in the puppy petting. 'Usually a bit foggy for a minute or so. But it doesn't last. Of course *this* time it was worse, because our joints didn't work too well for a bit. I suppose fifty-three years in cryonic suspension's going to give anyone a bit of a dead leg.'

'So how is it all powered?' Uncle Jerome was pondering now. 'Your father must have laid power down deep underground somehow. What would it have been connected to? Maybe there's a generator somewhere here. Maybe it leads off the power from the house? Or—or solar energy panels somewhere. Or hydro-electric from the stream. I don't know. So much to study—so much to find out! I must get the department out—I must get this properly recorded and studied, and—'

'NO!' Freddy shouted so loudly that Bess whined and Polly glared at him.

Uncle Jerome blinked and stood up from examining the base of the nearest chamber.

Freddy stood with his arms folded, lifting his chin. 'You *can't* let anyone else in! Father always told us this was *top secret*!'

'But—but, my dear boy, he worked for the government! They must have known about his research!'

'Not *this* research!' insisted Freddy. 'We know. We were *there*. He didn't share this with *anyone* at the government. Me and Poll were the only ones who knew about it. He said it was more than his life was worth to let anyone else know about it.'

'But, Freddy, that was fifty-three years ago,' said his nephew, taking off his glasses and rubbing them with his handkerchief. 'The government today is not the same as the government back *then*! They will be astounded by all this. Your father will be a *hero*! Think of it. We could carry on with his research—I—I could carry on with it . . . don't you think? Don't you?'

'And we *could* clear Father's name,' said Polly, unexpectedly siding with Uncle Jerome. She gave Rachel the puppy to hold and stepped across to stand next to her brother. 'It's beastly that everyone thinks he's a murderer! It's not right.'

Freddy frowned. 'Of course I want to clear Father's name . . . but . . . well, I think we need to wait a bit. It's only been a few hours since we got defrosted. I don't like the idea of rushing into anything with govern-ments. Father *did* work for the government and he was jolly proud of it . . . but he also said he didn't trust everyone there. That's why he didn't do all his research in *their* labs. He didn't even tell his closest colleagues that he'd done all this—not even Uncle Dick, and he was his best friend. He came to the house sometimes, but Father *never* showed him this.'

'I suppose Uncle Dick's long gone too,' sighed Polly. 'Or an old man now. He was fun.'

'Well, he was younger than Father,' said Freddy. 'I reckon he'd be about eighty-five . . . maybe.'

Uncle Jerome sat down opposite Freddy, replaced his glasses, and sighed. He nodded. 'You're quite right, Freddy. I was just getting carried away. This is so exciting. But we need to think carefully about this. You need time to get used to the twenty-first century, for one thing, before all this gets out. Once the government knows, there *could* be a leak. Then the tabloids would be chasing you in days.'

'Tabloids? What are tabloids?' Polly looked anxious. 'Are they some kind of—some kind of robot?'

Freddy nudged her. 'Newspapers, silly. The small ones like the *Daily Sketch*. Not robots!'

Ben laughed. 'Far worse than robots!'

'I suppose you must have heaps of robots,' sighed Polly. 'Do they really do everything for you—like metal servants? Do they talk? I saw something about them on Hilary's television set. They said robots would run the world in the future.'

'Yes—there are robots, Polly,' said Uncle Jerome. 'They make cars and so on, and defuse unexploded bombs, even do certain types of surgery—but almost nobody has a robot servant. Robots just aren't that clever yet. They certainly don't run the world.'

'So—these *tabloids*? How are they worse?' said Polly, looking serious. 'Do—do they print beastly things?'

'Only if you're a footballer's girlfriend or have boobs the size of China,' giggled Rachel, and both Uncle Jerome and Polly gave her a reproving look. 'Well—it's *true*!' said Rachel.

'Tabloids are somewhat worse than they used to be,' explained Uncle Jerome. 'They have very tenacious reporters who would be fascinated by your story. They tend to be a little—sensationalist—in their reporting. But you don't have to worry—no tabloids will come after you, because nobody is going to know about your past.'

'How, though?' said Ben. 'We can't hide them in the cellar every time someone comes—and what about Mum and Dad? They'll have to know! They're back in a couple of weeks! And what about school and stuff? And—well—inoculations! Medical things . . . I bet they haven't had an MMR!'

Uncle Jerome nodded and smiled. 'All in good time, Benedict! All in good time. There are ways and means. I agree, it's most important to first acclimatize

94

your great-aunt and uncle to the ways of the twenty-first century. Gently, of course. Most of your unlovely generation will shock them rigid. We can tell everyone that they are your cousins—come over from . . . um . . . South Africa?'

'But we don't know anything about South Africa!' protested Freddy. 'Come *on*, JJ! There's got to be a better cover story than *that*!'

'I know! I know!' Rachel jumped up and down. 'A commune! A hippy commune! They were brought up in the remote woods somewhere and—you know—taught at home. There are some children who are, you know! I read about it. They don't know anything about *anything*—not even *EastEnders*!'

'What's *EastEnders*?' asked Freddy.

'It's a soap,' said Ben. 'It's a waste of time.'

'Oh,' said Polly. 'Well, you should try Knight's Castile. It's jolly nice and keeps your complexion youthfully clear. And it's got lovely paper wrapping which you can draw on.'

Ben and Rachel looked at each other. 'Another time,' said Rachel, and Ben nodded.

'I say—can we get out of here now?' said Freddy. 'I'm dying to see what the twenty-first century looks like! Have you got a television set we can have a bit of a squint at?'

Ben sighed. 'We have got one—but it's broken. It blew up this morning.'

'Well then—a wireless?'

'A wire—? Oh—a radio? Yes. We've got two or three of those,' said Ben.

Uncle Jerome gave a cry of joy. He had just found the notebooks which Ben had looked at before the door locked, earlier that day. 'Shall we leave you to it for a bit, Uncle J?' Ben offered. 'Get some tea on for Freddy and Polly?'

Uncle Jerome was flipping through the note-book pages madly, pushing his glasses up the bridge of his nose and going 'Aha! Aha . . . aha . . . ' He glanced up quickly at Ben and Freddy. 'Yes . . . yes, of course. Get some decent food into them. They've not eaten for half a century. You can leave me here for a while.' Ben grinned. He knew that 'a while', in Uncle Jerome's case, might very well be days. *Literally* days. When he got *that* excited he was liable to forget to eat or sleep. They must remember to pop down with food for him.

'You boys go on ahead,' said Polly, as they went through the bunk bed room, 'and take Bess out into the garden for a few minutes. Rachel and I will pack some clothes to bring.'

'Righto,' said Freddy and scooped the puppy out

of Rachel's arms. She pulled a face. She didn't want to stay behind and pack.

Polly pulled two battered leather suitcases out from under one of the lower bunks and then went to the shelving on the far wall. There were drawers in the lower parts of the storage racks, filled with neatly folded shorts and blouses and dresses and jumpers, which Polly deftly gathered and pressed into the open cases. Rachel tried to help, but Polly shook her head at once. 'No! You can't put a jumper on top of a blouse! The heavier items are packed first . . . then the lighter items, such as blouses and petticoats, go on top. Or else they'll get creased!' She carefully placed the jumper under the lighter items of clothing. 'You do Freddy's. He won't mind creases so much.'

'Polly—we're only going up the garden!' said Rachel but Polly lifted her chin.

'If a job's worth doing, it's worth doing well. I could do with some tissue paper, really, to roll up my frocks in . . . Didn't your mother ever teach you to pack properly?'

Rachel had a vision of her mother, blonde and pretty, wildly flinging sparkly magic act outfits into a large trunk from across the other side of the room. Her method of packing was more like playing volley ball. The idea of her rolling anything up in tissue paper actually made Rachel laugh out loud. Polly looked a little offended, so Rachel coughed and answered: 'Um . . . well, we don't go away that much. Who taught you, then? Uncle J's mother?'

'Oh no, I learned all I need to know from *Girl*,' said Polly, snapping shut the top of the little brown suitcase. 'From the Mother Tells You How pages. They're frightfully good. Only last week I made my own laundry bag from an old pyjama jacket. It hangs up in the wardrobe and is really rather good. At least Father thought so.' At the mention of her father Polly fell silent and Rachel feared she might start crying again, but the girl just took a sharp breath, lifted her chin and stood up with her case. She gave Rachel a shrewd look. 'It's quite all right, you know. You needn't worry that I'm going to start blubbing again. I'm really not that kind of girl. It's just been a rather shocking day. I think I've got it out of my system now.'

Back in the house Ben and Freddy were looking for a working radio, Bess following them on unsteady legs, which hadn't had its batteries nicked to power their hand-held computer games. Rachel and Polly went to the kitchen to sort out tea. While Rachel rifled through the freezer for ready meals, Polly attempted to lay the table.

'Where are the place mats?'

'Place mats? Um . . . you could try the second drawer down,' suggested Rachel, hauling out some packets of Indian convenience meals.

Polly went to the second drawer down, opened it, reeled back a little in shock at the tangled mess she found there, and then gamely began to search through it for place mats. At length she retrieved some raffia weave things which someone had given their mother for Christmas some years ago. They were still in their box. It would simply never occur to Ben and Rachel's mother to put place mats out on a table. Having cleared the rectangle of scrubbed pine of mugs and odds and ends of junk, Polly swiftly wiped it down with a wet cloth and laid out four mats. She guessed at the cutlery drawer—correctly—and began the next stage of sorting out knives and forks that didn't have smears on them.

'Sorry, Polly,' said Rachel, glancing across at the girl's dismayed expression. 'The dishwasher ran out of salt and it always makes stuff go all smeary when that happens. It's quite safe though.'

'You have a dish washer?' Polly raised her eyebrows in surprise. 'And she ran out of salt and just didn't bother to go and get any more? Mrs M would have sacked her on the spot.'

'Umm . . . not a dishwasher *person*.' Rachel bit

her lip and tried not to giggle. Polly really was very funny—and she had no idea of it. 'A machine.'

'Like a tabloid?'

'No—no that's a newspaper, remember?'

'Oh yes.' Polly turned back to the knives and forks, found a tea towel, and began to polish them furiously, while Rachel turned her attention to violently stabbing the plastic seals of the frozen ready meals with a kitchen knife. After a few seconds she became aware of Polly at her shoulder, watching. 'Is that . . . food?'

'Yes,' said Rachel. 'Chicken tikka massala and rice. You'll like it. It's great. We have it all the time.'

Polly looked doubtful. 'It's a TV dinner, isn't it?' she said, unexpectedly.

'Um—yes. I suppose so.'

'They have them in America, all the time.'

'Well, they have them in England all the time now, as well.' Rachel stacked the plastic punnets inside the microwave, calculated the time, entered it on the greasy control pad and then set the microwave going. It hummed tunefully and shone a little light out through the spatters on the glass door.

'This really is a dirty kitchen,' said Polly. Rachel couldn't disagree. Housework wasn't a big concern at Darkwood House, although they did clear up from time to time. Usually about once a week, when Uncle J couldn't get past a pile of rubbish and got cross. Most of the time he didn't really notice. Rachel did make a point of not preparing food on mucky surfaces—she had learnt that much from health and safety lessons at school—but as most food preparation only involved heating stuff up in plastic tubs, it really wasn't much of an issue. Now she saw the kitchen through Polly's eyes and she was embarrassed. The kitchen in the underground chamber was much better than this, and nobody had cleaned *that* for fifty-three years.

'Come on,' said Polly, briskly. 'We've got twelve minutes before the microwaving is finished. Let's set to!' To Rachel's amazement, Polly was rolling up her sleeves and then emptying out the washing-up bowl (a swamp-like mess with orange scum floating around the edges) and stacking dirty crockery up on the side and running the hot tap. 'I'll wash—you dry,' she instructed, handing Rachel the tea towel. She briskly scrubbed the plastic bowl clean under the tap before filling it with hot soapy water. 'Washing-up water should be just hot enough to sting,' she said. 'Any cooler and it won't do the job. Now. Dirty cutlery— fill this jug, like so, and put it all in, handles up, to soak, while we get on with the rest. Always wash the least dirty things first—that way you make your hot water last longer. Do you have a long-handled washing-up mop?'

'A long-handled *what*?' gasped Rachel. 'Look—you don't have to worry about all this. We'll just sling it in the dishwasher.'

'Has it got any more salt?' asked Polly, crisply.

'No. Not yet.'

'Then it won't do. Come on. Start drying. And putting away. We've only got nine minutes now. We want everything on the table for when the boys come in, don't we?'

'Do we?' Rachel asked, faintly, but Polly gave her a look which silenced any further protest. She got wiping.

When Ben and Freddy and Bess came in ten minutes later, with a radio but no batteries, Ben was astounded to see four hot meals laid out in bowls on place mats, forks to one side, dessert spoons along the top, clean tumblers of water and a small vase of hand-picked honeysuckle gracing the centre. Polly looked pleased and Rachel, as she put Ben's dish on his place mat, looked as if she'd been abducted by an alien.

The food made Freddy and Polly cry. It was only a mildly spiced dish, but it had them reaching for their cotton handkerchiefs (neatly folded in their shorts pockets) almost immediately.

'What do you think?' grinned Ben. 'Twenty-first century food all right then?'

'Oh! It's marvellous!' spluttered Freddy, and loaded his fork again immediately. 'I've never tasted anything like it!'

'And there's so *much* meat,' said Polly. 'This must cost half your housekeeping!'

'Not really,' said Ben, giving a morsel to Bess, who was under the table, to stop her nibbling on his socks. 'Everyone eats chicken. Loads of it.'

Polly and Freddy exchanged awed glances. 'We only get it on Sundays, a few times a year,' said Freddy.

'Elbows off,' said Polly, and Ben and Rachel did as they were told—and sat up straight as well.

Polly sighed. 'Father loves roast chicken. If only we knew what had happened to Father,' she said, scooping up the last of her food. 'If only there was some way to be there, on that last day, and see what *really* happened. I can't bear to think we won't find out. It would be just too awful.'

Freddy suddenly put down his fork with a clatter and stared at Polly. She raised her eyebrows at him and said: 'What?'

'You said . . . ' He gulped and blinked. 'You

said . . . if only there was some way to see what happened . . . well . . . what if there was? Polly! What if there *was*?'

'I don't know what you mean,' she said, putting her own fork down and gulping some water from the glass tumblers she had polished clean a few minutes earlier.

'Polly! Have you forgotten the Ampex?'

She froze and then put her hand to her mouth. 'The *Ampex*!' she whispered. 'Do you think it could . . . did he? I mean, could it be . . . ?'

'What *are* you two on about?' demanded Ben and Freddy turned to him and grabbed his arm, his dark blue eyes gleaming with excitement.

'Ben, old chum,' he said. 'I'm going to take you back in time!'

LONDON, FEBRUARY 2008

The man in the grey trench coat was surprised to see someone else come to the graveside. As the priest muttered something in Latin, anxious to be off to his lunch on this cold winter's day, there was a crunch of frosted grass and another man arrived, wearing dark glasses and an unreadable expression. The only other mourner was a woman who had been Richard Tarrant's cleaner in the last few weeks of his life. She gathered her blue nylon coat around her, shivered, and then stepped forward to throw a handful of dirt onto the coffin before smiling at the priest and walking away.

Sad, that a man who had once been so popular should have only a cleaner, a resentful old work colleague, and someone else from the government attend his funeral. Because the newcomer certainly was government, no question.

Now he walked across, nodding respectfully to the priest who was making a swift exit. 'For a moment back there,' he said, 'I thought I might have got extremely lucky.' He held out his hand. 'David Chambers.'

'Ernest Granville,' said the man in the grey trench coat, and shook the proffered hand. 'I suppose you were hoping I might be Henry Emerson.'

Chambers laughed. He looked slightly embarrassed.

'We have no reason to think the old boy's even alive. But at least we know he wasn't a traitor. Tarrant did that much for his old friend. Cold comfort though—telling us fifty-odd years after the event.'

'It would be nice to let Emerson's family know that, wouldn't it?' said Chambers, taking off his spectacles and regarding Granville closely.

'Yes,' he agreed. 'But I don't think either of us are going to do that just yet, are we? Just in case . . . '

'In case they're hiding the return of an old genius scientist?'

'Or his son or daughter?'

Granville sighed. 'Let's stop playing games, shall we? None of us has a clue. He could be dead or alive, in Russia or in Peru for all we know. And his children too. We'll probably never know. I suppose you've a sleeper in place in Amhill, even so.'

Chambers smiled. He stooped down and threw the dirt on the coffin.

'Treacherous old goat,' he said. 'Doesn't really deserve

to Rest In Peace. Emerson could have taken this country into an astonishing future. But I suppose if he had done anything for the Soviets we would have seen some evidence of it now. He probably refused and paid with his life.'

'Like I said,' Granville threw his own handful of dirt and they both turned away from the grave and began to walk, 'we'll probably never know.'

Chapter 9

Ben knew this wasn't possible. There was no way he could travel back in time. But he couldn't suppress a shiver as Freddy led him back down into the vault for the third visit that day. They had hastily finished their food and were now descending the metal rungs once more.

Freddy jumped the last few feet and was away down the corridor and opening the first chamber door before Ben and Rachel and Polly had reached the bottom rung. They followed him into the main sitting room and saw him fiddling with one of the boxes of Izal toilet paper on the metal shelving to the right of the door.

'Don't worry,' quipped Rachel. 'The curry wasn't *that* hot!' But Freddy didn't pay her any attention. Now he was twisting something on the wall behind the cardboard packets and then he grunted with satisfaction as there was a hollow rattle and the entire shelving unit swung towards him. Ben and Rachel gaped as a bright glow shone out in a fattening column in the wall behind the shelving. It was a hidden room.

'Good. Light still works,' said Freddy.

'Freddy,' said Polly, doubtfully. 'Father said we weren't to go in! We weren't allowed!'

'That,' said Freddy, 'was before he froze us and disappeared for fifty-three years. I reckon he would have let us in by the time we turned sixty. And I'm sixty-six.'

Polly shrugged and followed him into the brightly lit chamber. Ben and Rachel looked at each other. 'Should we get Uncle J?' breathed Rachel. 'Shall I get him?' She gulped.

'If you like,' said Ben, 'but I'm going in.' He stepped into the room behind Freddy and Polly. It was small. About the size of a garden shed, with grey walls and more of the green swirly carpet. There was hardly any dust in it. Set into one of the walls was a small rectangular screen—perhaps fifteen centimetres across and rounded at the edges. It was dark green; showing nothing. Beneath it was a monstrous machine of grey metal. It was the size of a piano, but bulkier and had large buttons and stubby black sliders on it. On the top of the machine, on a black spindle, sat a large reel of what Ben recognized as old oxide tape in a metal wheel—the kind of thing early reel-to-reel tape machines used; much bigger than the little reels in the recording machine which had greeted them in the other room. At the front of the machine the proud letters **AMPEX** stood out. Beneath them more letters read: **Mark IV VTR.**

Ben peered at it, fascinated. He thought he might have seen something like it at the London Science Museum. 'Is this . . . is it a . . . video recorder?'

Freddy looked round, his hands resting with excited reverence on the buttons and faders. 'Yes! It is! Isn't that amazing?'

'It certainly *is*,' came a voice from the door, and Uncle Jerome drifted in, yet more amazement on his face (a look which threatened to burn into his features for ever after today, thought Ben). 'How on earth did your father get hold of *this*? These weren't even commercially available until the autumn of 1956! And they cost an absolute *fortune*!'

'Oh well, Father had a lot of connections,' said Freddy, breezily. 'He was a good friend of Lodge—the man who helped develop this for CBS. This was a prototype. He only got it last month . . . ' Freddy turned his attention to the many ducts and wires that fed into the back of the huge machine. 'I think it's still connected up—I wonder if the camera still works. Probably not.'

'Do you mean to tell me that your father set up a video surveillance system?' gulped Uncle Jerome. 'His own CCTV?'

Freddy blinked. 'CCTV?'

'Closed circuit television! His own camera—recording something around here?'

'Well—yes. That was what it was for,' said Freddy.

'It was a spy camera!' said Polly, widening her eyes theatrically. 'Like in spy films! He said we had to know who was lurking around outside the house, in case they were spies!'

'Did he really?' asked Rachel, who had come in now, behind Uncle Jerome.

'Well, not exactly,' admitted Polly. 'But it was jolly close to that! He thought the meat man spent too long peering down the driveway and started to wonder if he was a Soviet. Father was a bit funny that way.'

Uncle Jerome had now joined Freddy in running his hands over the mammoth video recorder. 'The very first Ampex!' he was murmuring. 'Just astounding!' He looked at Freddy and, quite oddly for Uncle Jerome, asked: 'Can I?'

Freddy grinned and shrugged. 'Go ahead. I don't really know how it works. Father never let me have a go. I just watched a couple of times.'

Uncle Jerome beamed at him and then turned back to the machine. After a brief pause his fingers moved to the grey metal reel of oxide tape and picked up one end of the wide brown ribbon which ran off it. He swiftly threaded it up and down through all sorts of metal rollers and pulley wheels which bobbed smoothly in their settings, as if they were a few weeks rather than half a century old. Uncle Jerome fed the end of the tape into another—empty—grey metal reel and moved the spool around a couple of times until the tape caught and began to pull against the reel next to it. Now the tape tightened and with a single balletic bob of all the rollers and pulleys, the reels turned together. Uncle Jerome pressed a button on the machine—everything clunked and bobbed again and both tape reels wound faster and faster.

'Got to rewind the tape first,' he said. 'It must have rolled on and then come off the spool when time ran out. Must have flicked around a few times and then the power probably cut out automatically.'

The huge plate of reddish grey tape grew smaller and smaller on one side and larger and larger on the other, and Uncle Jerome stopped it just as one side shrank to the size of a saucer. Then he looked up at the screen above and reached over to it to turn a button. A discreet click was followed by a pinprick of light in the centre of the green screen.

They waited in silence. After a few seconds Rachel said, 'Is that it?'

Polly gave her a pitying look. 'It's got to warm up, silly!' she said.

'TVs in the 1950s took several minutes to warm up,' explained Uncle Jerome, not taking his eyes from the little screen. 'The cathode ray tube would heat slowly and gradually radiate across the screen. You had to be patient. Something you children of today are not used to at all.'

At last something was happening on the screen. The dot had become a column and the column was widening out into a speckly white and grey rectangle. A couple of minutes later the whole screen was lit. Uncle Jerome took a breath and then pressed a button on the Ampex. There was a heavy clunk and a gentle hum and the tape spools began to move again, in the reverse direction. Up on the screen a grainy image began to gather.

'Yes!' said Freddy. 'It still works! That's the gate!'

Ben squinted at the screen, not sure what he was seeing at first but gradually beginning to recognize the view. It was the road outside Darkwood House. Darkwood Lane with the hedgerows on either side, June blossom, bright in black and white, blowing in a gentle breeze. Exactly the same view that you would get if you climbed the chestnut tree by the gate— except that the road was rough shingle, rutted and unmade up, whereas today it was smooth grey tarmac. Everyone stared, rapt, at the view. It was the least dramatic thing they were ever likely to watch on TV and yet quite thrilling.

'Could this be the same day?' asked Rachel. 'The same day you went to sleep?'

'It looks like yesterday,' agreed Polly. 'It was bright and sunny and a bit breezy and there *was* blossom out in the lane.'

'Did your father run this camera continuously?' asked Uncle Jerome.

'I think so,' said Freddy. 'Well, during the day at any rate. It was all a bit new. I don't know if he'd totally got the hang of it. He would come in to change the reels every couple of hours, so I don't suppose he could have run it all through the night. It was more of an experiment than anything else.'

'Look! Look!' cried Polly. 'The meat man! This must be about half past eleven—he always used to come before lunch.'

On the small screen an old-fashioned van rolled into view and a young man wearing a peaked cap and an apron got out. He disappeared around the back of the small vehicle and then reappeared, carrying a large covered basket.

'He used to bring our chops and lamb and pigs' hearts every week,' said Polly.

'Pigs' hearts? Oh, yuck!' said Rachel.

Polly frowned. 'What's wrong with that? Everyone knows pigs' hearts make your brain grow. Mrs M poaches them with onions. Oh, look—there he goes.'

The meat man had walked towards the screen and then on into the driveway, out of view. For several minutes they stared at the van and then the back of the meat man's head went past and they saw him return his basket to the rear of the van, walk around, get back in and go.

'It'll be you next, Freddy,' said Polly. 'You came back from youth club right after the meat man came, I remember.'

She was not wrong. Uncle Jerome sped up the reels and two minutes later Freddy suddenly shot across their view on a large, old-fashioned black bicycle with a basket on the front. Uncle Jerome wound it back—Freddy zooming backwards this time—and then played it at normal speed. Ben felt a shiver run through him.

The tape showed a time so obviously fifty-three years old, with the unmade-up road and the 1950s delivery van. But Freddy, jumping off the saddle and wheeling the big black bike in past the gate, looked exactly the same as he did now, standing right here next to them. He was wearing the same clothes. In his basket on the front of the bike was a striped paper bag and a comic of some kind. Ben squinted and made out *Eagle* on the top of it, in bold, angular letters.

'Blast it! I never did get to read that!' muttered Freddy. 'I suppose it's long gone now. Never got to eat those bull's eyes either. Rotten luck!'

'Oh no—don't tell me you ate bull's eyes too!' grimaced Rachel.

'They're sweets, you goose!' laughed Polly.

After Freddy had gone in, nothing else happened. After a while Uncle Jerome wound the tape forward at high speed. 'What time was it when your father put you into stasis?' he asked, eyes still on the screen and hands poised above the buttons.

'Just after lunch,' said Polly. 'We had chops. I cooked them! Mrs M was off that week.'

'So . . . about now then.' Uncle Jerome was watching a dial of numbers. 'This is the time code,' he said. 'We've been watching for about ninety minutes-worth now and if your meat man and Freddy here came in just before lunch, I believe you would have eaten by now.'

'Yes, we ate around one, I should say,' said Freddy, glancing over Uncle Jerome's shoulder at the spinning time code numbers. 'So I reckon we'd be down in the chamber about now. Maybe . . . maybe we'll see Father going off somewhere . . . do you think?'

Ben eyed the spool on the side that was getting smaller and smaller as the tape wound on. There wasn't much of it left. He really hoped they would see *something* else before the tape ran out completely, but as it went on shrinking, there was nothing else but the lane and the blossom blowing in the wind and the occasional bird flitting in and out of the hedgerows.

'Not much more now,' sighed Uncle Jerome. 'Sorry.' But even as he said this a shadow was thrown across the lane at the top right corner of the screen. A young man walked into view. He was wearing a jacket and tie and a trilby hat. He paused at the gate, leaning on it while he did something with his shoe— pulled a stone out of it, Ben thought—and then glanced down the driveway before walking on up the hill. Something tugged at Ben's memory, but this was clearly just his imagination. He didn't know the man. This was forty years before he was born!

Now the tape was clicking and whirring on the spool, filling up to almost full. Uncle Jerome prepared to stop it.

'Wait!' said Rachel, just as he went to stop the tape. 'Look!'

As soon as she said this the tape ran out, flicking madly like a whippet's tail as the spools spun on at speed and then began to gradually slow. 'There was something else! Something dark came in. Look—you have to look again!'

Uncle Jerome stopped the spools, re-threaded the tape and wound it back slowly. Just as the tape began to flicker, where it was a little squashed from being threaded at one end, something dark *did* come in. The bonnet of a car. A black car, gliding up to the gate. Only the first glimpse of windscreen rolled into view before the tape ended.

Freddy and Polly looked at each other wide-eyed. 'A car!' gasped Polly. Freddy nodded.

'So? A car! Whose car? Could be anyone's,' said Ben, exasperated and disappointed. 'What does *that* tell us?'

'You don't understand, Benedict,' said Uncle Jerome. 'Cars were not that common an occurrence in 1956. Even on through roads, and Darkwood Lane only goes up to the woods and downs. Anything other than the delivery van was very rare. Someone came along that day—almost certainly for a reason.'

'But who?' said Polly. 'Who drove up to us? Can't we see something?'

Uncle Jerome held the image of the car steady on the screen. It had a high black bonnet and a metal grille like long teeth between two round headlights. The number plate was only partially in view, obscured by part of the five-bar gate.

'The man before,' said Polly. 'He would have seen it, wouldn't he? He can't have been that far on—just seconds on from it, don't you think? He would know!'

'Yes—brilliant, old girl!' snapped Freddy. 'All we need to do is put a notice in the local newspaper asking for anyone who might remember seeing a black car while he was passing in 1956! Easy!'

Polly gave him a furious look and turned on her heel and walked out of the room.

'Come on,' said Ben. 'It's really late. You need to get some sleep. We all do.'

'Quite right,' muttered Uncle Jerome. 'Off you go now. Early to bed! Off to sleep!' Ben knew he was desperate to get rid of them so he could examine the Ampex undisturbed.

'We've slept a lifetime!' grumbled Freddy, but he *was* looking very tired.

Ben patted his shoulder. 'Come on, mate. Honestly—it'll all seem a lot better in the morning.'

He steered Freddy and Rachel out and Uncle Jerome stared up at the screen for a long time. He wound back the tape a little way and squinted at the man with something in his shoe. Then he looked at the car again. Then the man again.

Then his mouth fell open and his hand went to his temple. 'No,' he breathed. 'No . . . it *can't* be.'

Chapter 10

The next day began sunny. With screaming.

Rachel was hurtled out of sleep by the sound of Polly waking up and realizing that yesterday *hadn't* been a dream after all.

'It's OK—it's OK!' She grabbed Polly's arm, still dealing with her own sense of unreality. 'You're all right! You're safe!'

Polly stared at her and then shut her eyes. When she opened them again she looked more composed. 'Sorry,' she said. 'Oh gosh—I'm *really* sorry! Bess has wet the bed. And—oh no—she's eaten a bit of Ritzy!'

Rachel winced. Her Chatz doll was still pouting and smirking despite having her left leg gnawed off at the knee. And being covered in puppy drool. Bess thumped her tail and looked very proud.

'I think we'll have to get her a basket and lay

down some newspapers in the kitchen or something,' suggested Polly, looking very guilty.

'Yes—we can do that today. Don't worry about it,' said Rachel. She lay back in bed and felt her brain stretching and flipping like a mad gymnast as she tried, all over again, to believe that she was sharing a bedroom with a girl—and a puppy—from 1956.

A second later the door burst open, with only a hint at a knock beforehand, and Freddy and Ben spilled in. 'The sun's out again!' said Ben. 'And I think we might be able to go out on bikes—all of us!'

'We've only got two bikes!' pointed out Rachel. She couldn't imagine Polly doing a doubler, somehow.

'No! We've got four!' beamed Ben. 'Freddy and I have been right through to the back of the old garage and guess what? Their bikes are still there!'

'Really? After fifty-three years? Aren't they just a heap of rust?'

'No,' said Freddy. 'They've been under a heap of old sacking, so they've stayed quite dry. Just need a bit of oil and a pump up! Come on, you two lazy-bones! Stir your stumps! We've already had breakfast.'

Half an hour later, after eating boiled eggs and toast, with cups of tea (which Polly had insisted on neatly laying out on the table once more), and feeding Bess with some food scraps, the girls were outside by the garage, helping Ben and Freddy work on the old bikes. It was utterly weird, thought Rachel, seeing the very same bike that Freddy had ridden across the old video screen before their eyes only hours before—still here fifty-three years later. The bike had *not* worn as well as its rider. In spite of the sacking over it there was a fair bit of rust on its wheels and the basket was mouldy. Rachel poked at it with a revolted finger. 'We'll have to chuck this away.'

Polly looked appalled. 'Why on earth would we throw it away? All it needs is a good clean.'

'It's mouldy!' protested Rachel.

'It'll be perfectly all right after we've given it a wipe down with carbolic,' maintained Polly. 'You do *have* carbolic these days, I suppose?'

'What's carbolic?' asked Ben.

'Soap, you dolt!' laughed Freddy, pistoning the old black bicycle pump with vigour.

'Well—we've got antibacterial cleaning sprays,' said Rachel. 'I'll go and get one from under the sink— and some hot water and cloths.'

She expected Polly to be unimpressed, but in fact, as soon as she'd got the hang of it, she was quite pleased with the spray. 'It really cleans ninety-five per cent of all known bacteria . . . *dead*?' she marvelled. 'That's jolly good!' And she was right; the mould on the basket was only a thin layer and after they'd sprayed and scrubbed at it for a few minutes it looked fine. 'See,' said Polly. 'Good as new! Waste not, want not! Oh, Bessie! *Don't* try to drink the dirty water, you silly goose!'

Polly's bike was smaller than Freddy's but very similar in shape, also with a basket on the front. It creaked and groaned as they wheeled it out from under all the junk at the back of the garage, but after they'd all set to work again, pumping up the tyres, oiling and cleaning, it too was in good working order.

'I'm amazed the tyres haven't crumbled away,' said Ben. 'But they seem OK. We'll probably need to replace them soon, though.'

Their own bikes didn't need so much attention. Just a quick wipe down and pump up. Polly and Freddy stood back in awe as Ben wheeled out his black and red *Volcano* mountain bike, with its twenty-one gears, shock absorbers, and chunky all-terrain tyres. Rachel's was a bright green *Lizard* with eighteen gears, shock absorbers, and glistening discs set into the spokes of each wheel, which glittered and spun wildly as she pedalled.

'Oh heck,' said Freddy, glancing at his own bike with less appreciation now. 'We are going to look so . . . so terribly old-fashioned.'

'No—no—it's kind of . . . cool,' said Ben, although he had no idea what any other kids in the small town would make of it.

'Right then,' said Freddy. 'Where to?'

Ben considered. He needed to protect these strangers to the twenty-first century. Like Uncle Jerome said, they had to be introduced to it all gradually. 'I know,' he said to Rachel. 'The farm shop. We could go out there and definitely get what we need for Bess—and it's a nice ride on country lanes. We go up the hill, across a track and onto a really quiet road. We don't have to go into town just yet.'

'OK,' nodded Rachel. 'Good idea. How long do you think it'll take to get there, though? I think it's about five miles away, isn't it?' She looked at her handlebars doubtfully.

'Five miles? Pish! That's nothing!' said Freddy. 'We go twenty miles or more in a day, don't we, Poll?'

'Yes—but not without a good picnic,' said Polly. 'We can't go off without our lunch.' And with that she rested her bike on its little kick-down stand and went back inside, Bess at her heels, to the kitchen.

'Come on, Rachel,' she called back. 'We can't let the boys starve, can we?'

Ben snorted with laughter and Rachel narrowed her eyes. 'Don't think you'll be getting this kind of treatment for long!' she muttered at him, while Freddy looked mystified. 'It's only while she gets used to things. You can both do the next picnic—and don't think you're getting out of it.' She stomped off after Polly with a toss of her blonde ponytail.

Freddy pulled a face at Ben. 'What's up with her?'

Ben shrugged. 'Um . . . things are a bit different these days with girls. You can't go round expecting them to sort out all your food for you and iron your clothes and stuff.'

'Why not? I fix her bike for her and get spiders out of the bath and all that. Fair trade, I say! And girls are good at cooking and laundry and sewing and all that. They all want a nicely run home, don't they?'

'Nope.' Ben shook his head. 'Not any more.'

'Oh lord,' said Freddy. 'Things really have gone badly, haven't they? I say—can I have a crack at your bicycle?'

The sun shone down brightly as the four pedalled vigorously along the lane. Two of them carried backpacks. One had a red-checked cloth tucked across the top of the basket hanging from her handlebars and one had a puppy sitting up in his.

'Hurrah!' shouted Polly. 'How I *love* the hols! Just weeks and weeks without any school! We're going to have such fun and such adventures!'

'Stop hurrah-ing and keep pedalling,' shouted back Freddy. 'I nearly went into the back of you then. I say—sit down, Bessie! You're too little to run along with us. You might get squashed!'

'Oh, won't it be lovely when she *is* big enough to run along with us?' sang Polly. 'She could be our guard dog too, just in case we ever bump into any bad sorts. You'd protect us, wouldn't you, Bessie?'

Wuff, said Bessie, and Freddy and Polly laughed.

Ben and Rachel would have laughed too, but they were having difficulty breathing.

'C-could—could you just—slow—down—a bit?' gasped Ben, feeling as though someone had dumped a small truck on his chest. He'd never seen any other kid race up Poppycock Hill with such speed and *still* be able to speak. As soon as they'd started out from Darkwell House, Freddy and Polly were away and shooting past old Percy, as he ambled on up the hill after his usual rest on their gate, so fast that his peaked cap blew off. He was still dusting it off and looking shocked when Ben and Rachel strained past, clicking desperately through their many gears.

'Oh, Ben, don't be such a girl!' shouted back

Freddy. 'You've only just been going for five minutes and you're already coming over all queer!'

'Really—must—remind you,' puffed Ben, 'not—to say that . . . '

'Well, honestly, with all your clever tyres and unshockable suspension, you'd think you and Rachel would be *miles* ahead of us!' Freddy glanced back, scornfully.

Ben gritted his teeth. 'Just wait—till we go off road!' he gasped out. 'Then we'll show you!'

At last they reached the top of the hill and could speed down the other side, catching their breath. Even here Freddy and Polly outstripped them, their narrow road tyres slick across the tarmac.

'Jolly good roads!' shouted back Polly. 'Not nearly as many ruts and holes as there were yesterday. I say— can we get ices at this farm shop? Oh, do say we can! There's nothing quite as lovely as an ice after a bicycle ride on a sunny day!'

'Yeah—I think so,' shouted Rachel, finally getting enough breath back to speak. 'And I think they sell Magnums.'

Freddy's brakes screeched and Bessie's ears, which had been flattened, inside out, to the side of her furry brown head, flopped back forwards. 'You mean they sell *guns* alongside ices these days?'

'No, you doofus,' laughed Ben. 'It's a kind of ice cream lolly thing—loads of chocolate on it. Revolting, I think, but Rachel loves 'em.'

The farm shop car park had only three cars in it. They were enough to bring Freddy and Polly screeching to a halt again; Freddy only just grabbed Bess before she was catapulted out. The brother and sister looked at the cars—a new Mini, a Ford Mondeo, and a VW Golf—in awed silence.

'Blimey O'Reilly!' murmured Freddy, eventually. He got off his bike, rested it on its stand and ran his fingers lightly over the shiny green bonnet of the Mini. 'I didn't think they could get a motorcar to be this neat and small. Where do they fit the engine?'

'This one's got a window in the roof!' cried Polly, who had also rested her bike and gone to peer at the Golf. 'Gosh—and a television set in it too! How on earth can they do that? Surely you don't watch television *and* drive!'

'No—it's a SatNav,' explained Ben.

'A SatNav? What's that?' Freddy went to look in the Golf's window.

'Satellite navigation . . . it sends information into the car—on to the screen. From a kind of giant camera in space which can track you wherever you go.'

Freddy looked appalled. 'Sounds ghastly! Like something out of *Flash Gordon*.'

Polly nodded: 'Yes—like you're being spied on by the Galactic Bureau of Investigation. How dreadful!'

'Well, no—it's really just to help you to get to places without fumbling about with a map book,' said Rachel, resting her bike against a telegraph pole and unwinding her lock and cable.

'That's what they *want* you to think,' said Freddy, darkly.

'OK—moving on,' said Ben. 'Ice cream—remember?'

'Ooh yes—ices!' Polly clapped her hands.

'Bring your bike over to mine, Polly—we need to lock them,' said Rachel. 'Freddy can lock his to Ben's.'

'Lock them. Why?' asked Polly.

'Well, they might get stolen . . . ' Polly looked astounded. 'By bad sorts,' added Rachel. Polly's eyes shot wide open.

'Bad sorts? Do you have them around here?'

Rachel smiled at her. 'Welcome to the twenty-first century. Bad sorts are around everywhere.'

Polly was still looking fearfully about her when they went into the farm shop. It was a modest place with tools and animal feed at one end, and more general hardware and some snacks and sweets at the other. They found a metal bowl, a bag of puppy food, and a small, squashable dog bed which Ben could fit into his backpack (he'd got an empty one with him for just this purpose) and then went to the big freezer chest with ice cream and lollies in it. Next to it was a glass fronted fridge filled with cans and bottled water.

'So much *choice*,' Polly was muttering, peering into the freezer chest. 'What to have! Gosh, look at the twinkly wrappings, Freddy. Oh, look—this one looks like a helter skelter.'

'Better steer them away from the really colourful ones,' Ben muttered to Rachel, who was carrying Bessie. 'They're full of E-numbers and they'll probably go bonkers after they eat them. They're not used to it.'

'Go for a Cornetto,' advised Rachel. 'You'll love those. Mint or strawberry or vanilla. The helter skelter ones aren't that good.'

Ben got a couple of cans of Coke for them all to share and some water for Bessie, and Freddy looked on, dazzled by the array of 7 Up and Sprite and Dr Pepper and Tango. A rainbow of cans glistened through the glass in a way that Ben had never really noticed before. At the till a sulky girl in a stained green apron slouched on one elbow. Ben and Freddy gathered up the Cornettos and Cokes and went across to her.

'No—look, I say, let me get these,' said Freddy, digging his hand into his shorts pocket and extracting some clunky old coins. Ben stared at them in fascination. They were shillings, he was sure of it, and a sixpence, and several huge old pennies. 'How much, miss?' asked Freddy, politely, while the girl chewed noisily and looked at him with immense boredom. She got up and rang the Cornettos and Cokes through the till and said '£5.75,' with a flash of tooth-imprinted gum across her tongue.

Freddy looked astounded. 'Um . . . *how* much? I mean . . . is that . . . five *shillings?*'

She stared at him as if he was an idiot.

'Stop messing her about.' Ben gave him a nudge with his elbow and handed the girl a fiver and a pound coin. He and Rachel had built up quite a bit of pocket money that summer, having nowhere to go and nothing to do. Freddy and Polly tried not to look amazed at the money. Of course, thought Rachel, they didn't know anything about decimal coins. And five pounds or more would seem like a *huge* amount to them.

The girl snatched the money from Ben and glared at Freddy and as she turned her head Polly clapped her hand over her mouth to stifle a scream, while her eyes stretched wide with horror.

Chapter 11

The shop girl stopped chewing and let her mouth hang open for a few seconds while Polly squeaked and struggled to get herself under control.

'Oh my goodness! Oh my goodness!' she breathed. 'You—oh gosh—you've got—you've got something *awful* stuck in your eyebrow! Oh, Rachel—hurry—look for a first aid kit!'

The girl at the till was narrowing her eyes at Polly now, and slapping the change down on the counter. In her right eyebrow was a sharp silver stud—the kind that pokes through on either side. Ben and Rachel saw them on people's faces all the time in town. Rachel thought they were pretty nasty—especially the lip or tongue ones—but was certainly not shocked by them. Who *was*, these days?

'Iodine! Or Germolene—that's what we'll need. And some sticking plaster,' went on Polly, grimacing at the offending eyebrow with great concern and sympathy.

The girl curled her lip dangerously as she thumped a carrier bag of their goods on the counter. 'Are you taking the—'

'Polly's just a bit . . . um . . . odd,' said Ben, hurriedly picking up his change and propelling Polly away, while Rachel snatched up the bag and yanked a gaping Freddy along by one arm. Ben made a twirling gesture with his finger at his temple and grinned at the glowering shop girl. 'She doesn't mean any harm.' He shoved Polly out through the door and Rachel dragged Freddy swiftly outside too.

'What? What? I just wanted to help that poor girl!' squawked Polly. 'She was horribly injured—didn't you see? It was awful!'

Ben and Rachel looked at each other. There was going to be so much explaining to do.

After the ice cream and Coke (the cans also caused great amazement—apparently Coke only came in bottles in 1956) they decided to go back up Poppycock Hill and then go off road, along a winding track to the top, where a small clump of trees offered some shade and a good view of the Amhill valley spread out below them. It was just as well to do another bike ride. Freddy and Polly, even without any E-numbers in their ice cream, had experienced a bit of a sugar rush and were both buzzing with amazement and excitement.

'They *want* a spike through their skin? They actually *want* that?' Freddy kept repeating as he put Bessie back into her basket below his handlebars. 'And through their *tongues*? Are they lunatics?'

'Girls *really* get tattooed?' Polly was shaking her head and there was mint ice cream on her nose—her pupils were wide and glassy. 'Really? *Girls?*'

'Twenty-first century overload,' Ben said to Rachel. 'Ice cream, cars, Coke in cans, and piercings—they're freaked. Let's get them cycling again.'

Once again, fuelled by more sugar than they normally consumed in a week, the brother and sister stormed ahead up the road, but Ben and Rachel finally got to be smug when they reached the off-road path. While Freddy and Polly had to get off and push their bikes almost immediately, Ben and Rachel were able to show off and ride easily up the stony track for some way on their chunky all terrain tyres. It was lunchtime when they reached the little clump of trees and all four, plus Bessie, gratefully sank into the tall cool grass beneath the branches. Ben had to explain that, yes, you really *did* buy water in bottles these days, as he poured it into the bowl for Bessie to drink. She lapped it up eagerly and then scoffed a whole sachet of puppy food while they got out their own lunch.

Polly laid out the checked cloth (Rachel had absolutely *no* idea where she had found such a thing—their mum was more likely to bring bin bags to a picnic than a cloth!) and set out foil-wrapped sandwiches of corned beef and pickle. Little wax-wrapped round cheeses came out with them ('*I* put those in,' said Rachel) and a plastic tub, full of diced cucumber and tomato from the fridge ('I *didn't* put those in,' added Rachel). The Tesco delivery had come earlier that week and the salad stuff hadn't yet gone off. Amazingly, Polly had also managed to find a couple of flasks, which she had washed thoroughly and filled with hot tea—*and* four tin mugs, which were also strangely clean and shiny.

'There's ginger cake and apples to follow—but only *after* the sandwiches,' said Polly, patting the cake package primly. Ben grinned. It was like having a miniature mother with them. Polly, wearing beige shorts and a blue, high-necked blouse, and her wavy dark hair held neatly back with matching blue clips, was so funny. Freddy clearly didn't think anything of it. He just grabbed a couple of sandwiches and started to munch. '*Ahem!*' said Polly.

'Fanks, shis,' he mumbled, his mouth stuffed. He gulped. 'I'm absolutely famished!'

Polly beamed as they all got stuck in to the food, Ben and Rachel taking care to say thank you. She bit into her own sandwich and sighed happily. 'I don't know why it is,' she said, after a gulp, 'but food eaten outdoors always tastes heaps better!'

'Unless there's a wasp in it,' observed Ben. He'd nearly eaten one once. It had hidden in a Jammy Dodger.

'Oh—just *feel* that sun!' went on Polly, ignoring him. 'We shall all be brown as berries! We'll look just like little Indians!'

'Um . . . two things,' spluttered Ben. 'First—now really, pay attention—you can't say we look like little Indians.'

'Whyever not?'

'It's—well—disrespectful to Indians. Especially little ones.'

Freddy and Polly looked at each other, mystified.

'And we can't get brown as berries because we'll end up with a deadly skin disease,' added Rachel. 'We should have put cream on before we left, really. When Mum's home we can't get outside the house any time after March without being coated in goo. The sun's much hotter than it used to be in 1956. More dangerous.'

'Seems just the same to me,' said Freddy.

'Tell them about the ozone layer, Ben,' sighed Rachel. She was only just beginning to realize what an enormous task lay before them. How on earth were they ever going to explain everything that Freddy and Polly needed to know? There was more than fifty years' worth of stuff to catch up on. Ben was explaining the ozone layer and his great-aunt and uncle were looking very sceptical. Polly, though, pulled her bare legs back into the shade.

'You've got a lot to learn,' said Ben, echoing Rachel's thoughts.

'Fair enough,' nodded Freddy. 'But we'll catch up soon. You see if we don't!'

'It'll have to be soon—we haven't got much time, you know.'

'Before what?' Freddy screwed up his foil and threw it expertly at Polly's head.

'Before you go to school. We go back next week. And if you're going to get signed on to all the registers and everything, you'll have to be coming with us.'

'Well, it's not as if we've never been to school before!' said Freddy. 'I mean—how different can it be? You still get masters, I dare say? You don't get taught by robots or anything?'

'Teachers, not masters,' corrected Ben. 'And

to be honest, some of them are about as human as robots . . . '

'All right then. Teachers. And desks and blackboards and chalk . . . ?'

'Tables, *white*boards and markers . . . oh, and interactive screens, smartboards, Powerpoint, internet access, computers . . . and so on.'

Freddy and Polly, now on their ginger cake, glanced at each other and back at Ben.

'You'll have to have some lessons in all this stuff,' he said, looking at Rachel, who nodded. 'I mean, even if we do pretend you've been off living in a hippy commune all your lives, you have to know about *some* of this stuff. You just *have* to.'

'The internet's amazing. You can learn about anything on it,' said Rachel. 'And get almost anything from it. We might even be able to find you a Miss Rosebud, Polly—on eBay, maybe. Uncle J might let us use one of his computers.'

'What's eBay?' asked Polly, cuddling Bess close to her.

'Oh, it's a thing on the net where people buy and sell stuff.'

Polly looked blank. 'On the net?'

'Yeah—a website. Sorry, you won't know anything about websites, of course.'

'Well, my father's study was a dreadful web site,' said Polly, stroking Bessie's ears. 'I used to have to tidy it up, because Mrs M wasn't allowed in there. The duster would get *covered* in webs because he wouldn't let me in for weeks sometimes, when he was really in the thick of some research. I can't abide cobwebs in corners. It's really poor. When I'm a housewife I'll never let cobwebs build up in my home.'

'No—no—quite right too,' muttered Rachel. She didn't have the first idea how to explain the internet to Polly. She thought she'd leave that to Ben.

Ben lay back in the grass and watched the clouds passing overhead. His brain hurt just trying to *think* about all the stuff Freddy and Polly needed to understand. He flopped his forearm over his eyes and tried not to panic. He pictured all the kids in his year—sneery Jim Lewis and obnoxious Roly O'Neal. The Pincer twins with their habit of doing wrist burns to anyone they'd just met and beefy Lorraine Kingsley, who smoked like a chimney in the girls' toilets and had once head-butted a teacher. He thought of all these glorious examples of modern youth waiting to meet Freddy and Polly, and shuddered.

'We'll get some magazines and newspapers and stuff, and some batteries for the radio,' he said, from under his arm. 'And see if Uncle J can mend the telly and get the satellite dish back up—and for the next week you're going to have to learn everything you can. If you can't do that and you turn up at Amhill Secondary like you are now—well, we might just as w-well put you back in your sleeping chambers, b-because, trust me, your life won't be worth living!'

Freddy rolled onto his front and sank his teeth into his apple. 'Benedict, old chum,' he said. 'You worry too much.'

Ben exhaled and thought maybe Freddy was right.

'Honestly,' said Freddy. 'We'll be right as rain and gay as ninepence! You'll see.'

The deepest vaults of the Kremlin storehouses were as bad as anyone's cellars. It fell to a young intern to sort them out late that spring. He re-labelled and re-shelved boxes and boxes of documents from another time, before *glasnost*, before the welcoming of McDonald's into Russia's capital city, from long before he had even been born. If he'd had the time to rummage through them, they might have been fascinating, but there were far too many. They were to be catalogued and sorted, that was all.

At the end of his second day of housekeeping, Ivan paused in his work. Lying alone on one of the highest metal shelves was a white oblong envelope. On it were the intriguing words: 'To be opened only by the Leader of the Soviet Union in 2007'.

Ivan put down his pen and clipboard and flipped the envelope thoughtfully. He'd always wanted to deliver something to the president.

Chapter 12

They found Uncle Jerome in the front garden as they all skidded to a halt by the gate later that afternoon. He was up the chestnut tree and gave them a shout of excitement as they got off their bikes.

'Look! It's still here! Well . . . what's left of it. Not working, obviously.' And he reached down from a low branch which he'd been balancing on (a paint-spattered stepladder was set up below it) and in his hand was a rusty box, about the size of a small shoebox. A lichen-encrusted circle at the front had once been a glass lens and a metre or two of kinked and ivy-clad wire trailed from the back of it. 'This was the camera!' shouted Uncle Jerome, his voice high with excitement and altitude. Climbing a tree was not something they'd ever seen him do.

'Do get down, JJ, before you break your neck!' laughed Freddy. He was quite cheeky, really, thought

143

Ben—but then he *was* Uncle J's uncle. It still made Ben's brain bend to think of it.

Uncle Jerome handed Ben the camera and came carefully down the stepladder. His eyes were glittery; dark lines underneath them. It was entirely possible he had not slept at all since yesterday. They had seen him like this before, when his work in the attic got very exciting.

'You need to eat,' said Rachel. 'I bet you haven't had anything at all, have you?'

'What? Oh, nonsense. Don't worry about that,' said Uncle Jerome. 'Time enough, time enough. I want to talk some more about what happened on Wednesday the sixth of June. I have one or two leads to follow up.'

'Well, you can do it over some cake and tea,' said Polly, firmly, arriving at Rachel's side. 'You'll make much more sense of it all then.'

'What leads? What have you found out?' asked Freddy, clearly not remotely worried about how under-nourished Uncle Jerome was.

'Well,' said Uncle Jerome, taking back the camera and turning it lovingly in his hands. 'That man—the one Polly spotted on the film, walking by just before the car came that afternoon. I've studied him on freeze frame. I couldn't believe it at first—but now I really think I know who he is.'

'You do?' breathed Polly. 'Who? Who could it be?'

'Well, if I'm right, it's very good news, because he's still alive. And he knows a lot about the investigation into your father's disappearance. On the other hand, talking to him could be trouble.'

'Who? Who?' squeaked Polly, sounding like an anxious owl.

'Percival Shaw,' came the reply. But it didn't come from Uncle Jerome's mouth. Uncle Jerome's mouth was wide and his eyes were blinking in shock through his glasses. The voice came from behind them all. They spun around and there, leaning on the gate as he so often did, was old Percy.

Normally old Percy just stared away at the trees behind the house, his rheumy eyes distant and his face impassive, as inscrutable as an ancient Japanese warrior. Today, his eyes were fixed on Polly and Freddy, his elderly teeth gnawing on his lower lip and his head shaking in amazement. 'It is you. It *is,* isn't it? I saw you this morning and I thought I'd gone senile. But no . . . here you are. Frederick and Pauline Emerson. Maybe I *am* senile. Maybe I'm in a bathchair now, down at Sunset Mansions where the old folk get put out to pasture . . .'

Uncle Jerome stopped his gaping, strode across to the gate and grasped Percy's arm. 'No—no, Percy.

It's real. Didn't I tell you? Didn't I always say? He didn't do it! He didn't! And now we have proof. Well . . . sort of. I mean . . . nobody's ever going to believe it, I suppose. But yes . . . this is Pauline and Freddy. The professor managed to suspend them—cryonically—truly! They've been frozen for fifty-three years! Can you believe it?'

Ben felt very uneasy. He could see Freddy and Polly did too, and Rachel was raising her eyebrows at him urgently. What should they do? Percy was still staring at the sixty-six-year-old boy and his sixty-five-year-old little sister.

'Tea,' said Polly, suddenly. 'Everyone come inside and we'll have a pot of tea.'

'For fifty-three years I've not been able to get the Emerson case out of my head,' said Percy, formerly Detective Inspector Percival Shaw of the North Hampshire Constabulary. 'For fifty-three years I've known that it didn't add up. None of it made sense. It's needled and needled away at me—all my career I wanted to crack it. And even when I retired . . . well, it just wouldn't let go of me.' He picked up his teacup and sipped at the hot brown brew, his eyes continually roaming from the brother to the sister, and back again.

146

'Uncle J,' said Ben, quietly. 'What now? What if he goes and tells people? What if—you know—the authorities and all that come along? They'll take Freddy and Polly away for testing and stuff and we might never see them again.'

'Is that why you keep coming up to the house and leaning on the gate?' Rachel asked Percy.

'Well, this always *was* my constitutional—walking up to the wood on the hill,' said Percy. 'Kept me fit. I didn't think anything of it. But in the summer of 1956 that changed—for ever. You see, I was the last one to see the house before—before the suspected murders were reported. They even had *me* down as a suspect for a while—but not for long. I met Clara up along the track, you see. We were courting. She was my alibi—and her brother John. And anyway, we all knew, in the force, that it was fishy. Suspect. Nothing run of the mill—all very hush hush. It never sounded right. Never rang true. A cracked bell—that's what it was. Never rang true.'

'But don't you see!' Uncle Jerome, stuffing down a bit of ginger cake left over from the picnic, sprayed crumbs across the table as he began to get agitated again. 'Don't you see—*you* might be the key! You were the last person to pass on the security camera. You may have seen something—you see, there was a car.

A car that came along only seconds later. You may well have looked back over your shoulder and seen it. Did you? Can you remember?'

Percy screwed up his face and ran an age-spotted hand through his thinning grey hair. 'It's too long ago now,' he said. 'Some things I remember better than last week . . . but . . . ' He looked hard at Uncle Jerome and shook his head. 'Truth be told, Jerome, I don't even know if I'm here right now, or gone ga-ga, down at Sunset Mansions, after all. How can this be, eh? How can these two *be*?'

'I'll have to take him down—show him the film,' said Uncle Jerome.

Freddy was on his feet instantly. 'No! You promised. Absolutely not!'

'But if he sees the film, he may remember. This could make all the difference!'

'Father said we must *never* let anyone else in. It's top secret. I won't hear of it, I tell you!'

Polly touched his arm. Her eyes were full of hope. 'Freddy, it might be the only way to find Father. Let him see the film! Please! What good is it to us now, keeping everything secret, if we can't get Father back?'

Freddy stared at her for a long time, biting his lip. Then he sat back down and sighed. 'We have to

148

make him promise—*really* promise. He can't go around blabbing about it. That won't do.'

'Percy, will you give us your word that what you are about to see you will not speak of—to anybody?' asked Uncle Jerome.

Percy shrugged. 'Nobody listens to an old codger like me anyway. Why would I bother?'

'But you were a policeman—a detective inspector!' said Ben, and the old man smiled and nodded sadly.

'*Was* a detective inspector,' he said. 'Just another old codger now. You'll see, lad—in another sixty years . . . you'll see.'

Percy struggled a bit with the rungs down into the shaft, but his daily walks up the hill had kept him reasonably fit for a man nearing eighty and he made it to the Ampex room in one piece, staring in amazement around the time capsule sitting room as he passed through.

They discovered that Uncle Jerome had carefully attached another length of blank oxide tape to the first lot, making it easier to weave the film back onto the spools and move it back and forth while he scrutinized the grainy image of the young man with the stone in his shoe and the black car's arrival. Percy leant on the front of the huge video machine and peered at the tiny screen above it intently. He chuckled and shook his head as he watched himself, fifty-three years younger, walk by, stop to sort out his shoe, and then walk on again.

'And you don't remember seeing anyone here, while you did that?' prompted Uncle Jerome.

'No, it was just normal. The front door was open a bit, I remember that much. Someone had been cooking; I could smell lunch. Made me feel a bit peckish. Of course, I only remember this now because a week later I was making a statement about it—and then getting everyone else's statements too. For what they were worth—which was nothing.'

Now the black car rolled into view, on the last few images. Everyone waited while Percy looked at it, screwing up his eyes and tilting his head—trying to read the number on the registration plate.

'A 5 3—that's all I could make out—after hours of trying,' sighed Uncle Jerome. 'What do you think? Is it a car you recognize?' Percy was straightening up again now, and frowning. 'Is it? What do you think, Percy?'

'I don't need to see the number, Jerome. I know what car that is,' he said. He stepped away from the Ampex, shaking his head. 'Better give it up now, unless you want a whole lot of trouble.'

'What? What does that mean?' demanded Freddy.

'It means you're not ever going to find out what you want to know, young man, that's what it means. That car came along for a purpose. It didn't just happen by. And if I'd remembered seeing it on the day, chances are *I* wouldn't ever have happened by again.'

They all stood, staring at him, waiting for him to make sense. Percy regarded them all gravely. 'It's a government car.'

Freddy shook his head. 'But—but Father *worked* for the government! So that's probably why they came to see him. He worked for them.'

'Did they ever come by before, lad?'

Freddy swallowed and shook his head. 'No,' he said. 'Never.'

'I thought not,' said Percy. 'I saw that car—or one like it—a few times in my career. Whenever it drove through, misfortune and confusion weren't far behind. It was a Clean Up car—that's what we used to call it back then. Whatever happened here to your dad, it was cleaned up. That's why we kept turning up nothing but dead ends on our investigation, I'll warrant. Somebody at the top sent in the Clean Up car.'

Ben felt a chill creep into him. 'But—surely not his own government . . . ? The people he'd been working for . . . ?'

151

'Ah well—our government, someone else's government . . . much the same thing back then,' said Percy. 'You have to understand, lad, it was very bad times in the world. Nobody trusted anybody. Spies were going east and spies were going west and terrible weapons were being made so we could all kill each other much more efficiently. Professor Emerson knew a lot of people and a lot of people knew him. Moving in his world, you could find yourself connected to some very bad people and not even know it. And look—here it is—he *did* have something to hide, didn't he?'

Percy looked around him and back through the open door to the sitting room. 'Reckon it's about time you showed me the rest, don't you?'

Uncle Jerome took Percy on a tour while the rest of them sank onto the dusty chairs and sofa in the sitting room, trying to absorb what the old man had told them.

'He always did say they weren't to be trusted,' muttered Freddy. 'But he said that about *everyone*! I never thought they might . . . they might . . . '

'Well, we don't know, do we? It's no good worrying about it—we just have to keep trying to find out. Emersons don't give up,' said Polly. As she'd promised Rachel, there was no more 'blubbing'.

'It's why he didn't tell them about our sleeping chambers,' went on Freddy. 'He didn't trust them not to do something terrible while testing them.'

Ben and Rachel exchanged glances. It seemed to them that Freddy and Polly's father had done something pretty terrible himself while testing them. They didn't say so.

'Did the government have *any* idea what he was doing here?' asked Ben, at length.

'I don't know,' admitted Freddy. 'He was working on all kinds of things up in London—and cryonics was just one of them, but I think it just involved insects and rodents and so on. It didn't work well in the labs up there. The rats used to bleed afterwards and sometimes lose their claws and teeth. They'd go blind too—and then die. Horrible. They stopped the research after a while—said it would never work, but Father didn't agree. He always felt sure he could crack it—and he did. He found a different method and the rats survived. But he wanted to test it thoroughly before he let anyone know, so he started working on it here instead. I don't think they knew—or had any idea of how much further he'd taken it. He froze himself, first. He had to show us how to put him in the chamber and then get him out again. That was jolly scary, but we soon got used to it. The problem was, he needed to be taking notes, too, so he needed someone else to go in. So we volunteered.'

Percy re-emerged in the sitting room, looking stunned. 'Say what you like about him,' he said, patting Freddy's shoulder as he passed, Uncle Jerome close behind him, 'but your father was a genius. No mistake. A genius.'

Freddy sprang to his feet before Percy could move on to the door to the shaft.

'Your word! I need your word!'

Percy held out his hand, which was trembling slightly, and looked Freddy straight in the eye. 'I give you my word I won't speak to anyone else about what I've seen today.' Freddy nodded gravely and shook his hand. 'But I will try to find out more about that car—and look back through my old case notes. See if there's something I missed which could help. And there's also the thirty year rule now.'

'The thirty year rule? What's that?' asked Freddy.

'Well, in theory, government secrets get opened up after thirty years have passed. It's the law . . . or supposed to be. Of course, some of them get made right back into secrets as soon as they're uncovered. A judge extends the rule for up to a hundred years sometimes. But that could be something you could look into, Jerome . . . with your connections. If there was a cover-up in 1956, they might be ready to uncover it again now. Especially thinking there's nobody left to care.'

Uncle Jerome nodded. 'Yes, I think I should. Discreetly, of course. I know one or two people who might be able to help. I have a good friend in Whitehall . . . he can be trusted.'

'Thank you,' said Freddy, to Percy. 'Thank you very much.'

After tea that night—macaroni cheese from the freezer which both Freddy and Polly thought was awful—they listened to the radio, which Freddy and Polly also thought was awful. Ben had taken care to tune to Radio 2, to be kind, but Polly was still shocked rigid by the rude jokes of the presenter and the words in the songs. 'Why do they want us to keep shaking our ass?' she queried, dismayed. 'That would be cruel. I hate cruelty to animals.'

Ben and Rachel tried to explain, but the truth was even more shocking to poor Polly.

They got to bed early, exhausted, intrigued, and worried by the talk of government clean up men. Freddy was quiet and Ben could tell this was on his mind.

'We could go into town tomorrow, if you think you're ready for it—do some research at the library,' Ben offered, hoping to cheer the boy up. 'They keep all the newspapers in the vaults from way back—we can follow all the stuff that was written about your dad, and see if there are any more clues. Maybe find out if Mrs Minstead knew anything . . . ? She might still be alive?'

'I doubt it . . . she was pretty ancient even fifty years ago,' said Freddy. He sighed and dropped his head respectfully. 'But yes . . . into town. That would be whizzer,' he added, lying back in the lower bunk. Just as Ben was about to reach over and switch off the lamp there was an urgent thud on the door and Polly and Rachel almost fell into the room. Ben and Freddy shot up in bed when they saw their faces. Both girls looked white and scared.

Polly held Bessie and whimpered, 'Freddy—oh, Freddy, look!' She turned the puppy's furry brown snout around and pulled her handkerchief away from it.

On the hanky was a blurry rose of blood.

Chapter 13

'Bleeding first, then teeth and nails . . . blindness, then . . . ' Freddy stared down at his hands, which were wringing the bedclothes into a tight bunch. 'But look—she could just have scratched her nose with her claws. Puppies have very sharp claws, don't they? It doesn't mean what happened to the rats is happening to her or . . . or . . . '

'Or *will* happen to us,' said Polly. She hugged Bessie to her and peered down at the puppy's wrinkled brown muzzle. She dabbed at it again and they all stared at the hanky. 'Doesn't seem to be any more blood now, at any rate,' said Polly. 'And we never had this happen before, did we, Freddy?'

'We didn't stay frozen for fifty-three years before,' pointed out her brother.

'We should go to Uncle J,' said Rachel. 'We should.'

'No,' said Freddy. 'It's just a scratch, you'll see! Father sorted out the problem which killed the rats, I tell you. We're not going to panic about nothing. I mean—yes—if we all wake up tomorrow with our noses gushing like Niagara Falls, fair enough—but right now I feel fine, don't you, Polly?'

'Yes, I'm quite all right,' said Polly. 'I think you're right—it's just a scratch. Sorry I was such a goose about it. Let's all get some sleep. We can plan what to do next to find Father in the morning.'

Rachel was impressed. She was seriously frightened by the bleeding and the awful thought of what could happen to Polly and Freddy—and Polly must surely be terrified. But the girl was now getting up with a smile and tucking Bessie back into her arms.

'Good plan,' Freddy was saying. 'Let's get some decent kip. Tomorrow we can shake our gravy asses into town and do some sleuthing.'

'I knew the radio was a bad idea,' sighed Ben, pulling his pillow over his head.

'Sorry, you really can't wear those.' Rachel firmly removed the little pink grips from either side of Polly's dark wavy hair.

'But they keep me neat!' protested Polly.

'Or *that*.' Rachel surveyed the pale yellow pinafore dress that her great-aunt wore.

'But this is one of my best dresses! You always ought to try to look decent when you go into town!'

'Polly, you look like a six year old! Nobody over seven wears that kind of stuff nowadays! Nobody! You'll have to borrow some of my stuff. Look, these will fit you.' She rummaged in her wardrobe and pulled out a pair of newish blue jeans, with a chain of silver stars threaded through the belt loops, and a pale blue T-shirt. Polly stared at them in awe, and then sighed and shrugged out of her pinafore dress.

When they reached the hallway, Freddy was also dressed twenty-first century style, in a pair of Ben's jeans and a white T-shirt. 'Not bad, eh, Polly? Really rather gravy, I reckon!'

'*Groovy*,' corrected Ben, with a sigh. 'Or cool. Cool is better.'

'I say—you look jolly nice, too, Poll.'

Polly smiled, slightly doubtfully, but she did look great in Rachel's gear. Much less little-girlish. 'I like these,' she murmured, playing with the little silver stars on a chain around her waist. 'But what *have* you done to your hair?'

'Wax!' grinned Freddy, whose neat parting had

159

now been messed up. 'Isn't it ghastly? Ben says it's "cool" though. Which means good. I think.'

'Still have to sort out their shoes,' Rachel said to Ben, and they nodded, like anxious parents, as they looked at the old-fashioned, round-toed leather sandals with buckles that Freddy and Polly wore. 'We'll have to ask Uncle J for some money to get them trainers, or they'll be laughed out of Amhill.'

'Got some from him already,' said Ben, patting his jeans pocket. 'Right, back on the bikes then. But I think we should leave Bessie behind today—just to be on the safe side.'

'She's fine,' said Polly, bending down to play with Bessie's ears—and Bessie did *seem* fine. There had been no more bleeding when they woke up that morning, much to everyone's relief, but Ben was adamant.

'No, town is too busy, full of cars. And we need to go into places which won't let dogs in. She's too little to stay outside on a lead on her own. Someone might nick her.'

Freddy and Polly exchanged worried glances. 'All right,' said Freddy. 'We can't risk her being dognapped!'

They left Bessie in the hallway with her basket, a bowl of water, a Chatz doll to chew, and plenty of newspaper laid down. Uncle Jerome said he'd look in on her when Rachel took a sandwich down to him in the vault, but they doubted he'd remember. 'We'll have to get back by lunchtime,' said Polly.

It was downhill into the town, so Freddy and Polly didn't shame Ben and Rachel quite so much this time.

'We can't let them bike all the way in—they won't be used to the traffic,' Rachel said, as she cycled alongside Ben. 'If we chain up the bikes in the park we won't have to go too far in. We can walk from there.'

The park was on the outskirts of the small town of Amhill, alongside the pretty River Am which ran through the valley. They reached it in ten minutes and locked the bikes up together against some chain-link fencing.

'It's very colourful now,' said Polly, gazing at the swings, the roundabout, the slide, and the little horse-y things on springs that the toddlers rode on. 'It was all just red and grey when we used to come here. The witch's hat has gone. And the pirate ship too . . . '

'What were they?' asked Rachel, following Polly as she stepped out onto the playground and gave a little squeak of surprise when she realized the ground, which looked like black tarmac, was actually spongey underfoot.

'The witch's hat was jolly good fun—my favourite.

Like an upside-down cone made of metal—a sort of cage with a wooden seat all around the bottom edge, hanging off a metal pole up through the middle. It spun and swung around. I loved it!'

Freddy was crouched down, poking the rubbery ground with fascination. 'The pirate ship was the best. It wasn't really a ship, of course—just a long log-type thing with seats on, and we all sat on it and it swung back and forth until it went so fast we started to fall off. One time it cracked Gus Blaine in the back of the head and knocked him out cold! It was hilarious! He went down smack on his face. I wonder why they took it away. It was heaps better than this. This is all little kids' stuff!'

'Um . . .' said Ben, 'I think with this stuff people tend not to get knocked out so much.'

'Safe,' said Freddy, kicking the multicoloured roundabout. 'But jolly dull.'

Ben felt slightly embarrassed. 'Come on,' he said. 'Let's get into town.'

On the modest high street of Amhill, Freddy and Polly were once more open-mouthed with astonishment at all the cars, the shiny shop fronts, the vending machines, the buses with their digital number and destination displays, the perspex BT phone hood next to the Post Office, the colours—everywhere—luminous, glaring, iridescent colours. 'It's so . . . so *bright*,' murmured Polly, staring all around her. 'And it smells . . . funny.'

Ben and Rachel couldn't really work out how it would smell different—except perhaps for more traffic pollution. The cars held Freddy mesmerized. 'How can there be so many cars on one road?' he gasped.

Ben shrugged. 'You should see it on a Saturday— this is nothing.' And in fact, only ten or so cars had passed them. It was a fairly quiet high street.

'Is there a *band* playing in that one?' Freddy stared, incredulously, at a BMW which cruised by, pumping out a chart hit so loudly it made the pavement vibrate beneath their feet.

Ben laughed. 'Just a really loud sound system, that's all.' Freddy looked blank. 'He's just playing a CD and pumping up the volume.'

Freddy looked pained and shook his head. 'A seedy? A seedy *what*?'

Ben glanced at the Woolworths across the road. 'Come on,' he said. 'I'll show you.'

'Oh, goody! Woolworths is still here!' said Polly. 'How lovely! They do super frocks and petticoats.'

Inside, Ben took Freddy to rack upon rack of CDs, DVDs, CD ROMs, computer games—discs of all kinds. The display took up a quarter of the store. Rachel led Polly to the children's clothing at the back. Polly surveyed it, her smile fading. 'Not so much choice now, is there?' she sighed.

'Well—it's just children's stuff really,' said Rachel, apologetically, glancing down the rack of toddler's clothing and Marvel comic character pyjamas.

'But we *are* children,' protested Polly.

'Well . . . sort of,' said Rachel. 'We're nearly teenagers . . . kind of *tween*agers. We don't wear the same stuff as little kids, you know.'

They wandered back through the sweets aisle with its rows and rows of confectionery; Polly looked quite overcome. 'Is there some kind of . . . of . . . sweets festival?' she breathed, running her fingers along the rack of luridly coloured treats.

'Well, no. This is, kind of, normal,' shrugged Rachel. 'People eat lots of sweets.'

Polly stared up at her. 'It's a wonder you have any teeth left at all!'

Ben and Freddy arrived beside them and Freddy immediately went into the same routine of gasps of astonishment as he laid eyes on the sweets. It was getting to be quite tiring, dealing with the constant amazement, shock, and horror. 'Come on,' Ben muttered to Rachel. 'Let's get them to the library before they find the mega-sour jaw-breakers. Those'll make their eyeballs explode.'

They chivvied their great-aunt and great-uncle along the road quickly, hauling them away from shop windows and nudging them on past a cashpoint, where both were riveted by the sight of a *building* spitting out money. Then Polly got quite spooked by a man who walked past her, behaving, she said, like a lunatic.

'Did you see him? Oh, poor man!' She clutched Ben's arm and gestured over her shoulder, keeping her eyes firmly ahead. 'He was walking along talking to himself! All on his own, just talking to himself, and he'd poked a wire into his ear. How awful. Don't you look after people like that these days? He shouldn't be out on his own!'

Ben stared back along the road. He hooted with laughter. 'You'd better get used to *that,* Polly,' he said. 'He was talking into his mobile phone—using his hands-free kit. People do it all the time.'

And then, of course, they had to explain mobile phones. Goshing went off the scale.

At last they reached the quiet and calm of Amhill's library. Happily, it was an old-fashioned building with its old-fashioned interior lovingly maintained. It did have computers and internet access, but in a little side room. Apart from the barcode scanner when you took a book out, there was nothing too shocking about it. It smelled reassuringly old.

Ben approached the middle-aged lady librarian, as she stacked a pile of books at her corner desk. 'Excuse me . . . we want to do some research on old newspaper stories,' said Ben, in his best voice. 'Can you help us?'

'How far back?' she asked, not taking her eyes from her task.

'1956—ish,' said Ben.

'Hmmm, that'll be downstairs then. Microfiche, I'm afraid. They haven't all been uploaded to computer yet. What do you want to find?'

'Well . . . er . . . there was a sort of murder story, in 1956. Here in Amhill. It was never solved. We thought it would be interesting for our school project.'

The librarian looked up, smoothing back her brown hair and narrowing her eyes at him slightly. She smiled. 'Forgive me if I'm being dense,' she said, 'but aren't you still on holiday a couple more days?'

'Yes . . . well . . . um . . . it's f-for one of those school h-holidays projects,' said Ben, hurriedly. The librarian looked vaguely familiar to him, but he couldn't remember where from.

'OK,' she smiled at them all. 'Follow me. I'll set you all up. I must say, it's nice to see four young people interested in research. Mostly kids just look stuff up on the net and cut and paste it. There's no art to it, these days,' she sighed. 'It's a Wikipedia world.'

She led them down some stone steps behind the biographies section. Here it was cooler and quieter, the walls panelled with dark wood. It was a basement room but high up narrow windows gave a street level view at the top. They could just see people's feet and ankles and buggy wheels passing by. An old lady was working at one screen at the far end of the room, but otherwise it was empty. The librarian showed them to a table with another screen and then loaded something up into a machine below it, which reminded Ben of a slide projector. She hit a switch and a bright light shone from the screen, making them squint. The librarian showed Ben two twisting buttons on either side of the screen.

'It's very basic,' she said. 'But I've loaded the *Amhill Bugle*, 1956, so you can look through that. It was a weekly, so you'll only have fifty or so to look through—it's all on one reel. Careful though, not to spin it along too fast. It can make you a bit queasy. Have you got something to make notes on? You can't print off from here. It's just a sort of rolling slide show, really.'

'Yes,' said Freddy, pulling out a notebook and pen from his backpack. 'We're all organized. Thanks awfully, miss. It's jolly decent of you to help us.'

The librarian blinked and smiled at him, clearly charmed. She was not used to this kind of appreciation from thirteen-year-old boys. She looked at Freddy for a very long time and then glanced up into the corner of the room, looking slightly flushed. Then she said, 'You're very welcome, young man,' before stepping away and fiddling with something on one of the shelves.

The screen was now a blur of newsprint as Ben worked the controls and began to whip the images from the old *Amhill Bugle* from left to right across the screen. Page after page of stories edged past jerkily as they tried to spot anything important. Parish notices, council meetings, raging debates about a new road being built, a local girl winning a beauty pageant, a milkman discovering an old lady who'd fallen downstairs, a celebrated local athlete going out to the Melbourne Olympics . . . on and on it went. Often Polly or Freddy would give a shout of recognition. 'Sally Wilson! I remember her!' said Polly. 'She won the Singer's Sewing Susan contest! She made that dress herself and I saw her buying buttons for it in the haberdasher's! Gosh . . . she must be a grandmother now . . . '

'Shh,' said Ben. He didn't think anyone could hear, but the old lady down at the end might and the librarian was still somewhere around. She'd finished with whatever she'd been adjusting on the shelf opposite and had wandered off, but not up the stairs.

At last they found the cuttings about the strange events at Darkwood House and they all grew sombre and quiet as Ben paused his button twisting, so they could read the details again. Most of them they had already seen, in Uncle Jerome's folder of cuttings, but there were one or two which they hadn't read before. Just more fascination for what might have happened to the children and their respected but now doubted father. More comments from Mrs Minstead; a service held for them at the local church, where the junior choir sang the children's favourite hymns.

'Nothing from the family,' said Rachel. 'No comment at all. That's funny, isn't it?'

'Why is it funny?' said Freddy. 'Nobody wants to talk about their personal life to a newspaper, do they?'

Ben and Rachel looked at each other. 'Some people do . . . these days. Sometimes,' said Ben. 'If this happened today, you'd have the press camped on your doorstep and ringing the bell all day and night until you said something to them.'

Freddy looked appalled. 'I should call the police!'

They continued to look for clues, but after a while, during which Ben *did* begin to feel quite sick, with all the newsprint whooshing sideways, they realized that the story had tailed off.

'We're probably looking in the wrong place for clues anyway,' said Freddy. 'We should be looking for stuff that happened *before*. Stuff that might explain why Father did what he did. Perhaps we should look at the *Amhill Bugle* for 1955?'

Everyone else groaned. 'We really must go back for Bessie, now,' said Rachel. 'We'll have to come back and look some more another day. And we're also meant to be getting you some proper shoes and—oh, blimey—you'll need school uniform and stuff. There's hardly any time left. I think we might have to come back to this next week. Sorry, Freddy.'

Freddy stood up and ran his hands through his waxy hair, which had begun to fall out of its carefully constructed mess look and back to its smooth, neat parting. He set his jaw and looked hard into the distance, as if he could *make* the clues to his father's disappearance manifest themselves here in the library.

'I don't care about going to some stupid school,' he muttered. 'I don't care, I tell you! Finding out about Father is much more important. He could be in danger! He might need our help!'

'Freddy,' Polly touched her brother's shoulder. 'We don't even know that he's . . . that he's alive.'

He brushed her off. 'Of course he's alive! I know it! I can't believe you'd even say that!' And he stomped away from them all and then sprinted up the stone steps.

They followed him up, feeling flat. The research hadn't really helped at all, thought Ben. They were no nearer getting an answer, even after more than an hour of staring at the whooshing screen and feeling slightly motion-sick. While Polly and Rachel went to join Freddy, as he sat on the stone steps outside, Ben went to find the librarian. She was back at her desk, on the phone. She seemed to be speaking another language, in quite a low voice. She looked up and gave him a little wave, still looking a bit flushed, thought Ben. Maybe she really *didn't* get many kids in doing research these days. She covered the mouthpiece of the phone. 'You all done now, down there?' She smiled.

'Yes, but I didn't know how to switch it all off,' said Ben.

'Not to worry—I'll nip down and sort it out. Did you find out what you wanted to know?'

'Not really,' sighed Ben.

'Well, do come back again and tell me more about it,' she said. 'I might be able to help.'

'Thanks, we might do that,' said Ben, but she was already talking again to the person on the phone.

Ben realized now that she was the lady who had come to their house late last year on a mission to sign up more children to library events and stayed chatting to their mum for quite a while over a cup of tea. They never had gone along to any events, even though Mum had said they should. Ben wandered back outside where Rachel was promising Freddy something unbelievable.

'A whopper?' he said. 'Why would I want you to get me a *whopper*? A whopping what?'

'You shouldn't tell fibs,' admonished Polly. 'You tell whoppers and the truth will always find you out.'

'Oh, do stop talking like a Sunday school teacher!' snapped Rachel, clearly also the worse for the microfiche session. 'It's a kind of burger, you dummies! We'll go back past Burger King and get you some food. And look—do you think you could try to stop all the gasping and goshing for just five minutes? It's making my head ache.'

'Come on.' Ben put his arm around Rachel's and Polly's shoulders and gave Freddy a friendly nudge with his foot. 'We're all hacked off and hungry. Rachel's got the right idea. Let's stuff ourselves on glorious twenty-first century junk food.'

Polly and Freddy both began to query: 'Junk f—?'

'No goshing!' cried Rachel, yanking Polly along, around the corner to the Burger King. Minutes later they were walking back to the park, eating Whoppers from their cartons and holding cups of Coke in the crooks of their arms.

'Junk food?' said Freddy, uncertainly.

'Oh, just eat it!' wailed Ben.

'Eating while you walk isn't ladylike,' said Polly.

'You're *not* a lady,' said Rachel. 'Get it down you before I tip my Coke over your head!'

At the park they sat down near their bikes and finished the remains of the burgers. Polly and Freddy were quiet, intent on finishing every last scrap in their cardboard cartons. Then they stuffed down all the French fries in the battered paper bag Ben opened up, dipping them eagerly in the little punnets of ketchup. They sucked up the last of their Coke with a slight fluttering of their eyelids. Then they lay back on the grass, smiling and slightly glassy eyed.

'Do you eat this all the time?' asked Freddy.

'No—just once a month or so,' said Rachel. 'It's rubbish really.'

'It's *heavenly*,' said Polly.

Ben laughed. 'That's just the monosodium glutamate talking.'

'I don't know what you mean,' said Polly, with a yawn. 'But I'm *not* going to gosh.'

She closed her eyes and Rachel grinned at Ben,

guiltily. They had introduced two pure 1950s children to junk food. It was bad. But very funny. She leaned back against the fence and decided they could have a bit more of a rest before hurrying back to Bessie. Then Freddy wiped his face with his napkin and dropped it into the empty burger carton and Rachel felt sick all over again. On the napkin was something she wished was ketchup. But she knew it wasn't.

CHERNOBYL WASTELANDS,
AUGUST 2009

The Russian president's perspex face shield steamed up as he let out an excited gasp inside his protective suit. He had only visited Chernobyl twice before, and then far from the fall-out zone of the old, pulverized power plant. Both times he'd been surrounded by press, photographers flashing, as he shook the hands of the victims of the nuclear disaster who were still alive twenty years on.

Today he was deep in the wasteland zone, accompanied by just three other men—hand picked—including the young intern, Ivan, who had been present earlier that year when his leader had impatiently ripped open the letter addressed to The Leader of the Soviet Union, 2007. He had received it late, but its contents still stopped him in his tracks. It had taken some months' careful manoeuvring to get to this desolate place without being tracked by either their own or the rest of the world's press. Anything to do with Chernobyl rarely passed unnoticed.

'This is it,' said Gregor, as they arrived on the concrete bunker's lowest level. He hit a green button beside the thirty centimetre-thick iron door and to everyone's surprise, it worked.

'He's been here for fifty-two years?' muttered the president. 'Just waiting for me?'

'In the depths of his best research,' smiled Gregor.

Chapter 14

At Darkwood House, Bessie was in transports of delight to see them back. She'd drunk most of her water, gnawed through Ritzy's other leg and made thorough use of the newspaper they'd laid down for her.

'Ooh, Bessie, what a frightful pong!' Freddy held his nose and looked disgusted as Bessie leaped up at him and licked his knees.

'Come on,' said Ben. 'Let's get this cleared up before Uncle J sees it. He'll have a fit!'

'What JJ? No! He's a darling!' said Polly and Rachel and Ben nearly went into a 'goshing' session themselves. They'd never heard Uncle Jerome called *that* before.

As it happened, Uncle Jerome wasn't around to complain. He'd left them a note to say he'd gone up to London to sort a few things out. *'I've left some money in the breadbin in case I don't get back for a day or two,*' Ben read, from the note on the kitchen table. '*Spend it on school clothes for Frederick and Pauline, and do be sure to brief them as thoroughly as you can about what they should expect. I've already delivered a letter to your head teacher, to expect them next week. I used your hippy commune cover story, so you'd all better work on that too. I've called them Robertson, not Emerson—just in case there's anyone old enough on the school staff to remember. Hopefully I shall have some convincing papers and documents with me when I come back, so there won't be any questions asked. Tell them not to worry—I won't be giving anything away to anyone—but I might be able to sniff out a bit more detail about Professor Emerson. Will try out the thirty year rule. Thought I might try to look up Freddy and Pauline's "Uncle Dick" character too.*

See you all soon,
Uncle Jerome (JJ)'

Freddy read the note and nodded. 'I just hope he's careful,' he muttered.

'But, Freddy, whoever came from the government and "cleaned up"—if what old Percy says is true— well, they're probably long gone by now, aren't they?' said Ben. 'Nobody's going to be remembering you and Polly and your father now. It's long, long ago. I mean, even me and Rachel had half forgotten it—and we've *lived* in your old house for five years!'

Rachel was putting her bike back into the shed when Freddy came out to put his in too. She didn't know what to say to him. She was desperately worried about what she'd seen in the park. Freddy glanced over at her as he wheeled his old black machine up against Ben's. Then he looked again, harder. 'What's up, Rachel?'

She gulped and smiled and said, 'Nothing.' But as she went to walk away he stood in front of her, folded his arms, and put his head on one side, regarding her with his dark blue eyes narrowed.

'What *is* it? I'm not an idiot, you know. I've seen you staring at me since we left the park.'

She fumbled with her bike lock, feeling her face get hot. She didn't want to say what she'd seen. She didn't *have* to.

'You saw the blood, didn't you?'

She looked up, startled. 'Yes. Yes, I did.'

'Game of you not to say anything.'

'Game? What's *that* supposed to mean? I am *going* to say something! You could be ill—you could be . . .'

'Dying. Yes. I know. But you're not going to say anything.' His eyes were steely now and he was pressing his lips together.

179

'But—but what if it *is* . . . you know, like the rats and things?'

'Look—I'm fine. A little nosebleed after fifty-three years in suspension, well, it's not a bit surprising really, is it? You'd have to expect a few que—peculiar—things to happen! I'm *not* going to spend days on end in some sanatorium, having tests done. I'm *not,* I tell you. If you're my friend, you won't tell anyone!'

'But what if it gets worse?'

He looked down at his hands and then back up at her. 'If it gets worse . . . well, then everyone will know about it anyway, won't they? But Polly hasn't noticed yet—and I don't want her getting scared. Nor has Ben. Will you keep this secret? Will you?'

Rachel sighed. She did not like this *at all.* 'All right,' she muttered.

'Swear!'

'I swear!'

'Hands where I can see them—and swear again!'

That afternoon Ben and Rachel began to teach Polly and Freddy about modern life. They laid out newspapers and magazines they'd bought earlier in town and put the radio on again. It was fascinating and exhausting—there was so much to get through and Freddy and Polly were excited and amazed one minute, shocked and appalled the next.

As they flipped over the pages of the *Daily Mail* and *Now* and *Top Gear* magazines (publications they would never have dreamed of bringing home before) Rachel covertly watched Freddy and Bessie for any more signs of bleeding. There were no signs.

'So—an i-Pod . . . what's that?' Ben was testing them now.

'A robot?' said Polly (she was clearly a bit fixated on robots, thought Rachel).

'Noooo—it's the little box that holds recordings of tunes. Really small. About the size of a matchbox sometimes,' said Ben. He smiled patiently. 'It's like a tiny, tiny jukebox!'

'How many tunes can you fit in?' asked Polly.

'Oh, I dunno—hundreds—thousands sometimes.'

'In one little box? That's ridiculous!'

'But true.'

'But I thought you said all music was on discs now?' said Freddy.

'Well—yes—CDs too. But you can download tunes, too, from the internet.'

'Right-oh!' said Freddy, his eyes beginning to glaze over.

Rachel sighed. 'Look, I think we should work on their cover story. If we make that really good then everyone will understand why they don't know anything.'

'Yes, good idea,' said Ben. 'The hippy commune . . . '

'What is a *hippy*?' asked Polly, and Ben and Rachel both groaned. Of course, nobody was called a hippy until the 1960s.

'Oh, this is going to take *for ever*!' wailed Rachel. 'Can't we just make them both mutes or something? Then they wouldn't have to talk to anyone about anything.'

'Well, thanks a lot! I'd like to see how *you'd* like it, being shoved into another century,' huffed Freddy.

'Let's have a break now,' said Ben. 'I'm done in. Can we get some Pot Noodle on or something, Rachel? Oh, I *wish* the telly wasn't broken . . . '

They ate Pot Noodle, listening to Radio 2 again. Polly and Freddy seemed at first disgusted with the food and then madly into it. Rachel felt guilty all over again. First Burger King, now Pot Noodle. It really didn't say much for today's cuisine. She got apples from the fridge for afters, hoping to make up for it a bit. 'Um . . . ' she began, unsure how to say it in front of Ben, 'if you like, we can order in some ingredients and stuff and . . . um . . . maybe . . . you can teach me how to make a crock pot?'

'Hot pot,' laughed Polly. 'Yes—I'd be happy to.'

'But you'd have to teach Ben too.'

'Would I? Really?'

'Yesss,' hissed Rachel, glaring at Ben who was shaking his head wildly. 'If I'm going to learn to cook I should jolly well think you can too. Oh, what? Listen to me! I sound just like Polly! Help!'

'Get over it,' said Polly and they all exploded into laughter, spraying Pot Noodle across the table.

Chambers looked up from his papers, irritably clicking his ballpoint pen in and out, as a junior civil servant burst into his office without knocking.

'Yes, Travis?'

The clerk looked slightly pink—he'd obviously run up from two floors below. The Whitehall lifts were being serviced this week. 'Sir . . . I . . . um . . . remember you said to check on any movement in the old Emerson files?'

Chambers narrowed his eyes. 'Yes—yes, I remember. Something happening?'

'The Emerson records have been accessed, sir. Three times this week.'

Chambers put down his pen and sat up. 'Three times?'

'Yes, sir—somebody's poking around. Not old Granville's department this time. Someone else. What if they find something out, sir?'

Chambers smiled. 'If they find something out I shall be delighted. As long as we're the first to know. Better call Chapman. She's been bored out of her mind in that little backwater for the last nine months. We were just about to grant her a transfer. Maybe our esteemed scientist lives! Maybe he's bored with Russia too, and following his old friend Tarrant back home at last.'

Chambers would be glad to see the old man come home, even if he turned out to have been a traitor all along, and Dick Tarrant's confession had been a set up. He hated unsolved cases and nobody ever had found the children. And the children were the only reason he was interested. There was very wild talk of what *could* have happened to them. Few believed it, but Chambers was a man who could believe a lot.

'Sir, one more thing you should know. One of the access points for the Emerson files . . . well, it was inside this building. About half an hour ago.'

'What?' Chambers shot up out of his chair. 'Have you found out who it is?'

'Not yet, sir—but we know where they are. They're still on line. Three floors down.'

Chambers shook his head in amazement and grabbed his jacket. 'Shall we go?'

Chapter 15

'What *is* this stuff? Where are the laces?' Freddy was holding up a black school shoe and yanking the Velcro strap off it in fascination. 'Oh, bother! I've ripped it!' Freddy looked guiltily around The Foot Factory, which was busy with last-minute school shoe buyers on the last Saturday before the new term. The shop didn't have much in the way of lace ups. Ben showed Freddy how Velcro worked and he raised his eyebrows and seemed quite impressed. The school clothes had been easier—grey trousers and white polo shirts for the boys, with grey V-neck jumpers. Grey skirts or trousers for the girls with white blouses and grey jumpers; all available in the small clothing store on the Amhill High Street. Ben and Rachel needed new stuff as well, so they were all now lugging carrier bags full of school clothes.

There had been next to no goshing from Freddy

and Polly that morning—only a mild surprise that Polly could wear trousers, and that none of them had to wear ties.

'Jolly good thing too,' remarked Freddy. 'I hate ties.'

Ben paid for the shoes—his own as well as Freddy's—with the last of the money. He hoped Uncle Jerome had thought to place another food shopping order before he went off to London. There wasn't much left at home now and they'd heard nothing at all from him since he'd gone away the day before. He didn't carry a mobile phone and they had no idea where in London he'd gone.

Freddy and Polly continued to get better at not staring and gasping as they walked along the high street. Their eyes widened at times and they would blink and look at each other occasionally—like when three boys about their own age went by on roller blades. Freddy stared over his shoulder at them and gave a low whistle. 'Now *those* I would like to try!'

'Well, don't ask to borrow off *them*,' muttered Ben. The three boys had been Roly O'Neal and the Pincer twins. Roly O'Neal looked as if he'd grown a foot during the summer holidays—in height *and* width.

The weekend passed quickly with school preparations and more study of the twenty-first century, and on Sunday night Rachel got out the ironing board and got started on pressing their new uniforms. She did her own and Polly's things, while Polly busied herself with an evening meal. They had stopped at the butcher's the day before (for the first time, possibly, in Rachel's life) and got pork chops and beef mince and some stock cubes and then onions, tomatoes, carrots, and potatoes from the greengrocer's, along with strawberries and plums. Last night they'd had pork chops in gravy with carrots and mash and Polly was now making minced beef hot pot. It smelt wonderful. After a few minutes of ironing and feeling strangely relaxed and happy as her odd new friend made dinner, Rachel suddenly slammed the iron down on the board.

'OK—this has to stop now! It's gone far enough!'

'What?' Polly wiped her hands on a mystery blue and white striped apron that she had found somewhere.

'I was just about to start ironing *Ben's* shirt. *Ben! Ben!* Get in here and iron your polo shirt! Quickly! I've got a scary case of the Pollies going on here.'

Ben arrived at the kitchen door, hooting with laughter, but he took over at the ironing board, much to Freddy's amusement. 'Don't laugh—you're next,' warned Rachel.

Freddy *did* have a go at ironing, but was so useless

at it that Ben took over and did it properly. Rachel felt proud of her big brother. She knew a lot of boys his age would never even think about ironing. But they had both had to learn because their mum and dad were away so much, and Uncle Jerome wouldn't notice a creased jumper unless it bit him. Freddy had got a few more supplies out of the vault. Most of the clothes were only good for wearing at home—they'd get him laughed at, at school. But he had a good backpack-type bag which he could use. Ben and Rachel shared out their many notebooks and pens and pencils. The rest, they guessed, the school would give to Freddy and Polly.

The hot pot was wonderful. It beat frozen convenience food any day of the week, thought Ben. 'I could get to like this!' he mumbled, through a mouthful of gravy, mince, and potato. Polly looked delighted.

'Good,' said Rachel, 'because Polly's going to teach us all how to make it.' Freddy spluttered and laughed and Rachel gave him a very old-fashioned look for a modern girl and he coughed and looked down at his plate.

'You must have missed the bit about Women's Lib,' said Rachel. 'We'll have to go over that again soon! But for now just remember this—*girls* are not here to serve *boys*!'

After dinner they shared the washing up duties, although Freddy looked aghast when Rachel handed him a drying up cloth. Not long after, with Bessie fed and watered and put into her basket in the hallway, they went to bed. It was early, but they were tired out. Teaching modern history to Polly and Freddy was a full time occupation now for Ben and Rachel. And learning it was clearly pretty exhausting too. Their great-aunt and uncle looked done in.

Rachel and Polly fell asleep fast, even though they were excited and nervous about school the next day. But at around midnight Rachel woke up and noticed a light under the door. She got up, crept carefully past Polly's sleeping form, opened the door and peered across the landing. Freddy was in the bathroom, the door ajar. He was staring into the mirror above the sink, holding a tissue to his nose. Seeing Rachel, he screwed it up and threw it into the toilet, immediately flushing it away. He walked past her, back to bed, with a tight smile.

'You swore,' he said. 'Don't forget.'

MOSCOW, AUGUST 2009

'The question is, should I care about a promise made fifty-two years ago by Nikita Khrushchev?' said the Russian president. From the wall of his vast marble office, Khrushchev, leader of the Soviet Union in 1957, stared down at them all, along with Bulganin, Brezhnev, and Gorbachev. Ivan and Gregor said nothing. They were still in shock from what they had found in the bunker.

'Do we have all his work? All his notes?'

Gregor nodded.

'So then, perhaps we can work on without the man himself. But this . . . ' The president flipped his computer monitor around and looked at the grainy faces on its screen. Four children, clustered round a desk, somewhere in England. 'This makes it all so much harder to decide. I think we need to negotiate a new deal. I want to meet these children first.'

Gregor nodded to Ivan. 'Tell Tara to go ahead,' he said. 'With care . . . but quickly. We don't want to alert the British for as long as possible . . . in case they don't know already.'

'Do you think the British government has any idea?' asked the president.

'Tara says she can't be sure,' said Gregor. 'There has been . . . activity . . . in the town. A retired policeman has been looking up his old notes on the case. Jerome Emerson—who is the uncle of the fair-haired children— was seen in London, but our man lost him on the Tube. He may be back home by now. It's worrying. The British have been jumpy and curious ever since Tarrant crawled back to them last year. If we'd got that letter on time we would have known to stop him. We're sending three operatives to assist Tara. She'll make her move before the British work anything out.'

'Good. Good. Tell your agent, good work.' The president stood up and smiled. 'I will make time for a children's tea party for, shall we say, Wednesday?'

Chapter 16

'Polly is new—so I'd like you all to give her a warm Amhill Secondary welcome,' beamed Miss Janaway. The class murmured indistinct greetings and someone made a quiet farting noise, but Miss Janaway, sitting back down with a discreet smooth of her tartan skirt, did not notice. She was close to retirement age and very good at not hearing things after so many years' practice.

'Polly, perhaps you'd like to come up and tell the rest of the class a little bit about yourself,' said Miss Janaway.

Rachel groaned and she let her forehead flop into her palms as Polly skipped happily to the front of the class. Rachel raised her eyes fearfully as her great-aunt turned and smiled at everyone and began to speak in a voice like the queen (despite the many hours Rachel had spent trying to beat this habit out of her).

'Hello, everyone! My name is Pauline . . . er . . . Robertson, but everybody calls me Polly. I'm jolly pleased to meet you all. I know it's going to be frightfully difficult to catch up with you all, as I've not been to a school quite like this before, but I mean to try. I hope you'll all be kind and not think I'm a total clot when I get into scrapes with algebra. Algebra's probably my worst subject! I'm always getting into scrapes with algebra.'

There was a stunned silence.

Miss Janaway coughed. 'Um . . . perhaps you could tell us a bit about your last school, Polly?' she prompted.

'Oh—oh yes.' Polly went slightly pink. Rachel knew it was because she was about to make up a 'fib' about her last school. Polly was a hopeless liar. 'Well, you'd probably think it was a bit qu—peculiar, really. Not a bit like this. I grew up on a hip—hippy commune, I think you might call it. We all lived in a sort of camp in the woods and everyone sort of helped everyone else and we got taught by the grown-ups, in the big . . . um . . . well . . . we called it a wigwam.'

Everyone sat in yet more stunned silence, although Rachel very nearly moaned aloud. They had rehearsed and rehearsed this! And now Polly was making bits up. They'd *never* mentioned a *wigwam*!

'Everyone ate together and we all slept in hammocks and cooked over open fires.' Polly was getting into her stride now. 'We grew our own food and caught rabbits to eat. I can skin a rabbit like anything!'

There were gasps and the vegetarian girls clutched their friendship bracelets and whimpered.

'But, as you can probably guess, I don't know an awful lot about the twenty-first century . . . I mean, that is, I haven't had much to do with television and CD-Rons and DBDs and such like.' A titter ran around the class. Rachel tried to work out whether it was a mean titter or a friendly titter. Too early to tell. 'I've come here—with my brother Freddy—because Father thinks we need to get into a proper school now, so we can take proper CGSE exams. We're living with Rachel and Ben, because they're sort of related to us.' Rachel flinched, as several of her classmates turned to stare at her, and then felt guilty. She was going to have to look after Polly and it was no good pretending it wasn't going to be embarrassing.

'And they're both absolutely super!' concluded Polly, and the class collapsed into hysterical laughter. Polly beamed around at them all, her face awash with confusion, worry, and hope. Rachel reckoned her face could stop working so hard. It needn't bother with hope.

'First you get the skin off—you've got to use the right kind of blade or flint, or it'll just be a mess and you don't want to be eating clumps of fur,' instructed Freddy. The boys in 9C leaned forward in their seats. 'So you run the blade between the fur pelt and the sinews underneath and if you do it right you don't even spill any blood! Then, when the fur's out of the way you have to get its guts out. And let me tell you—that can be jolly messy if you don't know what you're doing.'

'Do you cut its 'ead off?' said one of the Pincer twins, much to Ben's alarm.

'Well, yes, of course!' said Freddy. 'You wouldn't want to eat baked eyeballs, would you?'

'Right—well . . . that's . . . that's been very interesting, Freddy,' said Mrs Ryan, looking slightly green. 'Not exactly what I had in mind by way of introduction, but—very interesting. Although please be aware, killing, cooking, and eating of rabbits or other animals during school time is strictly forbidden.'

'Of course, miss.' Freddy smiled at her. 'I absolutely wouldn't dream of it.'

'Please go and sit back down now,' said Mrs

Ryan. Freddy returned to his seat amid much whispering and narrowing of eyes. The boys of 9C had not made up their minds yet. Some of the girls had, though. One or two vegetarians were maintaining disgusted looks, but the majority of the girls were smirking at each other and widening their eyes and playing with their hair. Ben bit his lip. Freddy already had a few admirers. What would they think if they knew he was sixty-six?

Freddy's stories of life in the hippy commune had been quite exciting, Ben had to admit, even if he knew they had completely made them up the night before. Some bits were true, though. Freddy actually *had* caught and skinned a rabbit, as part of his boarding school's survival training. Some soldiers had come and taken his entire year out on Salisbury Plain for a weekend, to teach them basic survival skills. They'd set up snares and traps.

Mrs Ryan was handing out timetables and homework diaries, to prepare them for the term ahead, and soon everyone was filling in their details. Freddy had been seated next to Ben, and Ben glanced across to be sure his great-uncle was OK. Freddy seemed fine. So far, because of his gory stories of gutting rabbits, the other boys hadn't started going for him over the posh accent. Ben had tried to get him to drop a few aitches but as soon as he'd got into his rabbit story, he'd forgotten and was sounding like a visiting duke again in moments. For now though, he *looked* like every other kid in the class, his head bent over the homework diary, filling in details. Then again . . . Ben leaned over and jabbed his finger at the Date of Birth line. Freddy blinked and then nodded. He scribbled out 7 April 1943 and, after a little calculation, wrote 7 April 1995. He put the pen down gravely and Ben guessed he was, for a moment, lost in the weirdness of it all.

Ben gave him a sympathetic grin. Freddy nodded and smiled back. With his mussed up hair and ordinary school clothes, he really didn't stand out *that* much, thought Ben. They'd not done badly.

The door opened and the head teacher, Mr Gerard, came in. Freddy shot up from his seat and stood to attention. 'Good morning, sir,' he said. The head teacher stopped and looked around at this new pupil, his eyebrows raised. The rest of the class had, as usual, remained slumped over desks, continuing with whatever they were doing. Now though, they fell silent and sat up, staring from Freddy to Mr Gerard.

'Well . . . er . . . good morning, er . . . '

'Frederick Robertson, sir,' said Freddy, although he was beginning to look a little uneasy now.

'Good morning, Frederick. You must be new . . .

we . . . er . . . well, we don't stand on ceremony when I come into the room.' Mr Gerard fiddled with his tie and smiled.

'We don't, sir? Oh—I see. Sorry, sir. We did at my old school, sir, when a master came in.' There were sniggers now, rising and falling like a malevolent sea around the new boy.

'Well, it's very nice to be wished good morning, nonetheless. You may sit down now.'

Freddy nodded and sat. Ben looked uneasily around as the head teacher had a word with Mrs Ryan. The Pincer twins were making twisty shapes with their mean fists and Rory O'Neal was whispering, 'Good morning, sir—oh, good morning, sir! Jolly good show, sir! Really rather super to meet you, sir!' not very quietly. The girls were giggling openly.

'Just keep your head down and *try* not to say anything,' muttered Rachel, as she and Polly queued up for lunch. But Polly was staring, appalled, at what Rachel had just given her.

'You mean we *eat* off our *trays*? With no plate?' Her high voice, filled with disdain, rang out across the dining hall.

'The tray *is* the plate, you dummy!' hissed Rachel.

199

'*Please*—keep your voice down!' She led Polly along and thankfully the girl said no more other than, 'Yes please,' or 'No thank you,' as the dinner ladies dolloped mashed potato, carrots, and beef casserole into the correct sections on her tray-plate. A cellophane wrapped mini Swiss roll occupied the dessert dent and then Rachel plonked a knife and fork into the cutlery dent and a cup of apple juice into the cup bit. 'See,' she said. 'It works perfectly well. And it saves on washing up.' Polly nodded doubtfully as she sat down beside her great-niece.

Rachel had deliberately made for the table tucked into the corner furthest away from the dinner queue, and chosen seats which meant their backs were to everyone. She desperately hoped they wouldn't get noticed. Kids in her class had been whispering 'Absolutely *super*!' at her all morning. They were having a whale of a time; even Joanne and Carrie, who were normally her friends, were singing it out by break time. Poor Polly couldn't understand what was wrong with calling someone absolutely super.

'It's just—old-fashioned!' sighed Rachel, scooping up mash with her fork. 'I'm sorry, Polly—it was a really nice thing to say, but they'll be taking the—making jokes about it—forever now. That's what kids are like. You must know that.'

'I do know that. It's just that, in my school, they would have laughed at you for wearing a torn blouse or having something stuck in your hair. Here . . . ' she looked around and blinked mournfully, 'it seems you *ought* to have a torn blouse or something stuck in your hair. It's all topsy-turvy.'

'It's more to do with the way you *talk*,' said Rachel. 'You're just too—posh. I'm sorry, but they'll think you're stuck up. I know you're *not*,' she added, hurriedly, as Polly's face fell. 'I know you're great—brilliant—and really brave! But they don't understand that. They *can't*.'

'So I just have to change myself to make them happy,' said Polly, spearing a carrot with feeling.

'If you want to fit in,' said Rachel. It was a pathetic thing to say. It wasn't right. But it was true.

'Come on, then, let's get this over with!' Freddy raised his fists and danced from one foot to the other. He looked like the lion out of *The Wizard of Oz*.

The Pincer twins grinned at each other.

'L-look—j-just leave him alone!' said Ben, glancing anxiously around the playground and wishing a teacher would show up and save Freddy from the bashing that was lining up for him. He would be standing shoulder to shoulder with him, of course, but Roly O'Neal was sitting on his chest.

'L-l-l-leave him alone—p-p-pleeeeease!' mimicked Roly and leant his elbow on Ben's ear. Ben struggled and tried to hit out at him, but Roly was *huge* and he just couldn't get his arms free.

'Get your fat backside off him, you lout!' shouted Freddy. Roly shouted with laughter and the Pincer twins went in. Even from his squashed viewpoint on the gritty tarmac, Ben would never forget what he saw next. Freddy, still dancing about like a boxer, waited until the twins were nearly upon him, and then jumped up, grabbed their heads and bashed their skulls together with a clunk. They were poleaxed. They fell over with high-pitched screams. Freddy shouted 'Score!' and danced across to Roly. Roly headbutted him in the stomach.

The first sign of serious trouble in the dining room was the way the juice in Rachel's cup suddenly juddered—sending out little circular ripples—like that scene in *Jurassic Park* when the T-Rex is coming, thought Rachel. The T-Rex *was* coming. The T-Rex more commonly known, at Amhill Secondary, as Lorraine Kingsley. Lorraine plonked her considerable weight onto the chair opposite and slammed her tray down on the table. Her carrots hung briefly in the air before returning to their dimple in the red plastic tray with a plop. Lorraine didn't say anything, but she looked at Polly. She dug her knife into her mash and hooked it up into her mouth, where she spread it across her grey-tinged tongue, and all the while she looked at Polly.

She got through all her mash this way, and then went on to the carrots. She was nothing if not methodical. And still she stared at Polly. Once, Polly opened her mouth to speak, but Rachel elbowed her in the side and shook her head vigorously. So Polly continued to pick through her lunch with the occasional glance up to see if the girl opposite was still staring. She was. At length, when she had spread all her chicken casserole into her mouth and swallowed it (there was no sign of a fork in the cutlery dent) Lorraine Kingsley poked a sausage-like digit at Polly.

'Say "absolutely super",' she instructed, in a voice as thick as her finger.

'I—I beg your pardon?' said Polly.

'You 'eard. Say it. Say "absolutely super". Everyone's going on about it and I missed it and I don't like missing things.'

'Absolutely super,' muttered Polly.

'You takin' the—'

'Polly just said it!' cried Rachel in alarm. 'She just said it—like you asked her to!'

Lorraine Kingsley screwed her block-like face into a suspicious sneer. 'She didn't say it proper! She said it sarcastic-like, di'n't she? She didn't say it proper.'

Rachel sighed. 'Polly—please—just say it like you said in class.'

'Absolutely super,' said Polly again—this time with more feeling.

'Again,' sniggered Lorraine.

'Absolutely super.'

Lorraine bashed the table so hard that neither Polly nor Rachel could prevent a little scream. 'Oi! You lot! Get over'ere! She's doin' it! She's doin' it again!'

A tide of faces arrived around their little table. Rachel felt her skin heat up. This could be nasty.

'Do it again!' ordered Lorraine, poking her blunt, gravy spattered knife towards Polly.

Polly narrowed her eyes.

'Absolutely super,' she muttered, into the remains of her half-eaten meal.

'Again!' chanted Lorraine and a few of the others echoed her.

'Absolutely super.'

'AGAIN!' chanted everyone.

'Absolutely super.'

'Louder!' bawled Lorraine, her small eyes shining.

Polly stood up and took a deep breath as if she meant to project across the whole room this time. Then she picked up her food tray and upended it on Lorraine's head. 'Well, *that's* absolutely super, at any rate,' she said, with a smart rap to get all the gravy and beef out.

Chapter 17

'*Whizzer* first day!' said Freddy while the school nurse checked over his ribs one more time. His torso was red and purple. 'You all right there, old girl?'

From behind a wodge of bloodied tissues Rachel gave a cheerful thumbs up. They all very much hoped her nose would stop bleeding by home time. Polly tried to smile sympathetically, but her split lip was very sore. 'I know just what to use to get the blood out of your blouse,' she said, carefully. 'Cold water and a little salt rubbed in.'

Ben sat on a plastic seat in the corner of the school's medical room and watched his hand swell up a little more. The knuckles were violet and green already. He grinned. He wasn't a violent boy by nature, but he still felt a grim satisfaction every time he thought about the way his fist had connected with Roly O'Neal's chin. Just the once, of course, but even so . . . He hoped Roly's chin looked worse than his hand.

Mr Gerard came in and Freddy stood up again, but managed not to say 'Good afternoon, sir.' Mr Gerard looked thunderous.

'Well, this is a fine start to the year, I must say,' he glowered. 'And fine thanks for allowing you two in without getting in the full paperwork yet! If your uncle wasn't a good friend of mine, you can be sure you'd both be out on your ear again by now—all of you, in fact. I've never *seen* such a scrum! Two major fights in one lunch hour and *both* of them involving a Robertson! If this is what living in a hippy commune teaches you, then there's not much hope for any of us!'

'But it wasn't their fault!' protested Rachel, although nobody could really hear her very clearly through the tissues. 'They were being picked on.'

'Your cousin has just concussed two boys!'

'Yes, b-but, sir,' said Ben, from his corner. The head teacher spun round and glared at him. 'Th-think about it. It was Roly O'Neal and the P-Pincer twins . . . and Lorraine Kingsley . . . I m-mean, hon-estly . . . what do you *think* happened?' Ben felt a rush of nerves and excitement. He had never spoken to a teacher like this before, but he was quite convinced now that he was right to.

Mr Gerard opened his mouth to retort angrily and then closed it. He pondered for a moment. Then, to Ben's enormous surprise, he said, 'Well, you have a point, Benedict. Perhaps I will just send a letter home to your uncle this time. But I want you *all* to know that I don't tolerate stand up fights at Amhill Secondary. I advise you all to keep a low profile for a while!'

Ben hauled Freddy out of school as quickly as possible at the end of the day, and found Rachel shoving Polly along equally fast as he reached the gate. They were both looking fearfully around them. They knew the Pincer twins, Roly O'Neal, and Lorraine Kingsley well enough to expect a second round at any time. Although, thought Rachel, it had been absolutely glorious looking at Lorraine's astonished, casserole spattered face, and hearing the laughter growing among the crowd. Nobody liked Lorraine, after all, and it was much more fun to see her get a face full of someone's lunch than to watch the new girl being bullied. In the afternoon classes a couple of other girls had grinned at Polly and three boys at the back made 'salaaming' gestures to her as she went to her desk, next to Rachel. Lorraine wasn't in any of their classes, so they were safe until home time.

'Oh, do give over, Ben!' Freddy protested as his

great-nephew propelled him along to the bike sheds at great speed. 'Emersons don't run away!'

'No, I'm sure they don't. They don't run away. They don't give up. They don't have bodyguards, either—and that's our biggest problem right now.'

Ben looked back over his shoulder, but saw no sign of their enemies yet. They grabbed their bikes fast, just as a shout could be heard behind them. It was Lorraine Kingsley. There were brown spatters down her white blouse and her hair was wet from where she'd had to wash it in the girls' toilets. She was moving now, gathering pace, head down, like an angry bull. Rachel's fingers slipped on the combination lock on their bikes.

'I think you might want to look sharp, Rachel,' suggested Polly.

'You do? Really?' Rachel snapped the lock apart and hauled the chain out from between their wheels just as Roly O'Neal joined Lorraine on the path heading down to the bike sheds.

'Time to go, I think,' said Freddy, grabbing his handlebars. They all leaped onto their saddles, bags on their backs, and pedalled away at top speed, narrowly missing a dinner lady with a tray of bread.

'I'll getchooo! You wait! I'll getchoooo!' bawled Lorraine. Rachel glanced back and saw her punch

Roly O'Neal in the stomach. For no apparent reason. Roly was yanking Lorraine's damp hair in reprisal as she looked back again. Then they were round the bend in the road and cycling as fast as they were able, Polly and Freddy tearing along ahead of them. Rachel's heart clattered wildly in her chest but she gave a shout of excitement as they made their getaway. Of course, it would feel a lot different when they went back into school tomorrow, but for now—they had won!

Uncle Jerome still wasn't back when they got home, but a message was blinking on the answerphone and Ben pressed the button while Rachel and Polly made a big fuss of Bessie, who had been left alone in the hallway again for the day—and had managed to poo exactly where she was supposed to, on the newspaper under the stairs. Ben and Freddy held their noses as they listened to the message. It wasn't from Uncle Jerome.

'Hello, my lovelies!' sang out a woman's voice. 'It's me—Mum. I'm sorry—it's been days and days since we've been able to get a decent signal out here. Honestly, with all the ship to shore technology and satellite phones, you'd think it would be easy! Anyway, are you back at school today? I think it's today you go back—I do hope it's gone well and you haven't had any trouble.' Ben and Freddy snorted. Freddy had got down on his haunches and was peering into the answering machine, wrinkling his brow and trying, Ben guessed, to see a tape reel or something. 'Anyway, the season's gone really well and we've only got a few more days and we'll be flying back to you! Oh, I am so looking forward to seeing my little family again.'

They looked at each other, edgily. Mum was going to find out that her little family had grown a bit, thought Rachel. How on earth would she take it?

'We're already booked up for next year, and for a short spell at Christmas,' went on their mother, 'although we've said we won't go until *after* Christmas Day, you'll be glad to hear. Everyone especially loved the new fire act this time—although Daddy did lose his eyebrows the first time around . . . he's had to put them on with a felt tip pen ever since. Anyway, we hope you're having a great time and not getting into mischief. See you both soon!' There was a click and the message was finished.

'What—what do you think your mother and father will want to do . . . about us?' asked Polly, playing anxiously with Bessie's ears.

'You don't think they might call the police, or something, do you?' asked Freddy.

Ben and Rachel exchanged glances. They had absolutely no idea what their parents might do. Mum

211

and Dad were not normal parents . . . but maybe that was a good thing. They would not be returning to a normal family.

'No more messages?' Rachel asked, to change the subject. No. There was nothing else. 'I'm getting a bit worried about Uncle J,' she said. 'He's never left us alone for this long before. Where do you reckon he's got to?' There was a long silence. 'I mean . . . I don't want to worry anyone, but soon we're going to be out of food . . . ' said Rachel. 'We spent the last of our money today, on school dinners for the week.'

'Oh don't worry,' said Polly. 'We've got heaps and heaps of food down in the vault!'

Ben and Rachel winced. 'Yeah,' said Ben, 'but it's fifty-three years old!'

'Well, so are we!' said Polly. 'And we're all right!'

'Yes, but all the food hasn't been in a cryonic chamber *with* us, has it?' pointed out Freddy. 'Although I vote we go and have a rummage through the tins. They're meant to last for an age, aren't they?'

Rachel sighed. Half-a-century-old Spam really did not appeal to her. She went to the kitchen and poked around in the permafrost at the back of the freezer. It gave up five fish fingers and seven individual peas. They were completely out of bread and biscuits and there were only three apples left in the fridge. The tins they had in the larder all seemed to be chilli beans or rhubarb. Even Polly couldn't make a tasty supper out of *that*.

'We really do need money,' she said, as the others came in and Polly filled the kettle. 'It would be just like Uncle J to get caught up in something and forget to come back for a week!'

Ben sat down, straight-faced, at the cleanly scrubbed kitchen table, where Bessie immediately gnawed on his shoelaces. 'No,' he said. 'I've never seen him so excited as he was down in the vault. He couldn't bear to stay away from it for long. S-something . . . I th-think something is wrong.'

As soon as the words were out everyone was nodding gravely. They had all felt it but Ben was the first to say it. Where *was* Uncle Jerome? Rachel shivered. 'How can we find out?' she asked. 'We just don't know where he went. Or if anyone else at all *knows*. And if we go to the police or something, and report him missing . . . well, they'll be straight over here and with Mum and Dad away . . . well, we'll all get taken into care or something. And then what about Freddy and Polly? They'll want to know about them too . . . '

'He'll come back,' said Ben, wishing he felt half as certain as he sounded. 'And in the meantime we'll just have to think of a way of getting hold of some money. Is there anything we can sell?'

Rachel thought hard. 'Our bikes?'

'No, we need those. What else? Computer games? Books? CDs?'

'I know,' said Freddy. 'Antiques.' They stared at him. 'Well, don't look at me like I'm an idiot! What did JJ say? Our vault is a time capsule! There must be loads of old things in it that the antiques shop in town would buy. What about *our* records and our Dansette and stuff? I bet those would fetch a jolly good sum. And they're all in tip-top condition . . . as if they'd only just been bought.' He smiled, wryly, at Polly.

'Good idea,' she said. 'Let's go and see what we've got.'

Back down in the vault they switched all the lights and power back on as they pushed the inner door, and went to sit down on the chairs and sofa while Freddy slid a box of records out and a large navy-blue case-type thing from inside a sideboard. Dansette was written on it, in silver lettering. Freddy lifted the lid of the case to reveal an old-fashioned record player, with a big rubber turntable and a chunky arm which swung across it, a stubby needle poking out beneath, ready to run along the grooves of an old vinyl record. Ben and Rachel watched in awed silence as Polly flicked through the large square albums and slid them across the carpet, one by one. *Alma Cogan, The Four Aces, Dickie Valentine, Mantovani, Pat Boone, Guy Mitchell, The Crew Cuts, The Stargazers* . . . Polly chuckled and picked up one sleeve. She plucked out a wide black vinyl disc and carefully put it into the record player. She rested the needle into the groove and all at once the room was filled with the foot-tapping rhythm of Bill Haley & the Comets' 'Rock Around The Clock'.

'Oh, I love this!' said Rachel, and got to her feet.

'Do you? Do you know this? Truly?' beamed Polly, taking her hands.

'*Everyone* knows this!' said Rachel. They began to dance, twirling each other around and giggling and singing along. Polly grabbed Freddy and pulled him up too and then got Ben up as well. Soon everyone was singing, dancing, and throwing their arms about. As the record ended they collapsed back onto the carpet, laughing.

'Another one—another!' cried Polly and whipped off the first record to replace it with another from the Stargazers' sleeve. 'Close the doors. They're coming in the windows!' Polly sang along with huge enjoyment. 'Close the doors—they're coming down the stairs! Close the doors, they're coming in the windows . . . those ne-ne-ne-ne-ne-nehs are everywhere!'

'*This* was in the charts?' yelled Ben, looking both amused and horrified.

'Don't go there, Ben—*we* bought the "Crazy Frog", remember,' Rachel reminded him.

They sorted out a pile of thirty records, all beautifully kept in cardboard or paper sleeves. Most of them, it turned out, were Freddy's. 'Father liked some of it—his was the Mantovani and Jimmy Young and Humphrey Lyttelton,' said Freddy.

'*I* bought "Cherry Pink and Apple Blossom White",' said Polly, proudly.

'Are you sure we should sell them?' asked Rachel. It did seem a shame. She would hate to have to sell some of her CDs. Not that she had many and not that they were worth much.

'Yes, certainly we should,' said Freddy. 'It's a matter of survival. Anyway, you can always get them back for us on eBay one day, can't you?'

Ben and Rachel gaped. 'You *have* been paying attention!' said Ben.

Ben and Freddy decided they would walk back into town with the records. The antiques and collectibles shop was right on the edge of the town and not too far—and the records were way too heavy and fragile to carry on their backs while cycling, although Freddy was carrying something in his back-pack too—something he said he wanted to show Ben when they got to the park. They would both take a box with fifteen records each. Rachel and Polly would stay at home to feed Bessie and take her out in the garden for an hour. As they left the house Ben could hear Polly teaching Rachel that daft Stargazers song. 'Those ne-ne-ne-ne-ne-nehs are *every-where*!' he heard them both sing, collapsing into giggles, while Bessie barked excitedly. He felt bad that the record was in his box—but Polly, like Freddy, had insisted.

It was close to closing by the time they reached Past For A Present, the little shop which might want to buy the records. It was a small, dark emporium of all kinds of objects, from vases and china cups to elderly dinner suits and age-spotted mirrors. The old records, most of which *weren't* actually *that* old, were stacked across a display at the back of the shop. Ben and Freddy went to the counter where a middle-aged man with a bald head was leaning, flicking through the local paper.

'Excuse me, sir—we wondered if you might be interested in buying these seventy-eights,' said Freddy in his terribly polite voice. He rested his box on the counter and Ben did the same. The man peered inside and began to flip through the records, nodding and squinting, occasionally pulling one out and going, 'Hmm. Uhuh.'

After he'd been through Ben's too he sighed heavily and said, 'I'll give you fifteen quid for the lot.'

'Fifteen pounds! I say!' Freddy's eyes sparkled and Ben realized that, in his excitement, Freddy had forgotten about fifty-three years of inflation.

'You've got to be k-kidding!' said Ben. 'There's thirty records there—mint condition! Like they were bought last week! You trying to tell me they're worth fifty p each? D-do me a favour!'

Freddy looked shocked. 'I say, steady on,' he muttered, but the man was grinning at Ben and pointing a nicotine stained finger at him.

'I like your style, son!' he said with a wheezy laugh. 'All right—thirty!'

Freddy stared at Ben, excited all over again. Ben just sighed. 'Come on, we're wasting our time here.' He gathered up his box.

'Hold on, hold on—not so fast!' said the man. 'What do *you* think they're worth?'

'Well,' said Ben, 'considering you sell records of this age and in much worse condition for no less than a tenner, I would say they're worth about three hundred pounds—but I know you've got to make your money. So I'd settle for a hundred.'

'Get out of here! Sixty! That's my final offer.'

'Ninety!'

'Eighty—and I'm doin' you a favour!'

'Done,' said Ben.

Outside the shop Freddy stared in awe at the fan of ten pound notes in Ben's hand. 'That was whizzer! I can't believe you got him to pay up *eighty pounds*! That was most awfully impressive. Really . . . cool. I think.'

Ben grinned. 'He got a good deal. If we sold them ourselves we'd get a load more than that. But we needed the money fast, so we took a bit less. Anyway, let's get some fish and chips and get back. The girls can do the proper shopping tomorrow.'

'Don't let Rachel hear you say that,' warned Freddy. 'She's already called me a sexist three times today. I only asked her to press a shirt for me—honestly! You'd think I'd asked her to iron my entire wardrobe!'

'You *did* ask her to iron your entire wardrobe, actually,' pointed out Ben as they wandered towards the hot vinegary scent of the local chippy.

'Ah yes—well—won't be making *that* mistake again. Thank goodness Polly was decent enough to do it. Now, if a girl's all right about it and much better at it, that's not sexist, is it?'

'Yes it is,' sighed Ben.

'Well, it jolly well wasn't this time last week!' retorted Freddy. 'And I think 1956 was much better for it!'

'Hello, you two—how's your project going?'

Ben jumped and looked round. They were close to the library and right behind them was the librarian who had helped them with the old cuttings on the microfiche last week. She was standing, paused, on the steps to the old building, with some paperbacks in one arm. She smiled at them both, warmly—particularly at Freddy.

'Hello again, miss,' said Freddy. 'Yes, we're doing fine with it, thank you for asking.'

'You know, it's a funny subject to choose—the old Emerson murder mystery,' she said, brightly. 'What made you think of it? Nobody's talked about that for *years*.'

'Nobody knows it was a murder for sure,' said Freddy, heatedly. Ben elbowed him but he paid no attention.

'Well, no, I suppose not,' she said, smiling at him again. Too much, thought Ben. He felt uneasy. 'Quite an unusual topic for Amhill Secondary, though, isn't it?'

'Sorry—we have to go—we said we'd get back,' said Ben, before Freddy could say anything else. And he yanked the boy away and along the street.

'What *are* you doing? That was downright ill mannered!' protested Freddy. 'She was being friendly and helpful!'

'Yes. Wasn't she?' muttered Ben.

'What of it?'

'I don't know . . . I just . . . well, like *you* said, we need to be careful!'

'Well, we needn't be rude. Father says "manners maketh man".'

Ben gulped and grabbed Freddy's arm. 'Oh no!' Freddy glanced up quickly and saw what Ben saw: Roly O'Neal, weaving his way along the pavement in his rollerblades. A few feet behind him were the Pincer twins. A second later Roly had seen them too. This time it was Freddy yanking Ben along. He dragged him into an alleyway between two shops. 'Can you skate?' he said.

'You what?' gasped Ben.

'Can you *skate*?' Freddy was pulling his backpack off and now opening it. 'Quickly! It's important.'

'Um . . . yeah. I can skate. Not brilliantly, but I get by.' Ben had been given in-line skates last Christmas and had gone everywhere on them for a couple of

221

weeks before he got a bit bored. Now Freddy was handing him something with wheels on.

'Hurry—get them on. We don't have much time.'

Ben realized he was holding a very old-fashioned pair of skates—quad skates, with four little hard wheels attached to a kind of metal sole, with leather straps and metal buckles at the ankle and toe ends. He copied Freddy, still bewildered, and strapped them on tight to his shoes. Freddy had thrown his empty bag back on his shoulders and now looked around the corner. 'All right, you go right and I'll go left—let me go first and head them off. I'll catch up with you.'

'But—' said Ben, but Freddy was gone. 'You're heading straight for them . . . ' he added, dismally. He peered around the edge of the alleyway and saw Freddy skating like a bullet down along the wide pavement—right into the path of Roly and the Pincer twins. The boys were staring, open mouthed, as their quarry hurtled towards them. Ben saw Roly mouth 'Oh yeah!' with malicious delight as Freddy wobbled around a few feet in front of him and waved his arms about to stop falling.

'Geddim!' bawled Roly and Ben winced. Freddy was no match for Roly's skating—the boy was fast and confident. But even as he watched, preparing to see his new friend squelched into the gutter, Ben saw

Freddy give a whoop, leap up, arc around on his wheels and started hurtling back along the pavement towards him.

'Go—go, you idiot!' he bellowed, but he was grinning and now Ben could see why. Freddy was good—oh yes—Freddy was *very* good.

Ben turned and skated off fast and immediately noticed how much lighter his feet were in these skates than in rollerboots. It nearly spilled him at first, until he got used to it—but he began to realize why Freddy could outrun Roly and the twins. Glancing back he saw the boy powering along, his arms swinging with perfect momentum, hair streaked back from his temples, grinning like a loon.

'Go! Go! Go!' he laughed and Ben went. In seconds, though, Freddy had caught up with him. He seemed to be oblivious to the murderous shouts from their pursuers as he whipped along beside him. 'Better speed up a bit,' he advised. 'You can go like a rocket on these things now! Last time I used them it was flagstones and the gaps don't half mess up the axles! Good job I brought these along today, hey? Or we'd be mincemeat by now. Come on!'

Ben felt like a drunk daddy-long-legs in comparison to Freddy who was now powering away ahead. He'd never seen anything like it. But he didn't know how much longer he could outrun the others—they might be slower but they were determined and he was losing pace in spite of his light feet. He looked back over his shoulder and saw Roly mouth 'You're dead!' Being able to read his lips was *not* a good sign. What was up ahead wasn't much better when Ben whipped back around.

No! Pouring out of a gateway a few feet away came a sudden torrent of little girls in ballet outfits. Mrs Eagle's Dance School was off to a festival. Ben wailed aloud and then went 'Doof!' in a comedy fashion as he was grabbed and spun to his right, into a driveway that led to the town car park.

'This way!' said Freddy and hared along, wheels a blur, in among the cars. Only seconds later the trio in boots turned the corner and split into three wheel-based scouts, looping around the few remaining parked cars and shouting to each other like hunters. Freddy looked at Ben, wobbly on his aching ankles, crouched beside him between a car and a weed filled ditch, and grimaced. 'Sorry about this, old chum,' he said. 'You'll thank me later.' Then he shoved Ben into the ditch. Ben squeaked as he fell through the high weeds and seconds later was glaring up at Freddy through the leaves. 'Stay there—they can't see you. I'll come back for you,' said Freddy.

Ben scrambled back upright under the leaves and peered out, quite hidden, to see what Freddy was going to do next. To his amazement, the boy shot out in full view of the trio.

'Come on then!' he yelled. 'Do you want to beat me up or do you want to show me some *real* skating? Can you do this?' And he sped across the tarmac at immense speed before slaloming to the right in a tidal wave of grit and then leaping up and spinning in the air. He hit the ground, his knees bending like springs and swept into a tight circle, feet turned out, spinning faster and faster.

Roly immediately powered across towards him and also tried to slide to one side. His rubber wheels juddered against the tarmac and he nearly pitched over, his arms flailing madly. Enraged, he powered up again and jumped high into the air. He landed quite well, and managed a pretty good spin and then began to move meanly towards Freddy, bellowing colourful predictions of what Freddy was about to experience. Freddy laughed and pulled his skates smoothly in and out, in and out, toes and heels, toes and heels, *backwards* without once looking over his shoulder.

The Pincer twins—not great skaters themselves— stood off, watching the two boys in fascination. As Roly closed the gap, crouching low and ready, Ben guessed, to do his trademark headbutt on Freddy's chin, Freddy suddenly flipped around and made for the exit of the car park, just as a tow-truck passed by on the road.

'Hey, Roly!' he called back over his shoulder. 'Can you do *this*?' And he launched himself over the kerb, landed, still moving, on the road and grabbed the tow-truck's bumper, crouching low, holding his knees and wheeled feet steady and strong as the truck pulled him swiftly away. 'See you!' called back Freddy, and was gone.

In the car park the three boys stared, Roly's wheels juddering to a halt, his mouth open. 'Wow!' said one of the Pincer twins. His brother smacked him in the head.

'I'll get him,' Roly said, finally. 'You'll see. Tomorrow.'

Freddy came back five minutes later, his hair wild and his grin wide. Roly and the Pincer twins were long since gone and Ben had climbed out of the ditch to wait for him.

'Thanks. I think,' said Ben, handing him back his spare skates. 'I really think we should get our chips now.'

LONDON, SEPTEMBER 2009

Jerome Emerson sat very, very still and thought of Shakespeare. The words 'To be or not to be' and 'But soft, what light through yonder window breaks?' and 'Once more unto the breach' all rebounded around his mind as he tried desperately to remember as many Shakespearean speeches as he could.

It wasn't that he was into Shakespeare particularly—he was a scientist, not a creative—but he remembered a scene from a spy film where the hero managed to keep himself calm and focused while baffling his enemies by reciting non-stop Shakespeare in his mind.

A spotlight glowed in the dark, surrounding him in a pool of white as if he were indeed a player upon a stage. If so, there was only one man visible in the auditorium. A man who called himself Chambers.

'I wish you'd stop all this muttering and just relax, Mr Emerson,' sighed Chambers, from the dark side of the table. 'We're not going to torture you, for heaven's sake.

All we want to know, perfectly reasonably, is why you were poking around in government folders, on a restricted access site.'

'I've told you already,' snapped Uncle Jerome. 'I'm researching my family tree! What's wrong with that? Everybody's doing it nowadays. You can't turn on the TV or radio without somebody declaring they're related to Anne Boleyn!'

'Most people use the internet or parish census books,' observed Chambers. 'Not restricted government records.'

'I know, I know . . . it was . . . um . . . cheeky,' admitted Uncle Jerome. 'I have a certain level of access, as you know, and I just—well—tweaked it slightly to go a bit further. My family tree is more difficult than most, obviously, given the disappearance of my grandfather—Henry Emerson. I just *wondered*, as we're nearly twice past the thirty year rule, if anything about his whereabouts had been uncovered. Whether there were distant cousins in America or somewhere.'

'Or Russia, perhaps,' said Chambers.

'Possibly, possibly,' agreed Uncle Jerome. His lips went on moving. Chambers, who had lost his hearing for a while as a child, could read them. *Romeo, Romeo—wherefore art thou Romeo*. He smiled to himself. He knew that spy film too.

He also knew Jerome Emerson was lying.

Chapter 18

'It was good of you—you know—to give up your records,' said Rachel as she and Polly sat in the garden with Bessie, who was snoozing against Polly's legs. 'I just wish Uncle Jerome would get back or we might have to think of something else next.'

'I didn't give up all of them,' said Polly, looking a little guilty. 'I kept one.'

'Really? Which one?'

'I'll show you. You'll think I'm a ninny, but I didn't want this one to go,' said Polly, getting up and plonking Bessie's sleepy muzzle over on to Rachel's legs instead. The puppy snuffled a little, but didn't complain. Polly jumped over the stream and made her way back to the hatchway, while Rachel waited. She found herself checking Bessie's furry nose while she waited and was relieved to see no more sign of blood. She hadn't noticed anything else about Freddy either, since last night. Hopefully it was all going to be fine.

Polly was back quickly, a green and white and black record sleeve under her arm.

'Promise me you won't tease!' she said.

'Of course—why would I?'

'Freddy's always teasing me about it. It's just that—well, you know, it's a sort of a crush. I'm not the only one!' she added, hurriedly. 'Other girls like him too.'

'Oh, I see.' Rachel smiled. 'I get crushes too. What about Orlando Bloom, eh? You know—the one I showed you in the *Daily Mail* . . . in *Lord of the Rings*?'

'What, with all that long hair? Golly, I couldn't like *him*. He looked like a girl!'

Rachel sighed. 'Live and learn,' she said.

'Max is much better looking—really a bit of a dreamboat!' said Polly, flipping over the record cover. Rachel gurgled. She slapped her hand over her mouth. But she still couldn't stop a peal of laughter splurging out between her fingers.

'Oh really, that's too bad of you!' Polly sat down crossly and Bessie shot up with a small yelp. 'You said you wouldn't!'

'B-but . . . ' Rachel struggled to control herself. 'It's Max Bygraves!' And it was—admittedly much, much younger than the elderly crooner Rachel had seen on TV once or twice, here in black and white, raising his thumb and smiling cheekily from the record cover. The record was called 'A Good Idea, Son'. Even though it was fifty-three years ago the object of Polly's crush still looked like a cheery geography teacher. Polly was very put out.

'If you're going to be like that I jolly well shan't tell you anything, ever again!'

'Oh, Polly! Look—I'm sorry.' Rachel finally got control. 'It's just that, in my world, all my life, Max Bygraves has been . . . well . . . a golden oldie, I think they call them. He's really old now. He's still great, of course, and I know my nan thinks he's fab . . . but . . . Well.' She picked up the cover and tried to see what Polly saw. 'Of course, back in 1956 he *was* quite a—a *dish*, wasn't he?'

'Do you think so?' Polly picked at the grass, pink in the face.

'Well—yes—now that I come to look at it. And I bet he had a great singing voice too.'

'Oh yes! I loved "Meet Me On The Corner". I was going to listen in to him this week, on *Stars of Variety* on the Light Programme. He's got a super voice.'

'Well, there you are then,' said Rachel, nodding at the album cover. 'Sorry, I was being stupid. I can really see it now. Bring it up into the house with you. You can put it up on our wall in our room if you like. It's getting cold now anyway. The boys will be back soon, with fish and chips I hope.'

'Has fish and chips . . . changed . . . at all?' asked Polly as they went back inside and tucked Bessie into her bed in the hallway.

Rachel smiled. 'No. I think you'll find it's exactly the same as the fish and chips you had last week. Except they don't wrap it in newspaper any more— Dad told me they used to do that. Just white paper now.'

'That's an awful waste of paper,' said Polly. 'I couldn't believe how much paper they wasted at school today. There were perfectly good bits of lovely white paper, only used on one side, just screwed up in the bin! We could have drawn pictures on them. I was going to get them out of the bin but I thought you would probably say I was goshing too much again.'

'No, you're right. It is a waste,' agreed Rachel. 'It's just that paper's easy to get these days. Nobody thinks anything of throwing it away. We're a throw-away society, my dad says.'

Back in the kitchen they put the kettle on and made tea and Polly insisted they should put plates in the oven on the lowest heat, to be warmed and ready for the fish and chips. While she was laying out the table mats and cutlery and glasses the telephone rang. Rachel ran into the hallway and scooped up the receiver, hoping very much that it was Uncle Jerome, at last calling to tell them he was on his way back—maybe with information about Henry Emerson.

'Hello?'

'Oh, hello,' came a woman's voice. 'May I speak to Jerome Emerson, please?'

'Sorry, he's not here right now,' said Rachel, pulling a face and shaking her head at Polly, who was looking hopefully around the kitchen door.

'Oh dear—do you expect him back later?'

'Um . . . who is this, please?' asked Rachel.

'I'm just one of his work colleagues—needed to check something with him,' said the woman. 'When is he due back? Later this evening?'

Rachel paused. 'Yes—yes, I expect so. Shall I leave him a message? What's your name?'

'Not to worry—I'll call back,' said the woman, and then hung up. Rachel blinked. That was odd—Uncle Jerome hardly ever got calls from work colleagues. Maybe this was someone he'd been talking to while trying to find out something about Freddy and Polly's father. Rachel didn't know why goosebumps suddenly swept across her arms and shoulders. She put down the receiver, and then picked it up again to dial 1471. The number was withheld.

'Who was it?' called Polly, from the kitchen.

'Someone for Uncle J.' Rachel jumped violently as the door crashed open and then heaved a sigh of grateful relief as Ben and Freddy charged in, clutching a hot parcel leaking wonderful fish and chip fumes, and looking rather scruffy. Ben had leaves in his hair.

Over their warm fish and chips (they'd kept their tea well wrapped up as they hared back from the chippy at the top end of the town) Ben and Freddy told their story of Roly and the Pincer twins and how Freddy had outskated them all.

'I *wish* I'd been there!' said Rachel. 'Especially when you pushed Ben in the ditch! That was dodgy, though, hitching a lift on that truck! You could have been splattered all over the road.'

'I have to admit it did go a lot faster than the old meat vans we used to hitch up to,' said Freddy, digging into his cod and batter. 'It was a bit of a fright when it went to fourth gear! But I managed to get off at the next set of lights and make myself scarce. It's super skating on your pavements, though! Much, much faster! Our axles used to snap in half after a while, going over those flagstones all the time.'

'You wait till we get you down a skate park!' said Ben. 'You'll freak out!'

Polly sighed: 'There'll only be more trouble tomorrow, though. Oh, I do wish we didn't get into such scrapes. We're supposed to be keeping our heads down, aren't we? And when, oh when, will JJ come back with news of Father?'

Freddy paused, and thoughtfully waved a ketchup tipped chip on his fork. 'Hmmm—I really do think it's a bit qu—a bit odd—not hearing from your uncle for so long. Do you think we ought to try to find out where he's got to? I mean, I know he's a bit absent minded, but I'm certain he didn't mean to leave us on our own for quite this long.'

Ben had been thinking the very same thing. 'I know—but where would we start? How can we find out where he went without making people suspicious? There's nobody to ask, is there?'

'What about Percy?' said Rachel. 'He knows about us—and he was going to look into his old files, he said, didn't he? Maybe Uncle J has been in touch with him. He lives in Amhill. It shouldn't be too hard to find out where and go to see him.'

'We could look in the phone book,' said Ben.

Rachel shook her head. 'We haven't got one. Uncle J burnt them all in an experiment . . . something to do with the ink they use. We'll have to find out another way . . . or borrow one or something.'

'Top idea, old girl,' said Freddy. 'I vote we do that tomorrow—straight after school. That's if JJ hasn't come back by the morning, and he might have done.'

Everyone felt a bit better, now that they had some sort of plan. For two of them, though, the feeling didn't last. As they cleared up the remains of the fish and chips Rachel decided it was time Freddy arrived in the twenty-first century, and demanded that he wash up. Polly offered to do it, of course, but Rachel stood her ground.

'No! You mustn't encourage him, Polly. This isn't 1956 any more and boys do housework now—at least they *should*. I don't mind drying up, but *you're* going to wash, Freddy.'

Freddy sighed and then grinned. 'All right. I'll do my bit. And the next time there's a big hairy spider in the bath and Polly's screaming blue murder, *you* can get it out.'

'Done,' said Rachel, choosing not to think too hard about that particular deal. 'Go on, Polly—go and sit down with Ben in the other room. Go through the magazines and stuff again.'

Freddy washed up clumsily and haphazardly but eventually the drainer was stacked with dripping plates and cups and Rachel would have felt very smug about the whole thing if she hadn't then witnessed something quite awful.

As Freddy dried his hands on the dishcloth he winced slightly. He looked down at his hands, frowning, and then gulped two or three times. When he lifted his head his face was pale and set. He saw that Rachel had seen it too.

'Better get some sticking plasters,' he muttered and Rachel nodded, feeling sick. She didn't know if she could keep *this* secret. It was getting worse.

Two of Freddy's fingernails had completely fallen off.

When she had found some plasters she went upstairs to find Freddy in the bathroom. He was leaning against the window, his forehead on the cool pane. 'Come on—show me,' said Rachel and he turned round, keeping his face down. Maybe he was crying. She wouldn't blame him.

He wouldn't let her put the plasters on for him, but just took them in his good hand, which was shaking.

'We have to tell someone . . . call a doctor,' she said.

'No! Don't be an idiot,' he said. He glanced up at her and his eyes were red-rimmed.

'But this is serious . . . more serious than a nose-bleed,' she insisted. 'You could be . . . I mean . . . '

'Look, you don't have to pussyfoot around it,' he said. 'I'm getting ill, like Father's rats—that's what you're thinking, isn't it?'

Rachel bit her lip. She didn't want to say it. She felt sick and scared. Freddy scrubbed hard at his eyes and then turned his attention to getting the plaster on one of his fingers. He struggled one-handed and eventually Rachel stepped across and did it for him and this time he allowed her. The fingers without nails looked red and puffy and he winced as she wound the plasters around them.

'Look, Rachel, you're all right,' he said, when she'd done the second one. 'I'm sorry I called you an idiot. It's just that . . . I've *got* to find out what happened to Father. And if you call anyone to look at my fingers, the whole game will be up and I don't know *what's* going to happen to Polly and me then. Please . . . let's just wait until JJ gets back tomorrow. I'm *sure* he will be back tomorrow and then he can call a doctor and we'll see what can be done.'

Rachel nodded. 'OK. We wait one more day.'

'Good girl,' he grinned, wonkily, and she felt a pang. He was brave. Too brave.

Chapter 19

There was no question that they were in for it after school. Roly O'Neal and the Pincer twins made menacing noises and gestures at Freddy and Ben all morning. In the dining hall at lunchtime, Rachel and Polly came close to having their heads ducked into the warm grey-tinged water where the dirty cutlery was dropped. Lorraine simply grabbed them both from behind and dragged them along to it by their hair, intending to acquaint them with the bits of old baked bean and fish finger which drifted around beneath the soaking knives and forks. She would have managed it too, for both Polly and Rachel were too shocked to even squeak—and the dirty cutlery bowl was behind a screen and out of view of any teachers or dinner ladies. Happily for them, a Year Ten boy stepped around the screen and brought his hand down in a karate-style crack on Lorraine's wrists.

She let them both go and spun around hissing, but then stopped and simpered, 'Oh—hi, Wangu . . . ' before just shrugging and walking away.

Rachel and Polly stared in amazement. Wangu grinned widely and winked one of his dark brown eyes. 'Thanks, Wangu,' whispered Rachel while Polly just stared and stared and stared. She had never seen anyone from Malawi before. Rachel nudged her. 'Say thanks!' But Polly continued to stare, her mouth open.

'Watch out, Super Girl,' chuckled Wangu. 'Something'll fly in, in a minute.' He reached over a hand and helped Polly's jaw to shut with a little clunk, and then shrugged and went on his way.

'He—he—he,' gasped Polly, in a kind of slow motion titter. 'He's *really*, *really*—'

'Cute?' said Rachel, pulling her across to the lunch queue and keeping a careful eye out for the return of Lorraine. 'Cool? Black?'

Polly's eyes widened. 'You can't say that! You say *coloured*. Black isn't polite.'

'No—black is fine. And Wangu's the coolest guy in the school—that's why Lorraine went all soppy. Lucky for us! Polly, *don't* say "coloured" again. Please.'

'I've never seen anyone like him!' Polly looked quite pink. 'He's . . . he's *wonderful*.' She instinctively went to tidy her hair as she watched the Year Ten boy walk away.

'Oi! Where did *that* come from?' Rachel narrowed her eyes at her great-aunt.

Polly had just slid a neat pink clip, with a tiny rose on it, into the side of her hair. She pouted. 'It's nice. I like to look . . . tidy. Like a girl!'

'Hand it over,' sighed Rachel and Polly pulled the clip out and handed it over. She looked a little sulky.

'Now just remember—you're twelve! Not three!' Rachel shoved the clip into her trouser pocket. 'If anyone sees you with that in, they'll *all* be queuing up to dunk your head in the washing-up bowl!'

Ben and Freddy managed to keep a corridor or two between themselves and Roly and the Pincer twins and skidded into the dining hall in time to see Rachel and Polly eating spaghetti Bolognese at the teachers' table, talking a little too brightly to Miss Janaway, with the occasional nervous glance across the tables to the far corner where Lorraine Kingsley now sat staring at them, gnawing on a chicken leg in a threatening way.

'Keeping your head down then, are you?' Ben

muttered in Rachel's ear, as he and Freddy sauntered by to get their own lunch.

'What else could we *do*?' winced Rachel, stepping away from her food to talk to Ben and Freddy in a low voice, as Polly chatted on to Miss Janaway. She would never have dreamed of sitting at one of the teachers' tables before today, but anywhere else was just too dangerous. She told them about the cutlery bowl and their lucky rescue by Wangu. 'But it can't last! She's going to get us sooner or later. We've offered to help out after school—clear out the stationery cupboard. It should take at least an hour, so with any luck Lorraine and Roly and everyone will have pushed off and we'll get out alive. You need to do the same.'

'Nah—we've sorted it out already—*we're* getting off early!'

'How'd you manage that?!'

'Sports session. We get to go out in Year Nine, so we're going to do bowls. At the Crown Green.'

'*Bowls?* What—like those old people in white clothes?'

'Yep. It was the only one we could be sure Roly and the Pincers wouldn't sign up for. We're leaving our bikes here and going in the minibus, so they won't have a chance to get us. And they let you go straight home from the bowls club afterwards if you want to, so we can just nip into town and find out where old Percy lives. You two had better get back for Bessie.'

Rachel nodded. She didn't like being left out of looking for Percy, but she felt bad about poor Bessie being left alone all day. She sat back down with Polly just in time to hear her telling a bemused Miss Janaway that actually, Max Bygraves was really quite a dish . . . in his youth.

'Max Bygraves?' echoed the astonished teacher. 'Polly . . . I think it's a good thing you've been let out of the commune . . . Now, have you seen any posters of Johnny Depp yet?'

The plan seemed to have worked when Rachel and Polly left school an hour late that day. There was nobody left at the gate. Rachel wasn't that surprised. Lorraine Kingsley knew there would be another chance tomorrow. And another chance the day after that. Just how much injury she was planning for them was difficult to guess at. After all, actually killing or seriously maiming one of them would get her excluded . . . but a compass point through the hand or a swift nose-break could both seem like accidents . . . There would be hockey on Friday. Rachel sighed. She rather liked her nose the shape it was.

They stopped at a convenience shop and got more food with some of the old record money, keeping an eye out all the time for Lorraine, but she'd obviously gone home for tea.

Poor Bessie was whining when they got back home and the hallway smelt awful. Rachel insisted she would clear up this time, and sent Polly out into the garden with Bessie, but not before surreptitiously checking the puppy's paws. She'd had a nasty, uneasy feeling inside her all night and throughout the day every time she thought of Freddy's fingernails. As promised, she hadn't said a word to Polly about it, but had decided she *would* speak to Ben as soon as she got him alone. She just couldn't deal with Freddy's illness on her own any more. Bessie's paws looked fine but, alone in the hallway, Rachel felt sure she could see little splatters of blood on the newspaper around the dog basket. She leant her forehead against the cold radiator in the hallway and closed her eyes. 'Oh, Uncle Jerome . . . please come back soon. Please.'

LONDON, SEPTEMBER 2009

'Sir—we've just intercepted a message for Jerome Emerson.' Travis ran in once again without knocking, but Chambers let it go. 'Anonymous. We're tracing it now— but get this, it was warning him about *us*! That we're covering up something. Left on his work voicemail, would you believe?'

Chambers snorted. 'I don't suppose it gave any detail of *what* we were covering up? Jerome Emerson still isn't saying a word apart from that family tree research nonsense—or Shakespeare. It's really most unsettling when a secret service doesn't know what secret it's got!'

'No—no detail, sir. Chapman says everything's normal in the town too. Nothing out of the ordinary. But . . . but, sir.'

'What, Travis?'

'Something's a bit odd. I checked at the school where Jerome's nephew and niece go—just to see if there was any chatter—and they say they've got cousins who've just started there this week. Kids called Robertson.'

'Cousins? Where from?'

'Well, that's what *I* thought. I checked their family— the only cousins Ben and Rachel Corder have are full grown adults. The other thing is, the Corder kids' parents are out of the country—and Jerome is supposed to be their guardian. So what's he doing up in London, leaving them and these "cousins" on their own—just to research his family tree?'

'Well, I suppose it's time to ask him,' said Chambers.

'Sir—one more thing,' said Travis.

'Yes?'

'Isn't it a bit strange ... that Chapman hasn't reported any of that to you? I mean ... isn't that her job?'

'Yes ... what *is* Chapman's job?' Chambers picked up his pen and began clicking it ferociously. 'Travis,' he said, 'you're a clever young man. And I'm an idiot.'

Chapter 20

'We could ask that nice librarian to help,' said Freddy, as he and Ben checked in their bowling shoes and left the club. A few elderly men and women waved to them. Freddy, with his posh accent and perfect manners, had made quite an impression on them. They'd urged him to join the juniors.

'I don't think so,' said Ben.

'Why ever not? She liked us. She'd be glad to help—she said so.'

Ben shook his head. He didn't know why but he felt uneasy about the librarian. Her eyes were a little too sharp when she'd looked at Freddy in the high street yesterday. Of course, she couldn't possibly guess their odd secret, but even so . . . Ben's instincts about people were good. He was a fairly quiet boy, mainly because of his tendency to stammer, and while he was saying little he was listening a lot. And observing a lot. He didn't know why he didn't want to go back to the library—he just knew it.

'The town council building will have lists of people and where they live, for voting and all that,' he said to Freddy. 'Let's try there first. Or we might get a phone book—he might be in there, although loads of people are ex-directory these days, what with all the sales calls.'

'Sales calls?' said Freddy, hitching his schoolbag up on his shoulder. 'You mean salesmen actually *telephone* you now? That's a bit much!'

They arrived at the town council building, which was on the other side of the road from the library in a very similar building, and made their way first to the public telephone hood inside it. This was where a small magistrates' court was held, so the phones were there for the public to use, because mobiles weren't allowed in the building. To Ben's immense surprise he found an almost whole phone book chained to the shelf beneath the plastic hood.

'Shaw—that's his surname—Percival Shaw,' said Freddy, while Ben thumbed through to the Ss. He found quite a number of Shaws but only two P. Shaws. One was in a district some miles away, so he guessed the more local one would be where Percy lived. If it *was* Percy at all.

'Twenty-one Riverside Close,' said Ben. 'It's not too far from here—just the other side of the park. Come on.'

'You're sure that's him?' asked Freddy, prodding the phone book. 'Perhaps you should telephone him.'

Ben nodded. He punched the number from the book onto the grimy metal keypad and listened for ringing—but the number fed back one long note.

'Number unobtainable,' muttered Ben. He re-dialled to be sure, but it was the same.

'Well, it's the only P. Shaw there, and it's within walking distance of Darkwell House and the woods on the top of the hill, where Percy goes every day. What's up with your fingers?'

'Oh, nothing,' said Freddy, curling his plasters away into his palm. Ben stared at him. The boy was colouring up slightly.

'What? What did you do?'

'Just bent back my fingernails . . . doing that wretched washing up business, that's all. Come on— are we going or aren't we?'

Ben hesitated. They *could* ask to see the electoral rolls, to be certain where Percy lived, but again the nagging feeling of unease rose inside him. It would attract attention. Best hope that this was the right P. Shaw.

They set off again, along the high street. Ben noticed that Freddy didn't give all the twenty-first-century stuff a second glance now. He marvelled at how quickly the boy seemed to have adapted to it all. There was no denying it—Freddy was infinitely cooler than he was. Ben didn't mind though. He was definitely going to get Freddy to give him roller skating lessons. He'd always been a bit too cautious to do really well at skating— Freddy couldn't be more different. They reached the park beside the river inside ten minutes and would have been over the bridge and into Riverside Close in another four. But Ben stopped dead as soon as they got into the park. Quickly he pulled Freddy behind the public toilets. 'What?' said Freddy.

'Over on the bridge! Oh hell—it's Roly! And . . . ' he peered quickly around the brick corner and then pulled back again, 'yeah—the Pincer twins, Jim Lewis . . . and a couple of others, I think, from Roly's posse. We can't get over that bridge!'

'Is there another way we can go?' asked Freddy, also darting his head around the corner now, and bringing it back with a grim expression.

'No, this is the only way over to Riverside Close. We could go up the valley and backtrack along the A road from Silchester, but it would take us *hours*. We'll just have to wait until they go . . . although they hang

250

around there for hours sometimes. They like to throw things at the ducks.'

Freddy pursed his lips and narrowed his eyes. Then he grinned. 'Righto, then—we'll go across the river.'

'What? Didn't you see them? We'll never make it. We'll be mashed potato before we even get halfway. We haven't got skates on today, either!'

'Don't need skates—just bathers—or shorts,' said Freddy.

'You what?'

'Well, you have got some, haven't you? Your PE shorts? Let's nip in here and get them on. We're going across the river. Down by that bend there. It shouldn't take five minutes to swim it.'

'Swim it? Swim the river?' Ben gaped at him. 'Are you mad? We can't swim it!'

'Why ever not? We used to swim it all the time in 1956.'

'But—but . . . ' Ben stared down to the river bank on the far side of the park. The river was not fast but it was very wide along the Amhill valley and quite deep in the middle. People did paddle at the edges sometimes, but kids were always being warned not to bathe in it. There were big signs forbidding it. He didn't know why. Probably so the local council didn't have to worry about being sued if somebody stood on a broken bottle. Freddy had already nipped inside the public toilets and was even now coming back out with his black PE shorts on, stuffing his clothes and shoes into his school bag.

'We can leave these here, till we get back,' he said, swinging his bag up on top of the toilets' roof. 'Nobody will see them there. Come on—what are you waiting for? I say, you *can* swim, can't you?'

'Yes—yes, of course I c-can,' gulped Ben and it was the stammer that made him do it. The second it twitched across his tongue he got angry. He was *not* going to let Freddy think he was afraid . . . even though he was.

Two minutes later they were at the river bank, ignoring the little kids and their mums in the play area and stepping down into the pebbly shallows of the River Am. 'Brrrr!' said Freddy brightly, wading in up to his knees. Ben followed, feeling goosebumps prickle up his legs. It was a very warm September day, but the river was still cold. 'Right then,' said Freddy, now up to his waist in rippling blue-green river, 'nice and quick does the trick!' And he launched himself straight out across the surface of the water and began to execute fast over-arm strokes through the water, causing some alarm to the nearby ducks.

Ben took a deep breath and followed him. The

shock nearly made him shriek, but he knew that the boys on the bridge could look round and see them by now, and if he made any noise it wouldn't help. He hoped he and Freddy were far enough downstream to be unrecognizable. Certainly, not one of them would ever expect to see *him* swimming across the River Am.

The current was worryingly strong by the time he reached the middle of the river and the first unwelcome tingle of panic moved in Ben's stomach—but through the splashes his hands were making he could see Freddy, still powering through the water like a champion, and he was determined not to be left behind. He'd just thrown caution to the wind, hadn't he? There was no going back. The far side of the river reached out to them now—a protruding bank with trees and shrubs, ready to hide them when they reached the bank. He heard a shout from the bridge—then a whistle. But he realized, even through the rush of the disturbed water all around him, that these were not hostile noises—they were curious, even impressed noises. He must remember not to look up towards those noises when he got to shore.

Freddy helped him out of the water at the other side and for a moment Ben just stood, shivering with excitement and delight. Keeping his back to the bridge, he glanced back to the other side—he had swum the

River Am! 'Good fun, yes?' said Freddy. 'Me and Poll used to do it all the time with local children, in the hols. We used to have races. Don't you do that here any more?'

Ben shook his head regretfully. 'Council doesn't allow it.'

Freddy made a scornful snort. 'Sounds like your council members are a bunch of lily-livered old codgers to me! Where on earth did you get them from?'

'Well . . . er . . . most of them probably used to swim the River Am with you,' said Ben.

Freddy grimaced. 'Oh. Well, pretty poor show then, the lot of them!'

Dripping slightly, they picked their way through the little wooded area and across to a path that led into Riverside Close. Number 21 was a small red-brick house on the end of a terrace with a neatly kept front garden and late honeysuckle growing around its door. Hesitantly Ben lifted his hand and pressed the door-bell. Inside the house there was a distant jingle. They stood and waited. Nobody came. Ben rang again.

'Oh blow!' said Freddy. 'After all that he's not even in! It's too bad!' He leaned down and peered through the letter box and as he did so the door clicked and opened inwards. Freddy fell into the hallway with a surprised gasp and then scrambled to his feet.

'I say—I say, Mr Shaw . . . are you in?' he called. There was no reply.

'We should go,' said Ben, uneasily. 'It's not right to go in.'

'Mr Shaw! We need to speak to you!' called Freddy and wandered further into the hallway.

'You can't just—' Ben stopped and sighed. Freddy was already peering into the little front room.

'It's all right—I'm not going to burgle the place! Just having a bit of a squint around. I don't like this— I don't like it at all. First JJ and now Percy. Where is he?'

'He might just be up the shop or something,' said Ben, edging around the door after Freddy. The sitting room was tidy and smelled of furniture polish and old wood. The furniture was elderly but clean. The small fireplace held an old fashioned grille gas fire and the TV was a big square one, in a wooden cabinet. A clock ticked steadily on the mantelpiece.

'Come on, we should go,' said Ben.

'No. Not yet.' Freddy went past him back into the hallway and along to the little kitchen at the back. A glance through the dining room door showed him there was nobody there either and the kitchen, painted pale green and with furniture not unlike the stuff in the vault, was also empty. A dishcloth lay folded and dry over the hot tap nozzle of the old Ascot water heater on the wall. 'There's something odd going on,' said Freddy and Ben knew he was right. He could feel it. He didn't object when Freddy climbed the stairs and checked the bathroom, the small back bedroom, and the front bedroom. All were just the same really. Neat, well kept, clean—and empty.

'Do you really think he's disappeared?' asked Ben in almost a whisper as they padded across the highly patterned carpet on the landing. Through its small square window the sky was darkening. 'He was going to tell us stuff, wasn't he? He was going to look into the files again.'

'Maybe he found something out and had to dash off somewhere in his motorcar,' said Freddy.

Ben shrugged. He couldn't quite picture old Percy dashing anywhere, and he was pretty sure he didn't have a car. He was about to say they should give it up and go when he heard something scrape. A hollow, long scrape. He felt something fall on his shoulder.

'F-Freddy,' he whispered. His hair prickled from his neck to his forehead. Now he could hear breathing. Freddy looked back at him. 'What?'

Ben looked up and shouted out in horror.

Chapter 21

Polly sang old-fashioned songs in a sweet, breathy voice, as she rummaged through the many wiggly bits of cardboard and tried to find a corner.

Rachel smiled, in spite of her anxiety. Polly was quite happy at that moment, lost in the big thousand-piece jigsaw of a Swiss chalet which an aunt had given them for Christmas, and which would almost certainly never have been opened if they hadn't dug Polly up. She had cleared space on the dining room table and was ordering all the pieces into sides and non-sides, and, of course, the four corners. She sniffed a little and then went on singing. Rachel looked at her watch. It was gone six now. Where were Ben and Freddy? Surely they must have found Percy by now? She had been expecting them to turn up, or at least phone, at any time for the last hour, with *some* kind of information. Hopefully with news that Percy had heard from Uncle Jerome and that he was even now on his way back to Darkwood House. She looked wishfully through the tall dining room window, up to the gate. Clouds had rolled in across the warm day and it was getting dark. She thought she could hear thunder in the distance. She switched the table lamp on, so they could see the jigsaw better.

'*Don't go walking down lover's lane* . . . (sniff) . . . *don't go* . . . (sniff). I say, have you got a hanky, Rachel?' Rachel got loo roll from the downstairs toilet which Polly seemed slightly startled by, but she managed not to gosh and just blew her nose. She screwed up the tissue to tuck it into her sleeve and then stopped still. In her opening palm the scrunched up white loo roll spread itself back out, like a flower blooming. There was red in the centre of it. Polly gulped and raised her eyes to Rachel. 'It's starting, isn't it?' Rachel felt a chill pass through her. First Bessie, then Freddy—and poor Polly didn't even *know* about that—and now Polly too.

'It's just a little nosebleed,' gulped Rachel. 'Nothing at all to worry about. I get them all the time.'

'Do you think so?' Rachel knew Polly didn't believe her. She also knew that Polly *wanted* to believe her, desperately. What else was she to do?

'Yes. I do think so,' lied Rachel, unable to avoid

glancing at the girl's fingernails. She walked to the high sash window at the front of the room and pulled it down—she didn't like the feel of the clammy warm air funnelling through it. Outside it was very dark for so early in the evening. Where *were* the boys? She returned to the jigsaw. 'Come on—let's start joining up the edge pieces.'

They had connected three pieces when the phone rang and made them jump violently and mess up two lines of edge pieces. Rachel ran to pick it up. 'Hello? Ben? Freddy?'

Silence.

'Hello?'

Silence.

'Hello. Who's there?'

Silence.

She clicked off the phone and put it down on the hall table. She stared at it, remembering the woman who'd rung last night. Goosebumps broke out again. 'Oh stop it,' she muttered to herself. 'You're just being stupid.'

Then the phone rang again. She seized it and said, 'Yes, hello?'

Silence. This time Rachel could almost *feel* it pulsing out of the receiver and into her ear, like a toxic gas. She said nothing. The silence spoke back to her.

For several long seconds. Rachel pressed down the receiver but when the button clicked back up there was no dialling tone—just more silence. She gulped and put the phone down and went back to the jigsaw where Polly was concentrating just as hard as she could. 'Who was it?'

'Nobody. Wrong number, I suppose.'

'Twice?'

'Yes . . . I suppose.'

Polly went on with the jigsaw, barely glancing up. '*Close the doors,*' she sang, in almost a whisper, '*they're coming in the windows . . .* '

It made Ben feel better that Freddy shrieked too. The face above their heads was contorted and wild eyed and a spider fell from its shaggy grey hair right onto Ben's terrified upturned face.

'Oh, don't take on so, you pair of ninnies,' said the face. It was hardly what they expected. A groan or a bloodcurdling scream, before the sudden arrival of a bloodied axe or something, but not that. Ben realized in a second that this was just Percy, upside down and certainly not at his best, but still just old Percy. He found his hands were at his throat where his heart seemed to be beating at four times the usual speed.

'Sorry if I gave you a bit of a scare . . . but if you will go breaking and entering.'

'We didn't!' said Freddy, affronted. 'The door was open and we were trying to find you. We were worried about you—and I should jolly well think we were right to be.' His voice was slightly higher than usual and he was gabbling. He'd obviously had a huge fright too, thought Ben, letting out a shaky breath of relief. The hatchway above them moved further sideways and with a rasping metallic rattle, an aluminium stepladder swung down. Percy was on the landing beside them a few seconds later. The right way up he looked quite normal, if a little cobwebby.

'W-what were you doing up there?' asked Ben.

'What do you think? Hiding!' Percy shook the dust out of his hair. 'I thought they'd come this time.'

'Thought *who* had come?' asked Freddy.

'Why are you both half naked?' enquired Percy; not unreasonably, Ben realized.

'We had to swim across the river to get to you. Trouble on the bridge,' said Freddy, quickly. 'Now what on earth do you mean—who is coming?'

Percy went into the front bedroom and peered discreetly through a gap in the thick white netting. They followed, exchanging glances. 'I had hoped Jerome would have got you away by now. I left him a message,'

Percy muttered. There was a roll of distant thunder beyond the window. 'They're coming. You'd better not go back now. Better get straight away from here.'

Ben wondered if old Percy actually *was* a little bit senile. Almost as if he'd heard this thought, Percy turned round suddenly from the window and fixed Ben with a hard stare. 'The Clean Up car. Remember? I told you. I saw it back then, fifty-three years ago. Black. A certain kind of number plate. I've seen it again. I saw the Clean Up car in town this morning. Then I got the silent calls an hour ago. Two of them. Then I knew. It's only a matter of time before they come for me. And for you. You need to get away now.'

Ben swallowed. 'But—but why are you still here? If they're coming for you?'

Percy sighed and shook his head. 'I'm too old to run. Better to hide it out and hope they won't check the loft. Thought I might make it look as if I'd gone away.'

'What—and leave the front door open?' said Freddy.

'Open? Oh, blast that old catch! I thought it was shut. Chain usually catches it—but you can't put a chain on from the inside when you're supposed to have gone away.'

'Wait a minute—you said you'd left a message

for Uncle Jerome?' asked Ben. 'Does that mean you've got a number for him? We haven't! We can't find a number and we can't get through to him and he's been away for days and days now.'

Percy looked worried. 'How long?'

'Almost a week. And he's never left us that long before. It was only meant to be a couple of days. We had to sell stuff to get food!'

Percy shook his head and now looked extremely worried. 'I don't like it. I don't like it at all. I tried your house these last couple of days but nobody's been in—and he gave me his London office number but he's never there . . . finally I had to leave a message on the answerphone this morning. Stupid of me. It's probably how they've traced me.'

'What message did you leave for Uncle J?' asked Ben. 'Have you found anything out?'

'Not much,' said Percy, glancing out of the window again. 'But something . . . I asked one of my young chaps who still works in London on the Met, just about to retire—knows someone in MI5. He looked into it and told me more or less what I thought he would. It's not good for a country to know its top brains are running off to the enemy. So it seems as if the government believed your father did defect to Russia, but wanted to keep it quiet. I'm sorry, young man,' he added, seeing Freddy's thunderous face. 'But you see, they also thought that you children must have gone with him, and that's why you were never found. But I found out something else. Your father's friend, Professor Richard Tarrant, disappeared too, at the same time . . . although that didn't come out in the press either. He was a bachelor man and given to travelling, so nobody realized for a while. Then they thought maybe both men had gone across together . . . except . . . '

'Except what?' asked Freddy, coldly. 'I can't believe Uncle Dick would have gone either—I really can't. He was a good sort!'

'Well, he came back, you see. He came back two years ago. He was ill—dying. Wanted to make his peace with them. Gave the government some useful information and was allowed to end his life quietly in his home country.'

Freddy dropped his head for a moment, remembering the man they'd called Uncle Dick—but then looked back up and demanded, 'But what about Father? He must have told them about Father!'

'Maybe—but if so, my man didn't hear anything. Maybe there's nothing else to know. Maybe it's all still a mystery to them, even at the top. It's probably too long ago for anyone these days to care.'

'So how come you're worried about the Clean

Up car now then? If nobody cares any more?' said Ben. 'Why *would* they come along now, if nobody knows anything about Polly and Freddy except our family and you?'

'It's not only our lot have clean up cars,' muttered Percy. 'Just because our lot might not know what's what, doesn't mean someone else hasn't worked it out. Have you kept Freddy and Polly at the house all the time, up until now?'

'Well, no—they had to come to school with us. Uncle J sorted it out with the head teacher,' said Ben.

Percy stared at him and then pinched his nose and shook his head. 'So . . . two children from 1956, out and about in a modern school. No. They're not going to stand out, are they?' Ben realized he was being sarcastic and abandoned all thoughts of Percy being senile.

'But why should we worry if everyone just thinks Freddy and Polly are in Russia now?' said Ben. 'It makes much more sense than the truth, doesn't it? Nobody will ever, *ever* guess. I can't believe *anyone's* really coming for us—or you. I think you're just nervous.'

'I told you,' said Percy. 'Silent calls. I've had them twice today . . . and I know what that means, even if you think I'm just a daft old man. Someone, somewhere, is checking who's in—and who's not. Where are the other two?'

'Back at the house,' said Freddy. 'Oh, blast it! Ben—what if Percy's right? The Clean Up men could be going there now? We have to get back—we have to warn them!'

He made to run downstairs but Percy shouted, 'Wait! Use the phone first. And then get some ruddy clothes on. You can't go charging about like *that* and expect to not get noticed. I'll get you some clothes and shoes.'

Ben ran downstairs to the hallway, pushing the front door shut as he passed it, and picked up the receiver of Percy's phone. He paused as it reached his ear and then stared at Freddy.

'What is it?' asked Freddy. 'Can't you remember your own number?'

Ben held out the receiver. 'C-c-can't c-call them. The line's d-dead.'

Freddy stared back at him and then glanced across to the door. 'Get down,' he said. 'Get down. Right now.'

As they sank to their knees, Ben realized why. A flash of lightning flared through the frosted glass pane. The sudden light threw a shadow. Somebody stood, motionless, on the other side of the door.

Chapter 22

The warm, clammy wind curled through the garden as Rachel took Bessie out for a toilet stop behind the rhododendrons. The sky glowered dark grey and violet. Fine prickles of lightning lit up the eastern sky every few seconds. Thunder rumbled, still distant. Shadows moved in the corner of her eye but she knew she was just nervous and seeing things.

'Come on, Bessie.' She picked up the puppy, which playfully tried to nibble at her hands, and walked quickly back to the house. She firmly shut the door behind her with a shiver. Polly was in the kitchen, getting beans on toast ready for them. They were both worried about the boys and trying to get on with stuff, to avoid thinking about it too much.

'What were you doing by the gate? Did you see the boys coming?' called Polly from the kitchen.

'We weren't by the gate, we were round the side,' said Rachel.

There was a pause. 'Oh,' said Polly. Another pause and she walked into the hallway. 'Well, maybe they're back then . . . and just larking around in the garden still.'

'I didn't hear them,' said Rachel, stepping into the front room with Bessie at her heels and glancing through the high sash window at the front. The gate and drive could be seen from here, but nobody was there.

'Oh,' said Polly, again, following her in. 'I just thought I saw someone out there. Probably just the lightning playing tricks with me . . . I suppose.'

They looked at each other, saying nothing, but both gulping. For a moment, silence reigned and then Bessie began to whine. They stared at her. She was shivering and looking fixedly across to the other side of the room, where a second window gave on to the side passageway. The window here was slightly open at the sill. Rachel stepped across and shut it quickly, seeing nothing outside but the unkempt forsythia bush waving its tall twigs in the air. A flash of lightning made the twigs look like witch's fingers. She felt her skin prickle with fear.

'*Close the doors*,' sang Polly, picking up Bessie

and looking around with big, frightened eyes, *'they're coming in the windows . . . '*

'Will you stop that?' hissed Rachel.

Polly stared at her and mouthed, *'Close the doors . . . they're coming up the stairs . . . '*

Now there *was* movement in the side passage beyond the window. Rachel was sure of it. A shadow, shifting suddenly sideways as if it was scared of being seen.

'Is the back door locked?' asked Polly. Rachel nodded. 'Are you sure?' Rachel walked quickly into the kitchen where the beans were bubbling on the stove. The back door was shut and the bolts were across.

'We're just being silly,' she whispered, as Polly joined her, pulling the beans off the heat with her free hand. Bessie whined again.

'Yes, I expect we are,' she said, staring at the back door. And then they saw it—the dented brass doorknob very, very slowly turning. They both drew sharp, scared breaths, but managed not to scream. Rachel grabbed Polly's arm and hauled her back along the hallway and up around onto the stairs. They ran up, Bessie still whining in Polly's arms, but Rachel didn't go into any bedrooms; she moved further along the landing and to a door at the far end.

'It goes up to Uncle Jerome's study and lab,' she whispered. 'Come on!'

She pulled the door open and they ran up a steep set of wooden steps which turned at the top and brought them to the attic floor of Darkwood House. From gable to gable it was filled with Uncle J's stuff—a desk, several chairs, a high bench for experiments, all kinds of gadgets and bottles and books and tools and three different computers. It was hard to make it all out because Rachel stopped Polly putting on the light. The very last of the day glowed dimly through the four slanting windows in the roof, but Rachel ran down the centre of the room to the little window set into the gable. She looked through it, down across the front driveway and into the top end of the overgrown garden. Just along from the gate a large black car was motionless at the roadside. She could see nobody in it. Her heart began to hammer in her chest.

'There's a bolt on the door—I don't know if it will hold—but put it across,' she whispered to Polly, who put Bessie down on a desk and ran quietly to do as she was asked. Bessie snuffled around by one of Uncle Jerome's keyboards. She nudged the keys with her nose and the screen sprang to life, casting a pearly white light across the room. Polly caught her breath. *Honestly*, thought Rachel, irritated in the midst of her panic, *now really is not the time to start goshing over some perfectly boring computer*.

'Rachel . . . I think you should see this,' said Polly.

'What?' Rachel couldn't drag her eyes away from the scene outside, waiting tensely to see another dark shadow flit past.

'I think it's . . . some kind of message.'

'Yeah—that's email. Remember?'

'I know—you said—but . . . it's for us.'

At last Rachel spun round and saw what Polly meant. The screen was Uncle Jerome's permanent email connection. Several emails were stacked up on the lower part of it with the most recent one maximized at the top of the screen. He kept them very big, so he could glance at them in passing. The last one in always maximized automatically.

The email on display was entitled GET OUT OF THE HOUSE NOW!

'Keep right down and crawl to the back of the house,' said Percy in a low voice, from somewhere above them on the stairs. 'They might not know you're here. You can get out the back door and go through the hedge at the far end, to the alleyway.'

At the door, the dark shadow silently bent over as if examining the lock. There was a sharp click.

'Who *are* they?' whispered back Ben as he and Freddy began to crawl along with their bellies flat against the carpet.

'Black car men!' hissed back Percy. 'Our government or someone else's government. Doesn't matter which. Someone knows about Freddy and Polly—someone knows and they want them. They must have heard my message to your uncle. Now get out! I'll do what I can to keep them off your trail.' And suddenly Percy stepped down from the stairs and called out, 'Who's that? Who is that? I've called the police! I've called the police, I tell you!'

By now Ben and Freddy were in the little kitchen at the back. They got up and ran for the back door, unbolted it and hared out into the little lawned garden. As they reached the high privet hedge at the back, which was patchy and gappy, and began to push through it to the alleyway on the far side, they heard Percy shout. 'Oi! You can't just come in! Oi—get away!' Ben's thudding heart clenched; he felt he should go to help the old man, but he and Freddy had to get back to Darkwood House and get Rachel and Polly out and then . . . go somewhere. Where, he had no idea.

In the alley, which was paved with grey flagstones,

they looked quickly around and then ran off to the left, hoping it would take them back in the direction of the river. Ben could not imagine being able to swim back across it now, with the clouds low and dark and flash after flash of lightning above them. He winced as his bare foot struck a sharp stone. It was awful to be so under-dressed when they were in danger.

The alley did reconnect with the front of Riverside Close and only a little way past the path which led to the bridge. With any luck the bad weather would have sent Roly and his posse home for tea by now, thought Ben, but he was wrong. As soon as the bridge came into view he could see the collection of boys still hanging around on it, watching the brewing storm.

'Don't worry about *them*!' said Freddy, at his side. 'They're the very least of our troubles. Look!' Ben glanced back down Riverside Close in time to see two well built men in dark jackets running towards them with great purpose. A few yards behind them a sleek black car glided along the road. The men looked from left to right and one spoke into a phone or a radio in his hand.

'Don't run,' shouted the other. 'You need to come with us.'

Freddy grabbed Ben's arm and ran straight for the bridge. As soon as their feet struck the wooden boarding Roly and his posse looked round and then gaped at the sight of their foes pelting straight for them in nothing but damp PE shorts.

'Hello, chaps!' called Freddy in his most toffee-nosed voice. 'I say—I rather hope you can help us out! We're being chased by bad sorts. Any chance you can stop them for us?'

Roly was astonished. The Pincer twins looked at each other and then at the rest of the boys on the bridge. 'You what?' said Roly, and then his eyes shifted and he saw the men in pursuit.

As Freddy shot past the confused boy he called: 'Hey, Roly! Is it true you're actually a girl?'

That was enough. Freddy yanked Ben even harder by the arm and hissed, *'Faster now!'* and all the boys bundled after them, led by Roly who was shouting all kinds of colourful words—not one of them 'Bother'.

It was a desperate tactic. There was every chance they would be beaten to a pulp. But it *did* confuse their adult pursuers. Now they were chasing nine boys and in the fast fading light it was difficult to make out who was who. Ben couldn't see how they were possibly going to get away, though. His blood was thundering through his veins at the effort and he could hear his own heartbeat right up in his head. Good luck came their way a moment later, when Roly, leading the pack, tripped over, causing a domino-style pile up of cursing youths. The lull in the chase gave the men behind a chance to shout, 'Stay where you are! This is the police! Stay where you are!' They sounded really *like* the police and the boys got up in a confused knot, wondering whether to run or freeze.

By now though, Freddy and Ben had got around the corner of the public toilets. Once there Freddy vaulted up onto the roof, with the help of a low wall around the path to the gents side. Ben followed him up, amazed that he could. They grabbed their bags and then Freddy ran to the edge of the single storey building and leaped off it, landing on the pavement on the far side of the park's perimeter hedge. Ben quailed, wondering if his aching legs would just snap when he hit the ground. But they didn't. His poor feet howled though. At the speed of light he flung on his shoes and wriggled into his dark blue PE T-shirt, as did Freddy, then they were off again, screened by the toilet block and the line of hedging that surrounded the park. Along the road they sped, but Freddy caught Ben's arm again and slowed him down beside a small open-backed truck—a gardening vehicle used by the town's groundsmen. The engine was running and the driver was returning to the cab, having just delivered something to the park keeper's lodge, by the look of it. He was arguing intently with someone into his mobile phone. Freddy leaped into the back of the open truck and Ben whimpered slightly before following.

'Well, you tell Bill,' stropped the delivery man, flinging the driver's door open, 'that forty rolls is what was on my list and forty rolls is what I delivered! I can't deliver what isn't on the list! And you tell him I'm into overtime now, too!'

The door slammed and the man concluded his call with a grouchy goodbye, before pulling off the handbrake and grating the gears. The engine rumbled up a note and Ben shivered as they began to move. Across the park he could see a posse of boys scattering and two men walking purposefully towards the road, looking left and right. He ducked down onto the empty flat bed of the truck and anchored himself as best he could as it pulled away. Next to him Freddy was also flat down on his front. He was grinning.

'We've lost them! We've done it!' he called over the noisy rumble of the engine.

'Yeah!' called back Ben. 'Now all we've got to do is ask the driver to drop us home. I'm sure he'll be delighted!'

Chapter 23

Rachel stood, open mouthed, before the computer screen. She clicked the mouse for the full message.

GET OUT OF THE HOUSE NOW!

You're all in danger. We're on our way to get you, but we can't get through on the phone. The line has been tampered with. I just hope you disobey all my rules, go up to my lab and get this. Get yourselves out of the house as soon as you've read this message—down in the vault is the best place to go. Seal yourselves in. I'll knock seven times in a row so you'll know it's me.

I'm so sorry I've left you so long. And so sorry I said no to mobile phones.

So much to tell you. Now DELETE this message.

Uncle Jerome

Rachel stared at the time and date of the email. It had been sent about half an hour ago. She glanced at Polly who was looking wide-eyed and fearful. 'It's not just in our heads, is it?' she said. 'They really are coming up the stairs. We're trapped.'

Rachel ran back to the window and this time she *did* see the shadow. A black figure moved fast across the driveway, signalling to someone else behind. She heard a tinkle of glass and realized they must have broken the fragile coloured panes in the front door. They were in the house.

Polly was hugging Bessie to her. 'What can we do now? They're just going to find us, aren't they? They're going to come up the stairs and find us.'

'No!' Rachel took a deep breath and deleted her uncle's email. 'They're *not* going to find us. We're getting out.'

'How?'

Rachel strode across to one of the slanted windows and pulled a chair up beneath it. She stood up and undid the catch, before giving it a shove. The window pivoted open, the top swinging in and the bottom swinging up and out.

'We can't go up on the roof!' gasped Polly.

'We can,' said Rachel. 'And then we can get down. Uncle J put a fire escape ladder in here years

278

ago. It's because the stuff he does could be a fire risk. Mum and Dad insisted on it. It's half their house too.'

'But what about Bessie?'

Rachel gnawed on her lip. 'We have to leave her behind.' Polly looked stricken. 'I know! I know, it's horrible, but they're hardly going to hurt her, are they? And it's not like they're going to try to get her to talk . . . whoever they are. It would be too dangerous to try to take her with us. She might fall.'

Polly nodded and kissed Bessie's head. 'We'll be back for you soon. I promise,' she said, smoothing the brown silky ears. Bessie made a gruff noise and sat down and watched them as they climbed up out onto the roof. The stormy breeze made Rachel sway, but she quickly grabbed the metal curve of the emergency ladder frame below the window and eased down on to its narrow platform. There was a mechanism for releasing the long, lightweight ladder. She found it, undid the catch and wound the handle around once. With a whisper of nylon and aluminium it slithered down the roof and over the edge of the leaf-stuffed guttering. Rachel had not yet looked over the edge—she really didn't want to think about how high up they were—but as Polly eased down across the steep grey tiles above her, looking absolutely terrified (and with good reason), Rachel knew she had to look over to see if the coast was clear.

She gripped the ladder platform cage tightly and leaned out to look. Her head swam. The garden below looked as though it was on another planet. The tall oaks that lined their land waved their topmost branches at her . . . from below. It felt like a bad dream.

'Sh-shall I go first? Would it help?' asked Polly, her face pale in the dim light.

Rachel shook her head. 'No, it wouldn't be safe to try to squeeze past me. I'll be OK. I can't see anyone down there. I think they must be in the house by now.'

As if to confirm this, there was a thud from inside and they both jolted. Rachel lost no more time. She turned round and hung tightly onto the metal grip as her feet found the top of the ladder. It was quite steady, but as soon as she stretched her foot down below the guttering, the aluminium step beneath it twisted madly, three storeys of thin air beneath it. She had never been so scared in her life. Still, there was no waiting now. She gritted her teeth and put her other foot down. And then took the next step below that. Once she was clear of the roof her own weight held the ladder steadier and this would help Polly to climb after her. She moved rapidly now, glancing below, seeing no one. She was desperate that all this fear and struggle would be worth it—how awful to reach the ground only to be captured. And by whom? She wished Uncle Jerome's message had told her more.

It felt like an hour, but was probably less than a minute before she reached the ground. She held on to the ladder, anchoring it as Polly came down too. 'OK?' she whispered as the girl reached the ground. Polly nodded. They took one look around and then ran down the garden, keeping to the hedge until they were forced to dart from cover and across to the rhodo-dendron bushes. They scrambled down the slopes beneath and ran across the lower lawn, leaped across the stream and into the wood and as the trees closed in around them Rachel began to think that they would make it. They would follow Uncle J's instructions and seal themselves in until he came for them and knocked seven times.

They hurled themselves down the shaft, its light sending up a warm, welcoming glow and Polly hit the SHUT button, and pulled down the LOCK lever as she passed. The hatch cover slid smoothly across with a metallic rattle and they heaved shaky sighs of immense relief. They staggered down the remaining rungs and stumbled along the corridor and into the sitting room, collapsing on the old sofas, gasping with delayed shock.

'I—I can't believe we just did that,' breathed

Rachel. 'I never would have thought I could ever do that in my life!'

'I've never been so terrified,' breathed Polly. 'I feel absolutely dreadful that we had to leave poor Bessie . . . but, oh, it's good to get in here. JJ will be here any time, I know he will! I just hope those bad sorts don't come searching for us and find the hatch. I'm sure they can't get in, though. It's tough enough even when it's *not* locked from the inside. Jolly good thing we left it open, earlier. Although we really oughtn't to. It's jolly unsafe!'

Rachel felt a quietness drop around her. She stilled her breathing and tried to focus on something that niggled at her through all the excitement and drama. 'Polly . . . when did we leave it open?'

'Well, we didn't. It must have been the boys.'

'But they haven't been down here since yesterday. Do you think they would have left it open all night? I—I don't think they would do that.'

'They didn't,' came a voice behind them. 'I opened it.'

'We're going to have to jump off soon,' shouted Ben, over the engine noise, as he and Freddy clung on to the muddy shallow ridges in the back of the truck to try to stop sliding around. With every bump they went up and thudded back down and Ben's chin cracked onto the metal bed. He'd already bitten his tongue twice. 'I just hope the lights are red at the top of this road—if they're not we might have to jump for it anyway—we can't go too far past the entrance to our road. We've got to get back to Rachel and Polly . . .'

'Before anyone else does,' concluded Freddy. 'All right.'

Ben raised his head as high as he dared, peering up through the back window of the cab, to the front. The driver need only flick a glance in his rear-view mirror and one of his stowaways would be in full view. The engine note changed as he shifted down a gear and Ben hoped fervently that this meant the lights ahead were on red or going to red. He looked back down the road behind them and was relieved to see that there was no queue of cars; only one, too far back to see them. The engine note changed again and the truck slowed down to perhaps fifteen miles an hour. Ben saw the lights. They were red *and* amber and flashing—ready to return to green at any second. It was now or never.

'NOW!' he shouted and Freddy shot up beside him. They hurled their bags ahead of them on to the

283

kerb and then stepped up on the truck side and leaped for it. This time Ben's feet really did complain, even with shoes on. They had never been required to leap onto concrete from a moving vehicle before. Freddy pitched forwards and landed on his hands and knees. He winced and gritted his teeth and when he got up his knees were badly skinned and he was examining his palms and compressing his lips with pain. Only for a second though. As the truck pulled away, with a confused backward glance from its driver, they grabbed their schoolbags and ran back to the corner of Darkwood Lane. It would be at least another two minutes of hard running before they reached the house. Freddy got a few metres along the steep road before shrugging his school bag off and throwing it in some bushes. Ben did the same. They couldn't afford to be slowed down. His text books and school clothes would wait for him.

It was as if he existed in two layers, as they pounded along in the sultry, darkening evening, lightning throwing white streaks into Freddy's wildly flying hair. One part of him was whimpering with exhaustion and pain from his feet and lungs, while another part was utterly without compassion for the first part. The urgency of the situation demanded that not one second of slacking could be tolerated. He glanced back over his shoulder, expecting the black car to come gliding up behind them at any moment and the men to simply lean out and pluck them inside. He wondered what they had done with Percy. Had the old man managed to delay them or send them in the wrong direction? He doubted it. If they knew about Percy and they knew about Professor Emerson then they would certainly know where he and the others lived.

Freddy suddenly stopped, twenty metres or so before they would reach their gate. He leaned against a tree at the roadside and bent over, panting, his hand to his face. As he caught up, Ben saw, with horror, that Freddy's nose was bleeding. A lot. He touched the boy's shoulder and Freddy shrugged him off. 'Go ahead!' he said. 'Don't stop for me. You'll have to go on ahead.'

'You can keep going!' argued Ben. 'It's just—it's just a nosebleed. You'll be OK!' Freddy turned to face him, but he did not look right. It wasn't the blood on his face. It was something else.

'You have to go ahead . . . and then come back for me,' said Freddy. 'I'm sorry, old chap . . . it's just that I can't see.'

Chapter 24

'YOU!' Rachel was so flabbergasted that this was all she could say. Polly was also gaping with astonishment. After the terrors of the last thirty minutes: the silent phone call, the shadows in the garden, unknown people breaking in, their desperate escape onto the roof and down the ladder; the very last thing in the world she could have imagined was this.

'Hello again. Rachel, is it?' The woman perched on the arm of the sofa opposite them, smiling. She was holding a small metallic case with curved edges, about the size of a book, in her hand.

'You—you're the librarian!' Rachel's brain could hardly bend around this. What was the town librarian doing down in their vault? Visions of black shadows in her garden fought with the sight of this woman, here in her trousers and navy cardigan, smiling as if she'd just been asked for *Wind in the Willows*.

'Well remembered,' she said, smoothing back her neat brown hair. 'Hello, Polly. How are you?'

'What are you doing down here?' Polly demanded. 'You've jolly well no right to be down here!'

'I've been given permission. Don't worry your head about it. Everything's going to be fine. How are you finding twenty-first century life?'

Polly looked at Rachel. Could this woman *know*?

'How would you expect her to find it?' snapped Rachel.

'Pretty dreadful, I should think. Poor child. Has the bleeding started yet?'

Again Rachel and Polly gasped and stared.

'I see that it has,' sighed the librarian. 'Which makes it even more important that you come with me now. I can take you somewhere safe and make sure you get the care you need.'

'She's not going anywhere with you!' said Rachel, fiercely. There was something about the woman's tone that she hated. A smug, know-it-all kind of tone that made Rachel want nothing more than to punch her hard in the face.

'Oh, but she is—and so are you,' said the librarian. 'I wish I could leave you behind, Rachel, but there'd be far too much trouble if I did. Now, be good girls and come along with me. Making a fuss really won't help.' Rachel and Polly anchored themselves to the sofa and glared at her. 'Really, Polly, I'm surprised at you,' she said, getting up and walking to the door to the exit corridor. 'Don't you want to see your father?'

Ben staggered to the side of the road and tore great ragged gasps of air through his aching lungs. He had tried to drag Freddy along with him but the boy had struck out at him and insisted he had to go on alone. 'I can't help you! I'm no good to anyone now, blast it!' he'd said, with tears in his voice, which convinced Ben he was right. Freddy really could *not* see. Now Ben thought of the rats which had died in Professor Emerson's early experiments and shuddered. Just a few steps away was the fabled black car. It had to be a second one— the first would have passed them on the road if it had come here, and he knew it hadn't. It wasn't possible to make out if anyone was inside because the windows were mirrored, so he daren't dash past it. For the third time that day Ben dropped to the ground, this time to wriggle across the tarmac of the road on his belly. His only chance was to stay very low and hope no lightning flared to show him up as he went. A few drops of rain were beginning to fall now and the thunder rumbling in the east sounded louder.

As soon as he reached the gate he crawled around it and scrambled into the hedge to the right. Panting, he got up on his knees and stared along the drive to the front door of Darkwood House, which was wide open, with light flooding out. As he watched, a man clothed in black came out from the hallway, speaking into a hand-held radio or phone. The man signalled to another, who now joined him from the side alley of the house, moving with purpose towards the back garden. He shouted something in a foreign language, taking no care now to keep his voice down. Ben felt his heart thud hard inside his chest. They must have got Rachel and Polly then. And even if he had hoped against hope that they were actually just the local—or even London—police, sent by their own government after a tip off, the foreign language convinced him they were not. They sounded Russian. What should he do? They were too late. What would Freddy say? He felt fearful indecision settle on him like wet cement.

'You mean he's . . . he's alive?' Polly abandoned all pretence. The thought that her father was still on the earth knocked every other thought out of her.

'I can take you to him,' said the librarian. 'Come

with me and you'll see him very soon. I work for the same people your father works for.'

Polly took a step towards the librarian. 'You work with him?'

'For the same people,' she repeated. 'The government. That's how I know about you and about this place. So come on now—he's missed you so much, Polly. He told me he's looking forward to giving you a big hug and a kiss and telling you how much he loves you.'

Polly blinked, and then a coldness crept over her face. 'You don't know what you're talking about, do you? You're making it up!'

The librarian looked slightly uneasy, for just a fraction of a second. 'Why would I do that?'

'Because Father isn't like that! He's not a hugging and kissing sort at all and he certainly wouldn't ever say that to *you*. You don't know where he is at all and you certainly don't know *him*!'

The librarian sniffed and pursed her thin lips. 'I really don't have time for this. Look, I work for some very powerful people, who would really think nothing of it if I just finished off your friend here, Polly. We don't need her. So fine—come nicely or don't come nicely. It's all the same to me.' She walked briskly along the exit corridor as Polly and Rachel exchanged appalled glances, and then they heard her go up the metal rungs of the shaft and then press the unlock button.

'She might lock us in!' said Rachel, suddenly getting to her feet, and they both ran along the corridor and began to climb up the rungs. The librarian was sitting on the edge of the hatch and smiled tightly down at them as they climbed. She was talking into a phone or radio—yes, judging by the beeps before she spoke, it was a radio.

'I've got them,' she said. 'Come right now. No— I haven't sedated them yet—they're way too jumpy. I'll be needing your help.'

Rachel stopped climbing and looked down at Polly, who shared her frightened expression. 'Sedate us?' she whispered, and her words rang up through the concrete shaft.

'Yes,' called down the librarian. 'For your own good. It's going to be a long journey—tricky in places— better that you're asleep really.'

'What have you done with Ben and Freddy?' asked Rachel, climbing a rung or two higher.

'Nothing,' said the librarian. 'We expected to find them here with you. Where are they?'

'As if we'd tell you *that*!' said Rachel.

She reached the top of the rungs and a moment

later she was seized from behind by a blur of black. In the struggle and through flashes of lightning she saw another darkly-dressed man grab Polly. Soon they were both standing on the ground beside the hatch and the librarian was moving towards them. She had opened her little metallic case, which had several syringes in it. She drew one out, took the cover off its needle, and went towards Rachel first. As Rachel shouted out 'No!' and tried to pull against the iron grip that pinned her arms back, the librarian jabbed her suddenly in the shoulder.

'Sorry, dear,' she said. 'I didn't think I would ever really do this kind of thing . . . but the rewards are just so much better than government pay.'

Whatever was in the syringe was fast. Three seconds later, as Polly gave a little shriek, Rachel's vision turned black and white and then purple and then she knew nothing at all.

Chapter 25

Hiding low in the bush, Ben watched the men in black vanish down the garden. He wondered what on earth to do next. Where were Rachel and Polly? How could he help them? He'd just decided to get up and run into the house, in case he could find the girls hiding in a cupboard or something, when a third man came out of the front door, carrying Bessie. The puppy was looking around nervously from behind the big bulky arms of her captor. Ben felt rage shoot up through him and then caught his breath. He must try to stay calm and *think*. Rachel and Polly were in danger—and poor Freddy was blind. Now Bessie was being dognapped and here he was, shivering under a bush. He had to *do* something.

He crawled forward slightly, and his knee knocked into something cold and hard. Squinting down in the dim light he saw the old camera which Uncle Jerome had pulled out of the chestnut tree a few days ago. The aged flex wound off it like a tail, through the wet grass. An image sprang into Ben's mind. A warrior, swinging a flail. The man holding Bessie had taken her to the car and now returned, walking within feet of Ben's hiding place. He paused and pulled out his radio, his back to Ben. 'You got them yet?' he heard the man say, with a strong accent. 'Yes, drug the Emerson girl too. We have no time for hysterics. Your former colleagues will be here any moment. Hurry up.'

Ben felt the rage rise up in him again and this time he did not try to contain it. He needed it—this might be his only chance. He stood up with the bulky rectangle of the camera in his hands, wound the flex twice around his fist and began to swing the metal box from the end of its own tail. He swung it fast around his head, three times. The swooping noise it made seemed horribly loud, and he felt sure the man talking into the radio would turn around at any time. But he didn't. Which meant that Ben really would have to go through with it. He thought of Freddy, blind, bleeding, and possibly dying, shouting for him to run on and save the girls. Could he be the warrior? He must. He stepped forward and let the full force of the hurtling camera flail crack into the side of the man's head.

In the split second that the weapon connected Ben felt absolute triumph and absolute terror strike him. Now the man would turn and kill him. But the man did not turn. He fell over. And he didn't get up, but groaned, curled into an anguished shape on the wet driveway, and then his eyes rolled up into his head and he lay still. Ben stood rigid with shock. He felt a wave of overwhelming guilt—had he murdered him? But no, the man was breathing, in a snore-y sort of way.

'For goodness' sake, you clot!' shouted Freddy, in his head. 'You've brought him down! Don't just stand there! Save the girls!'

Ben shook himself out of his shock and ran down the garden on legs that trembled beneath him. He froze as soon as he reached the rhododendrons. He could see torchlight and a group of people heading up the garden. A woman and two men—the men were each carrying a lifeless form. He gulped. Rachel and Polly. Were they dead? No—he couldn't believe that. Unconscious then . . . drugged, of course—that's what his victim had said just before being rendered unconscious himself. Ben moved back up the garden and crouched around the corner of the porch, gasping for breath as terror pounded through him. Now what? Now what?

As the party reached the driveway one of the men shouted something in another language. They all drew up in shock at the sight of their comrade on the floor. Then both men dumped the girls on the ground and ran towards him. Thunder and lightning rolled and flashed all around them now. 'What's wrong with him?' shouted the woman and Ben, peering around the brick porch, realized with astonishment that it was the town librarian. 'Get him in the car! We have to go *now*! We'll miss our flight!'

Flight? Ben's panicked mind did not seem capable of squeezing any more awful things in—but here was a new one. Their home had been attacked, Rachel and Polly were drugged and being kidnapped, along with Bessie, and taken . . . out of the country? Ben groaned. He wanted to cry. Where was Uncle Jerome? Where was his dad? His mum? Someone who could help? He thumped his fist, painfully, against the wall, and stood up in despair, thinking he might as well give up. His head struck against something and he looked up to see the satellite dish which had fallen off the wall last week, just before all this madness started, dangling by its wire. If he could cut off the wire he might use it as a frisbee . . . see if he could take out another foe. But he couldn't, and besides, he knew he *wasn't* the kind of *Boy's Own* hero that Freddy probably was. The success of his camera flail was just a fluke.

The men were dragging their concussed comrade into the black car at the gate now. 'Put the girls in the boot—fast,' said the librarian. 'Then search the garden one more time. Someone attacked Anton—it could be the boys. But fast! If we don't get them on one sweep, we've got to go. I didn't turn traitor just to get caught!' A crash of thunder punctuated her words, theatrically.

Ben crouched low beside the porch. There was nowhere he could run without being seen. He glanced around desperately for some kind of weapon. A few feet away he saw Freddy's old-fashioned bicycle pump. He moved across in the shadow of the house and grabbed it. At least he could try to cause a bit more damage before they got him. Then his eye picked up something beyond the lightning flashes . . . he could see a beam of light hitting the broad trunk of the big oak tree across the other side of the road. He knew what this meant. Someone was driving round a bend in the road that led in to Darkwood Lane, maybe a third of a mile away. A car was coming!

'OK—forget the search,' called the librarian, who'd seen it too. 'We go now!' She ran for the car and the two men followed.

Ben stood up. He had to delay them.

'STAY RIGHT WHERE YOU ARE!' he bellowed and all three turned round. Ben tucked the bicycle pump under his armpit and held it like a rifle. 'I AM ARMED AND I WILL SHOOT!' bellowed Ben, trying to sound ten years older.

'It's a kid,' sniggered one of the men. They advanced—carefully—and one began to grin. 'Give it up, little boy,' he said. 'You can't shoot people!'

'No? W-well I can knock them out with a flail, c-can't I?'

The men faltered slightly. 'You?' said one. 'Not bad for a shrimp.'

'Just get him and go!' yelled the librarian. 'Now! There's a car coming!' Now the men were close enough to see that they were being held at bicycle pump point. They strode forward and grabbed it off him and yanked his arms back and up, doubling him over with pain. They propelled him to the waiting car and hurled him into the back where the librarian was already waiting with her syringe. Before she could inject him, though, the man who had jumped into the driver's seat shouted something in another language. His shock and anger were easy to translate.

He looked back at the woman. 'Keys! Someone has the keys!'

Ben laughed, in spite of his fear. He just *knew*

it! Freddy! And yes—there was Freddy haring across the garden towards the house. Unfortunately, Ben wasn't the only one to spot him. The men crashed back out of the car and gave chase and then drew up short. Freddy was holding the car keys out over the garden well.

'I'll let them drop!' he shouted. 'Get my sister and my friends out of the car now and you can have your keys back and go!'

Once again, two grown men stood, hesitating before a thirteen year old, unaware that the ornamental well only went down two feet. Ben, peering out of the window while the librarian grasped his arm tightly and drove the needle into him, couldn't imagine how this could end. And in fact, nobody else could ever have imagined it either.

There was an incredible bang and a simultaneous flash and a white hot rivet of lightning struck the satellite dish beside the porch, then threw jagged fingers of burning silver out in several directions, seeking an earth. It found two earths. A second later, two men were flat on the driveway, smoking slightly.

A second after that Ben blacked out.

Chapter 26

Rachel was bumped awake. Her head, which felt as if someone had vacuum-packed it with hot custard, slammed into something hard. She raised her hand to her stinging brow, trying to work out why she was being rattled about in the dark. Where was she?

Now she realized she could hear a car engine and smell petrol. The last few images before she was injected flashed into her mind and fear flared through her chest. She felt around her—yes—she was in a car. In the *boot* of a car. Her hand fell on something warm—Polly's face. 'Polly!' shouted Rachel, in a voice that sounded odd and slurred. Of course . . . she had been drugged. She took a deep breath and shook her head. She *had* to wake up properly. Oh! The car thumped her up and down, again knocking her brow on the low underside of the boot lid—they must be going over very uneven ground. 'Polly!' she called again, and this time sounded more like herself. But Polly only moaned and didn't answer.

Where were they being taken? The librarian had talked about a 'long journey'. Maybe . . . maybe she really *was* from their own government. Maybe they *were* being taken to Polly's father. But no. There would be no need to dump them both, unconscious, in the boot of a car, if that were so. And now she remembered the librarian threatening to kill her, if Polly didn't co-operate.

Suddenly the car lurched to a stop. The engine cut out and Rachel could only hear her own heartbeat and terrified, ragged breathing. What now? She tried to keep calm and listen. Now she heard a woman's voice—the librarian—talking urgently in a foreign language. She must have a mobile phone with her. She sounded angry and panicked but then there came another sound . . . a chopping noise, cutting through the night air. A helicopter. Or was she imagining that? It might just be thunder . . . but no, there was no thunder and no rain; she would hear it on the metal of the car. The storm must have passed. How long had she been lying unconscious with Polly in this boot?

'Yesss!' she heard the librarian say. 'About time!'

One of the car's doors slammed and Rachel had only seconds to think of what to do next, because she was certain the boot was about to be flung open. And she was right. There was a scrabble at the catch and a second later, torchlight flooded into their cramped prison; Rachel kept her eyes closed and her mouth open, hoping she looked unconscious.

'All right, sleeping beauties,' muttered the librarian. 'Time to go.'

The helicopter noise grew much louder and through her mostly closed eyes Rachel could see the librarian's brown hair whipping around her head. In the weird flashing light, she looked like Medusa. 'You first!' said the woman, reaching in and grabbing Polly. Rachel wanted to leap up and claw at the woman's eyes, but something told her to wait. Just a little bit . . .

Mistake. Three seconds later the boot lid slammed down and she was trapped again. Rachel bit her lip and tried not to cry. She wasn't thinking straight. She still felt so foggy. She pushed against the metal above her but it did not give. She began to fumble around inside the boot and after a while her hands fell upon what felt like a canvas bag. It had a zip, which she undid. Under her hands she felt a cool tin—some plastic packages—some material . . . ah . . . it must be one of those first aid kits. She rummaged further and then felt something round, like a plastic barrel . . . heavy . . . with a sliding switch. Rachel squeaked with hope and pushed the switch and at once light streamed out from the bag. She'd found a torch. She pulled it out and swung it around her. The boot was black metal with a black carpet beneath her. The catch on the inside of the boot lid was silver coloured metal and had little moving parts.

She emptied the bag, hoping for something metal . . . something she could try to pick the catch with . . . surely there would be safety pins or scissors. But there weren't—only wipes and bandages and plasters and the cool can of something. Antiseptic spray. She wailed with frustration and tried to turn around in the confined space. And as she did so, she felt a slight jab in her school trousers' pocket. She paused and then dug her hand in. Her fingers fell on something hard, pointed and metal. She gasped out a dry chuckle, despite her fear. Polly's hair clip! She pulled it out and stared at it. Was it strong enough? Hair clips she'd bought in years gone by would bend in seconds . . . they were pretty flimsy. But this, of course, was a Fifties hair clip. Built to last. It was strong and well-made with a pointed, sharp back-clip which would probably be outlawed by twenty-first century health and safety rules. On an impulse, Rachel tucked the antiseptic spray into her blouse and then turned to face the catch of the boot. Outside the chopper noise was steady, as if the aircraft had landed. She might have only seconds before the librarian returned. 'Well . . . here goes 1956!' she breathed and poked the clip into the lock.

Three seconds later there was a clunk and the boot lid opened a crack. Rachel could not believe it. She stared out through the crack and saw shadowy grass. The flashing light behind revealed that the helicopter must be off somewhere to the front of the car. She could hear voices. They were shouting.

'Leave them!' bellowed a male voice. 'We only need the girl and the dog. Leave the other two—we haven't got time.'

Rachel gasped and threw herself out of the boot a second later. She turned and pulled the lid back down quickly, and then ducked down, her heart beating a wild tattoo in her chest. Who else was in the car? Just as she peered through the window, the door on the far side was wrenched open and the lights all came on. She had just enough time to see Ben lying unconscious on the back seat before ducking down again. The car door slammed and the librarian called out. 'All right, he's too heavy for me on my own anyway—let's go.'

Now there was a different set of lights—car headlamps, several of them, and blue flashing lights. The police were coming, bumping over the grassland that Rachel now recognized as the downs above Dark Wood— just a mile from their home.

But the helicopter was ready to fly and the librarian was handing Bessie aboard. At her feet was Polly. And now she was lifting the girl up while the pilot reached down. It was too late! They would get away!

'NO!!!' screamed Rachel and ran faster than she had ever run before. The librarian looked back over her shoulder and gaped, Polly dangling, semi-conscious, in her arms. Rachel hurtled towards her and then took a great leap at the woman. She cannoned into her and Polly was dropped to the grass as her captor was knocked over. Rachel, falling with her, had never been so furious in her life. She pulled hard on the woman's hair but was slapped harder across the face as the librarian struggled to get up. Rachel felt something cool in her blouse and reached in to grab it as she was rolled over onto her back. Next she had the wind driven out of her by a knee hard in her chest.

'You really should learn when to *give up*, little girl!' spat the librarian, her eyes flickering in the helicopter's tail light and her face flashing blue and white in the light of the oncoming police cars. The closest runner of the helicopter began to ease up out of the grass beside them as the librarian lifted her hand and balled it into a fist.

'Corders don't give up,' croaked Rachel, lifting the aerosol can and pressing the button.

A strong jet of antiseptic shot right into the librarian's eyes. She shrieked and let go of Rachel, just as the helicopter tried to rise again. The librarian tried, blindly, to leap into it, but only staggered into the side. There was a volley of sound from the police cars— warning shouts through loudspeakers. Rachel grabbed Polly, whose eyes were now open, and dragged her away from the deafening aircraft.

Other arms closed around them. 'It's OK, you're safe,' said a voice. 'We've got you all safe now.'

Chapter 27

'Oh, not another needle! Why does everyone have to keep jabbing me with needles?'

Ben opened his eyes and stared across a white room, in time to see a man advancing on Polly with a syringe. He shot upright and shouted 'No! Leave her alone! Polly—*run*!' The man paused and Polly looked round, but she was smiling. Sitting next to her was Freddy, with his arm around her. He was smiling too.

All of a sudden a rush of images filled Ben's mind—the rain and the dark, the men in black carrying Polly and Rachel, striking someone's head with a flail, Freddy staggering along at the side of the road, bleeding and blind. The lightning strike . . .

'What's happening? What's happening?'

A hand rested on his shoulder. 'It's all right, Benedict. It's all right now.' He spun round and saw Uncle Jerome. Ben realized he was in a bed—a medical kind of bed in a small ward with a highly polished floor. Polly and Freddy were sitting on another bed across the room, wearing green pyjamas, and beyond Uncle Jerome, Rachel also lay in bed in green pyjamas, her eyes opening, grinning at him sleepily.

'You've been absolutely brilliant—all of you,' said Uncle Jerome, warmly. 'I cannot begin to say how proud I am of you. You managed to stop our country from losing something very, very precious.'

'So who is that?' said Ben, his nerves still jangling. 'And why are they injecting Polly? I thought we agreed—no tests, Uncle J—no tests!'

'It's quite all right, Ben,' said Polly. 'We have to have this. It's to stop the bleeding and the going blind thing. Freddy told me what happened on the road,' she gulped. 'They say this will stop it happening again and make us both well.'

Ben began to relax just slightly. 'Where are we?' he asked. A dark-haired man, who had been standing quietly by a pale green wall, clicking a pen in his hand, now walked across to him. He pushed back his rimless spectacles and smiled at Ben.

'You're in a special government hospital—quite safe, Ben. And I promise you, we won't *ever* do any kind of testing on Polly or Freddy without family consent. They are extremely precious to us.'

Rachel now sat up, looking around. 'Where's Bessie?' she demanded. 'She needs an injection too! Did you rescue her from the helicopter?'

'We did,' smiled the man. 'The pilot had the good sense not to try to take off, surrounded by British Special Branch. Don't worry, Bessie's already had her injection and she's just along the corridor, being looked after by a very delighted civil servant. We like dogs around here.'

'Ouch,' said Polly, as the man, in a medical uniform, gave her the injection. Ben held his breath but nothing happened—Polly didn't pass out and the man didn't suddenly advance upon them all, waving a syringe.

'Are you all quite awake now?' asked Uncle Jerome. 'Chambers and I have quite a lot to tell you. You've been out cold for just over a day, Ben . . . You must have got the biggest dose of knock-out juice! It seemed it was a bit hit and miss, because Rachel woke up very quickly after her injection.'

'Lucky for me,' smiled Polly and Rachel beamed back. She was still too exhausted to do much more.

'So you can make Freddy and Polly well?' asked Ben, looking at Chambers. 'They won't die . . . like the rats.'

'No,' said Chambers. 'We know exactly what to do to stop the bleeding and the other side effects. They will be absolutely fine. We've been given all the information we need. Now . . . are you all ready for a bit of a story? I think you've earned it.'

'It starts fifty-three years ago,' said Uncle Jerome, getting comfortable on the edge of Ben's high bed, and looking around at them all, 'but for Chambers here, it started two years ago—when Richard Tarrant came home. You see, fifty-three years is a long time in the government and pretty much nobody here even remembered the old Emerson case—not until Tarrant showed up one November day. He wanted to confess, to get some kind of pardon—to be left in peace to die back in his own country after half a century in Russia. He *had* defected you see . . . and he took Henry Emerson with him.'

'No!' shouted out Freddy, with a sob in his voice. 'No! I don't believe it! Father would rather have died than defect! He *loved* his country!'

'You're right,' said Chambers. 'He *would* rather have died. Tarrant betrayed him—took Soviet agents to his house to seize him.'

'Uncle Dick did that?' Polly looked shocked beyond measure.

'Yes—I'm afraid he did. Your father was overcome, abducted, and smuggled out of the country. And he probably would have killed himself once he was

310

captured, but he couldn't, you see. He had a terrible secret. The Russians imagined you and Polly were at school when he was taken—and later they got the idea that you'd been taken to a government safe house for your protection. They didn't really care either way—they just wanted your father's genius. He was an incredibly clever man and they knew he was a great advantage to Great Britain in the Cold War. They wanted him for themselves, if only to take that advantage away from us.

'But your father had this secret. He must have been absolutely tortured by it. He had left his beloved son and daughter in cryonic suspension—in a living death—buried in the woods behind his house. He had only just had time, when he realized he was being hunted, to shut you in and bury the hatchway in the woods,' Chambers went on. 'When he saw the men who were coming for him on camera, he was down underground. He should have locked himself in too, but he was desperate to hide some more of his work back in the house, if he could. Most of all though, he had to hide his children. If the Soviets had taken you two along with him, they could have made him do anything.'

'So what *did* he do for them?' said Freddy, almost whispering. He looked white and his mouth was trembling.

'For the Russians? Nothing they wanted him to at first—nothing to do with weapons, although he knew a great deal about them. He was sick of war and bombs. So, in the end, he shared with them the very thing he had tried to hide from us—his cryonic stasis breakthrough.'

'Why would he do that?' said Freddy. 'Why would he do anything for them at all?'

'He didn't do it for them,' said Uncle Jerome. 'He did it for you. It was the only thing he felt he *could* do for you.'

There was silence in the room and then Ben asked: 'How do you know all this?'

'Some of it came from Tarrant,' said Chambers. 'Of course, the minute he pitched up back in England we went into the files, and as thirty years had passed and it was no longer Top Secret, we got a lot more background on the case from other departments—found out about some of the early breakthroughs the professor had made in cryonics . . . all to no good apparently— the rats kept dying. And once Tarrant had returned we tried to find out, through our own network of agents in Russia, if there was any chatter about Professor Emerson. Tarrant hadn't seen him for fifty years, himself, when he came back—he'd just collected his money and retired to the Russian good life, such as it was. He couldn't tell us much more about what had happened to his old friend—or the children. I think he was quite haunted by what he did—to all of you—if it helps you to know that.' Freddy stared at his feet and said nothing.

'We couldn't find anything significant,' went on Chambers, 'so we decided to put a sleeper—an undercover operative—in place in Amhill, just on the off-chance that the professor himself was still alive and might one day come back. We placed her in the library. Her job was to keep her ear to the ground and report to us if anything occurred around Darkwood House or connected with the old Emerson case.'

'She was working for *you*!' Ben tried to stand up, on shaky legs, suddenly full of fear again.

'Yes, she *was* working for me,' said Chambers, while Uncle Jerome grabbed Ben's shoulders.

'Wait, Benedict,' he said. 'Hear him out.'

'She immediately noticed that you were interested in the Emerson history and so she made sure one of the library's security cameras recorded you all. She had studied the files for a long time—including family photos—and she could not believe what she saw, as soon as she laid eyes on Freddy and Polly. Just couldn't believe it . . . but she worked out that the only possible answer was your father's research—cryonics.'

'So you sent her with men to get us! Inject us! Kidnap us!' said Ben, through gritted teeth.

'No, Ben—of course not. We didn't even know ourselves until yesterday. Tara Chapman didn't send the tape to us—she sent it to Russia. She was . . . well, what you would call a double-agent. They'd convinced her to pass information to them, not us, not long after she was put in place. As soon as they realized what she was saying was probably true, they sent in their own people to help her find and abduct you all.'

'We did come for you!' said Uncle Jerome. 'As soon as I realized that I *had* to get help to you. Should have just been straight about it from the start. Would've saved a lot of trouble. We sent men to Percy's place too—he left me a message and we guessed he might be in trouble—and they ended up chasing you and Freddy across the town! We got to the house just in time to find three men's bodies on the driveway and Freddy screaming his head off.'

'That spy woman must have known how to start the car with its wires. Father showed me how to do that once, on our old Austin,' said Freddy. 'She jumped into the front seat and was driving off seconds later, even though I still had the key!'

'That was brilliant, when you took the key,' remembered Ben. 'How did you do that? You couldn't see!'

'Well, after a while my eyesight came back. Once I'd got my breath back I could see well enough to come on after you. I saw you crack that man with the camera. You were super cool! Then I hid behind the car when the others came up, and reached in and got the key while they were all distracted by you and your killer bicycle pump!'

Ben grinned as he remembered. Then he gulped. The lightning. 'Are those men dead?'

'Well, they were OK when we packed them off on a plane to Moscow this morning,' said Chambers. 'Some minor burns and concussion . . . I think the one you hit with the camera had the worst headache.'

'You did what? You sent them home?' Freddy looked aghast.

'We negotiated with the Russian president,' said Chambers. 'Turns out they had something we wanted rather badly, so we sent them back their men.'

'What did they have that you could possibly want that badly?' said Freddy, angrily.

'I guess you should see for yourself,' said Chambers and walked to a side door of the room. 'Come on in,' he said, to someone beyond it.

The door opened and a man who looked about the same age as Ben and Rachel's dad walked in. He wore a brown suit, and a grey tie. He looked dazed as he stared at Polly and Freddy. Ben couldn't work out who this might be. He had been hoping for an old man . . . Polly and Freddy's father. He felt a surge of disappointment.

Then Polly cried out and ran to the man, flinging her arms around him. 'Daddy! Daddy! Oh, Daddy! Daddy!'

Rachel and Ben stared at each other in amazement. Where was the ninety-one year old?

Then, of course, they realized what Professor Henry Emerson had done. He had built another cryonic chamber for the Russians—and then managed to get inside it himself.

The young man before them . . . because really, he *was* still a young man, knelt down and put his arms around his daughter and his face creased with emotion. He looked across the room at his son. Freddy's face was hard—almost angry—also holding back tears.

'Father,' he said, standing up and clenching his fists at his sides. 'I have to tell you something. Sir, I have to say this!'

'Go on, Frederick,' said his father.

'You oughtn't to have done it. You really oughtn't to have put Polly in there. It was jolly well not right— do you know? It's been the most awful week for her.'

Freddy gulped and bit back down on his lip. His eyes glittered.

His father got up and walked across to him, Polly holding tight to his arm. He put his hand on Freddy's green pyjamaed shoulder and nodded. 'Well said, my boy. Well said. I agree wholeheartedly. Can you forgive me?'

'Of course,' said Freddy, in a strangled voice, and flung his arms around the man. 'It's been all right really, I suppose.' He sniffed and gulped. 'Quite a hoot with Ben and Rachel—just wait till you try a Whopper.'

'And Pot Noodle!' piped up Polly.

Ben and Rachel had the good grace to look ashamed.

Chapter 28

'Can I help anyone, please? Who's next, please? You want fries with that? D'you want to go large for another thirty p?'

Professor Henry Emerson winced amid the racket of shouting staff, sizzling deep-fat fryers, and hyperactive children. 'You're telling me people come here . . . from *choice*?' he asked. He watched, mesmerized, as Polly proudly opened his carton in front of him on the plastic-topped table.

'Here you are—it's a Whopper! Not a fib, but a burger! In a round roll. It's super when you try it, honestly, Daddy! Try it!'

Professor Emerson reached into the carton as if he were about to de-fuse a bomb and retrieved the large burger. Polly nodded at him excitedly. 'Go on! Just take a bite!'

He paused and looked around. 'Can you not

get plates and cutlery here? It *is* a restaurant after all.'

'No!' said Polly. 'It's not that *kind* of restaurant. Oh, Daddy—you've got such a lot to learn. Just bite it!'

At last Professor Emerson did as his daughter told him and took a bite out of his Whopper. His eyebrows shot up while they all waited, breathlessly, for his verdict. After a few munches he nodded. 'Not bad,' he said. 'Certainly a lot better than Russian food.'

'Did you really meet the Russian president?' asked Freddy, poking his straw into the top of his Coke cup.

'Both of them—the one in 1956 *and* the one in 2009,' said Professor Emerson and there was a *hint* of pride in his voice, thought Ben. 'Khrushchev wasn't called a president back then, of course. Then it was the Soviet Union and they didn't have such titles, but that's really what he was. He was fascinated by my cryonic chamber research and personally asked me to work on it for the Soviets. I said I would build it for him, but only on the condition that he would let me go home afterwards. He wouldn't agree. He said not in his lifetime. So I suggested that he let me go home *after* his lifetime. We agreed that he would most likely be long gone after fifty years—and so when my work was complete, a few months later, he wrote a letter to the leader of the country, to be opened in 2007. In the letter he told whomsoever it might concern that my cryonically frozen body would be found in a research facility in an underground bunker in a province of Chernobyl, and I was to be woken and sent home.'

'Chernobyl!' gasped Ben, through a mouthful of chips and ketchup. 'You were in Chernobyl! But that's where they had the nuclear disaster! How did you survive?'

'So they *did* drop the bomb!' Freddy sat up, his eyes wide. 'Father—you were right!'

Professor Emerson smiled and shook his head. 'No, Frederick. They didn't. It was an accident in a nuclear power plant—quite close to the research facility I was sleeping in. It happened nearly thirty years after they put me into stasis. They had long ago abandoned the cryonic experiment, because I hadn't given them the final part of my research—the part that stops animals dying after they get re-animated. They couldn't solve that and so, like my old friends in Britain, they gave up and spent their money elsewhere. They left me in place, because they were told to, and because they didn't know what else to do. Then of course, after the Chernobyl disaster, nobody could get to me if they tried—not without great risk. And I was the least of their worries. I might be there still if someone hadn't found the old letter from Khrushchev. They put on their radiation-proof outfits and came to awaken Sleeping Beauty. It was the most extraordinary thing. It took me days to believe that I wasn't really still in 1957.'

'I know exactly what you mean!' said Polly, biting into her Whopper with feeling.

'But it is fantastic out there,' said Freddy, his eyes drifting to the expanse of glass at the front of Burger King and out onto London's Oxford Street where countless shoppers, tourists, and locals moved in a colourful, never-ending procession.

'They put spikes through their skin!' whispered Polly. 'Just because they want to!'

Her father's eyebrows went a notch higher.

'And they don't just pierce their ears—they pierce their tummy buttons! Truly! Girls of *my* age! Can you believe it?'

'I really don't want to.'

'*Everyone* has a motorcar and there are more sweets than you've ever seen in your life,' said Freddy.

'And Coca-Cola comes in tins,' went on Polly. 'And you can get money out of brick walls.'

'They're called cash points,' laughed Rachel.

'And people talk all the time on tiny, tiny little phones clipped to their ears and look quite, quite mad!' added Polly.

'And . . . ' Freddy looked reverent, 'I just saw a TV screen the size of a *door*!'

His father shot him a look. 'Oh really, Frederick. Now you're going too far.'

'We'll take him into Curry's next week,' said Ben and Uncle Jerome nodded, with a smile.

'Don't you worry, sir,' said Uncle Jerome. 'You're going to absolutely love it! Science is going off the scale! DNA, gene therapy, string theory, chaos—oh— a new planet, we have *nine* now, don't you know . . . unless you take away Pluto, which turned out not to be a planet after all . . . and then . . . '

The two scientists fell into a riveting discussion about DNA then and Freddy, Polly, Ben, and Rachel grinned at each other.

'Would you go back?' asked Rachel. 'If you could?'

Polly and Freddy looked at each other. 'I don't know,' said Freddy. 'It would be awfully hard now, knowing all of this is to come . . . and having to wait until I was sixty-six to get to it.'

'And we'd miss you two,' said Polly. 'I don't know what we'd have done without you.'

'I do,' said Freddy. 'We'd've stayed asleep for another fifty years! No—it's been super. You saved our lives—both of you.' Ben grinned at Rachel. By now they had shared their stories and he was as proud of her as she was of him.

'We can't thank you enough,' went on Freddy. 'And . . . well, it's going to be jolly hard to get along without you.'

'It's only for the term though,' said Rachel. 'You'll be back at home with us in the school holidays. You're both much better off back at boarding school. You won't meet anyone like Lorraine Kingsley where you're going. It's one of the country's best schools, too! And you're not far from us at all, so we'll be able to pop up and see you on weekends sometimes. We might be able to bring Bessie.'

'Oh, gosh, yes—that'd be super!' said Polly. 'Imagine! I'll be at the same school as Freddy! They have a girls' wing and a boys' wing. Would you ever believe such a thing? We'll be able to meet up and have a midnight feast!'

They finished up their junk food with enthusiasm. 'Isn't it the tops, Daddy?' said Polly, as her father screwed up his napkin and put it inside the burger carton.

'Polly—no! It's *not* the tops!' said Rachel, earnestly. 'You really should only eat it every so often. Your hotpot is miles better—and much healthier. Do remember that. Burgers and stuff are just treats. And look . . . not too many sweets or Pot Noodles, either. OK?'

'You're turning into Mum,' laughed Ben. 'Hey—they'll be home this weekend! What on earth are they going to say when they find out what's been going on—and who's coming to live with us?'

Outside, Professor Emerson blinked as someone went by on a unicycle, and handed him a leaflet for a Tattoo Parlour. Uncle Jerome took it off him and they all stood around, slightly awkwardly, until Polly hugged Rachel and then Ben.

'I'm not going to blub,' she sniffed. 'Because we'll see you all again in a week or so, to meet your mother and father . . . and I can't wait.'

Rachel hugged her back and *did* start to blub.

Freddy shook Ben by the hand. 'I want you to know,' he said, 'that I have never seen anyone do that flail thing so impressively. To see you knock out that bad sort was just so . . . cool!'

Ben grinned. Freddy thought *he* was cool. And well . . . maybe he was. He shook hands with his great-uncle and best friend and then gave him a blokey hug. This was the twenty-first century after all.

'I say, steady on!' laughed Freddy. 'No really,' he added. 'You've been an absolute brick!'

'Um . . . best not say that again,' advised Ben.

The refugees from the 1950s turned and walked along Oxford Street, a government minder discreetly a few steps behind them. Ben was glad the minder was there. London today was a big, startling place. Their new branch of family should be protected.

'Back to normal then,' said Rachel.

Ben grinned. 'Do you think anything's ever going to be normal again?'

'I suppose not,' smiled his sister. 'I'm really going to miss Polly's cooking, though. Do you think *I* could make a hot pot? In time for Mum and Dad coming back?'

'I'm sure you could,' said Ben, as they walked towards the tube station with Uncle Jerome. 'I'll help, if you like—but first you've got to try out Freddy and Polly's skates! They're super . . . way faster than in-lines . . . '

'Ben—did you just say "super"?'

'Me? Don't be daft.'

'You *did*. You jolly well did . . . '

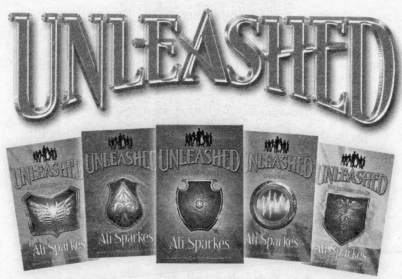

WHAT IF YOU HELD THE POWER OF THE UNIVERSE IN THE PALM OF YOUR HAND?

Ty Lewis is messing about in the woods when he stumbles upon something freaky—a glowing lump of rock or metal or *something*. Whatever it is, it gives him an amazing power.

Which is cool at first, until Ty's new powers start attracting attention, and soon he's being followed by two sinister agents who seem intent on 'collecting' him.

But Ty has no intention of letting that happen.
So now he's got to RUN . . .

OUT NOW!

To find out more about Ali Sparkes' books visit

www.alisparkes.com